AS THE
LOTUS BLOOMS

R. BRUCE LOGAN

BLACK ROSE
writing™

ISBN: 978-1-68433-102-4
PUBLISHED BY BLACK ROSE WRITING
www.blackrosewriting.com

Printed in the United States of America
Suggested retail price $18.95

As the Lotus Blooms is printed in Adobe Garamond Pro

For Victoria Lynn Logan

AS THE LOTUS BLOOMS

The Lotus Flower

Despite being born into dark, muddy conditions, where hope for a beautiful life seems dubious, the lotus grows, and rises above adversity. Ironically, this same dirty water washes it clean as it surfaces. As the lotus opens each petal to the air, not a stain or spot of mud remains. It is pure, and bright, and beautiful.

Paraphrased from "The Story of the Lotus Flower"

PROLOGUE — LIEN

I was tired of waiting for the pain to go away. The scare of the day before had brought back all the fears, ghosts and nightmares. Jacqueline Hartzog, my counselor, called moments like those regressions. She said it was normal for PTSD to be triggered by another traumatic event, but it wasn't normal for me. I didn't know what normal was anymore.

During the night I saw crooked, gnarled men coming after me from every direction, lust and desire written all over their faces. I ran to get away from them, but new men appeared from ahead of me, beside me, behind me, their vulgar grins widening into yawning cavities. They taunted me by calling my name repeatedly, until a cave appeared before me and I aimed for it, wanting shelter from their jeering and lewd suggestions. But suddenly, Colonel Khlot appeared in the mouth of the cave, blocking the entrance. He wore nothing but a filthy grin. I screamed at him, "Go away, go *away!*" until I awakened in a cold sweat, my skin crawling.

BOOK ONE

CHAPTER ONE — PHA

Pha stepped out of her two-room apartment on the fourth floor of a concrete block in Singapore's Geylang Road district. Encumbered by her tight miniskirt, she minced downstairs toward the street, her stiletto heels clacking on paved steps. Several hundred meters along, past the row of sixty-year-old, two-story shop-houses and two karaoke parlors, at the intersection of Geylang Road and Lorong 12, she took her position within a row of other young women, all attempting to look mature and worldly, none older than eighteen. It was just past six p.m.

A young stud with spikey black hair cruised past the lineup on his motorbike, eyeing the miniskirts and tight shorts just below eye level. Although made up to look alluring, the girls' faces looked as pasty as undercooked pasta, with slashes of red on their lips and eyelash extensions that fluttered like insects. The girls leaned forward and jiggled their bosoms or stroked their bare legs as he passed them, a catlike smirk frozen to his face.

Pha stood last in line, backlit by the red and white lights of a 7-11. His leering grin told her that he liked what he saw of her young body, her small breasts pushed up and out by a cleverly designed brassiere.

"How much?" he asked.

"Thirty dollars, thirty minutes. Fifty dollars, one hour."

The girl in a red miniskirt standing to Pha's left shoved her aside, saying, "This one likes me better. You go find someone else."

Pha gave her a hard push that knocked her sideways. As she did, one of the girl's heels snapped off.

"Easy there ladies," the young man said. "No need to fight over me. I'll take you both. I'm Ronald. I have a queen-size bed in my apartment. We can make a Ronald sandwich. I'll give you seventy-five dollars each for two hours."

The girls looked at each other, hesitant.

"*Địt mẹ mày!* That sounds gross," Pha said, and then she looked across the street and saw Chester Lim glaring at her. He stepped off the curb and started toward her. "Okay, Ronald," she said.

"Jump on."

Forced by their miniskirts to ride sidesaddle, the two girls slid on behind the driver, Pha with her legs dangling to the right side, the other girl's to the left.

***

At two in the morning Pha trudged up the concrete stairs to her tiny flat. Chester was waiting for her in the living room-kitchen, an open bottle of beer in front of him and a cheroot burning on a saucer atop the scarred table. His dark eyes glared. "How much?" he asked.

She pulled the wad of cash from her small handbag and clutched it, trembling. "A hundred and five dollars. Only two customers tonight. One for seventy-five dollars, one for thirty."

"That's not enough. I got expenses supporting you. Hand it over."

"Can't I keep some for food? And what about MRT fare? I go to the doctor for my weekly checkup tomorrow."

"You still have a kilo of rice, half a bottle of cooking oil and two cans of kippered fish. You can use my EZ-Link card for the MRT. Here." He tossed her the card.

She'd been trying to save a little each week, so her voice cracked. "But I told you. I need to go home to Vietnam. My mother …"

"With eight girls to look after I don't want to hear about your fucking mother. I can't worry about the personal problems of any one of you. Forget about getting home. Just live for the present. Isn't that how you Buddhists think? Now give me the money."

"Please Chester." She held the money close to her chest. "Can't I keep just a little? I need to eat. I want to go home to my family."

When he backhanded her across the side of her face, she stumbled and fell onto her hip. He pried the money loose from her fingers and shoved her into a sitting position on the floor. As he stormed from the room he said over his shoulder, "You better get more tomorrow night."

Pha sat on the floor and listened to the door click as Chester locked it from outside. She hugged her knees to her chest and wept.

CHAPTER TWO — LIEN

I approached the front desk with caution because I had only stayed in a hotel once before, and that time my grandparents, *Ông* Pete and *Bà* Catherine, had checked me in. This time I would do it alone. The clerk, neatly dressed in the hotel colors, looked about five years older than me, perhaps about twenty-three. She greeted me in English with a long, warm smile and tilted her head slightly sideways, as if trying to put me at ease. "Good afternoon, Miss. Are you checking in?"

"Yes," I said. My grandfather told me everyone here speaks English. "My name is ... " My voice caught and I cleared my throat to find a sturdier tone. "My name is Le Nguyen Thi Lien."

"May I see your passport please?"

I opened the little green booklet to the picture page, as Bryan from the Green Gecko organization had instructed me, and I handed it to her. Bryan was the representative for the NGO's office in Singapore, and he had picked me up at the airport. Moments before, he had dropped me off at the hotel.

As the clerk tapped computer keys, I looked around the modest lobby. On a settee near the door, a middle-aged Caucasian man sat with a young Asian woman. As I glanced in their direction, he rose and walked toward me. In passing, he looked me up and down, and such a shiver ran through me as he moved on toward the washrooms that a little sound escaped my throat.

The desk clerk looked up. "Is anything wrong, Miss Lien?"

I took a steadying breath. "I thought I recognized someone. I was mistaken."

This was how it often went with me. Some men reminded me of the brothel. Even after three years of rehab in Saigon, and two more years in a residential international school, I still had nightmares. I mistrusted men when I first encountered them, and even though everyone at Green Gecko had told me that Singapore was clean and safe, I was afraid.

A bellman carried my one medium-sized suitcase and took me in an elevator to the third floor. His uniform reminded me of Colonel Khlot, my first "customer" in the brothel, and I pushed myself against the back wall of the elevator, wishing I had a way to put even more space between us. But he just stood watching the numbers that lit over his head at the front of the car until we arrived on my floor. At my room I didn't let him enter with the bag but told him to set it down in the hall. I tipped him two Singapore dollars as Bryan had told me to, and then I quickly dragged the bag into my room and shut and bolted the door.

Out the window I focused on a green expanse of city park, its grassy spread the same color as the rice paddies outside my girlhood home in the village of Tuy Phuoc. I used to love watching the vast sea of emerald rice sweep into ripples as breezes from nearby mountains tickled the tops of young plants. In the mornings, when wisps of wood smoke from cooking fires mingled with tendrils of mist in the paddies, I imagined that the spirits of our ancestors were sending us good wishes for the day ahead. In the evenings, Grandmother Quy, Papa and I sat under the lean-to roof of our tiny porch, listening to crickets chirp and insects buzz. Papa smoked. It was a glad time for me.

In one corner of the park I spotted a small pond fouled with black muck, but home to several beautiful lotus plants. My name, Lien, means Lotus Flower.

I turned from the window and for the first time noticed a colorful bouquet of flowers on the writing desk. Beside the bouquet, a vinyl-covered file folder bore a post-it note with my name on it. The note read, *Lien, please look this over before I see you tonight — Bryan.* I opened the folder and considered the little packet of wallet-sized photos of a girl in her late teens. She wore that glazed expression of one who was serious and nervous at the same time.

The package also contained a typed memo outlining the circumstances under which the girl, Pha, was now, in all probability, an unwilling hooker working on the streets west of downtown Singapore. My assignment was to look for leads to where she might be living and working in that high-density warren.

I closed the folder and moved to the bathroom. After I splashed warm water on my face, I returned to the lobby for a cup of hot tea.

To my relief, the man with the young Asian woman had left. The woman behind the front desk asked, "Is everything satisfactory, Miss Lien?"

"Perfect," I said. I found a comfortable wicker chair and small table near the front window of the lobby, and a smiling porter brought my tea and a saucer of dainty cookies. The first sip was hot and oddly flavored, not bitter like the artichoke tea served in Central Vietnam.

Out the window, a lively cluster of schoolgirls in blue jumpers with white blouses stepped along the sidewalk, heads tossed back in laughter, juvenile smiles lighting their faces.

I used to walk to and from school like that with my best friend, Ha. At thirteen, Ha and I had shared all of our secrets with each other. Often, we would either erupt into giggles or share tears of sorrow. Side by side, we rode our rusty bicycles on the rice paddy berms and small dirt lanes to our three-room village school. I loved school. Sometimes when I finished my afternoon chores and had some free time, Ha and I played school, taking turns being the teacher or the pupil. I used to dream of becoming a teacher someday.

My grandmother Quy encouraged that dream, but everything changed when I was thirteen, when she had a stroke. Then our little family came apart and my nightmare began. I lost who I was and I lost what I thought my life would be like. Even five years later, I was still too embarrassed to contact Ha. Since leaving rehab, I'd had no one to talk with about my feelings. They just churned in my stomach.

When I returned to my room, it was dark and I lit three lights, but I was afraid to sleep. I longed for grandmother Quy and her wisdom and tenderness, but she lived in a care facility in Saigon. Whenever I saw her, I worried that I had shamed her by being a prostitute in Cambodia. Had I also dishonored my father and my dead mother? I believed I had. The counselors at the center constantly told me it wasn't my fault, but those words didn't change my feelings. I had no balm for the pain in my heart.

Near midnight, I thought I might find some peace of mind in a warm bath, so I filled the tub with water and added the contents of a little packet of salts and herbs I found on the counter. The salts would add comfort to my bath, instructions on the packet informed me. But when I loosened its belt and let my terrycloth robe drop to the floor, I glanced at the image of my body in the mirror and looked away fast. On my breast, the jagged red marks left by an old customer's bite made me feel dirty, used, broken.

CHAPTER THREE — PETE TRUTCH, CATHERINE TRUTCH

Pete Trutch ran a hand through his gray hair as he rapidly scanned the remaining lines of an email from Lien. "Damn," he said. "They want her to go to Singapore for her first assignment."

Seconds earlier he'd been delighted to open the email and learn that his granddaughter, now eighteen, had been hired by the Green Gecko Children's Foundation. He knew about Green Gecko, a Hoi An-based NGO that rescued trafficked children, and he had studied their website. When he'd learned that they enjoyed a modicum of success freeing children from sweatshops within Vietnam and from brothels in China, he had even donated money to their cause.

Catherine poured them each another cup of coffee. "What's wrong with that? Singapore's a progressive city. It's clean, with a marvelous café culture. It could be a good education for a former Vietnamese village girl. She's learned to speak English remarkably well over the past few years and almost everyone in Singapore speaks English."

"It's what they want her to do there," Pete replied. "They want her to hang out in the red light district so she can try to locate an under-age girl who was lured there to become the wife of a businessman." He read from the email. "The girl, Pha, stopped contacting her mother a month ago. The mother, who lives in Hoi An, is understandably frantic. When she asked an English-speaking friend to call the businessman, he said that Pha was no longer his wife. So the mother contacted Green Gecko."

"Pete, Singapore is safe. And an NGO as reputable as Green Gecko isn't going to just cast an eighteen-year-old into harm's way. They're not like your beloved US Army, which uses teenagers for cannon fodder, for heaven's sake."

"Damn it, Catherine, 'my beloved Army' has the best trained, best equipped and most highly motivated soldiers in the world. I happen to think Lien's too young and tender to be nosing around whorehouses in a foreign country."

Catherine added soymilk to their coffees. "She's a young adult. She's finished high school. She can make her own decisions. You're just back into your power bag. Some things are beyond your control."

Pete's voice rose an octave or two above normal. "It's not about power … and it's not about control. This raises a red flag for me. Will this foundation just buy her a ticket to Singapore and tell her to sink or swim, or do they have people on the ground in the city to support her? It's all very vague. Maybe I'm overreacting, but I still think of her as that traumatized thirteen-year-old we rescued on the Cambodian-Thai border."

Catherine set his coffee in front of him and put her arm around his shoulders. "It's a good first assignment for her, Pete, probably no more dangerous than riding a motorbike on a city street. I imagine they'll give her a benign, monotonous task, some routine like showing a picture of this Pha to business owners in the area, or … I don't know … making phone calls, taking notes at meetings. Maybe she'll be an assistant to an experienced investigator."

"Yeah, maybe." Trutch sat at the counter, his refilled cup untouched, and furiously tapped keywords into the search function of his iPhone.

***

On Sunday, Catherine studied Trutch's expression as they walked the loop trail in Seattle's Discovery Park, then she said, "What are you conjuring up, Colonel Trutch? I can hear your gears grinding."

He stopped walking and gazed out across the cerulean waters of Puget Sound to the snow crested Olympic Mountains beyond. "I'm making another trip to Vietnam — by way of Singapore this time. I'd like you to come with me if you want. But I'm going either way. I want to scope out this gig Green Gecko has Lien doing. I might be able to help in her assignment."

"You're being overprotective. On Friday night, after your Google search — which, by the way, abruptly closed the discussion we were having — you told me that Singapore has very little violent crime. And prostitution, while not illegal, is closely regulated. It's the cleanest, safest city in Asia. You read that aloud to me, Pete."

"It's not about being protective." He stopped on the path to face her. Five years ago he'd been unaware that he had a paraplegic son and a granddaughter. But Lien was only thirteen when her treacherous uncle sold her into slavery. His son, Ngoc, had reluctantly contacted him for help. "Well, maybe it is," he said, "but she's my flesh and blood and I want her safe. I'm sure Ngoc does too."

"You're seventy-three years old. You can't be rescuing children from red light districts. Rescuing Lien I understood. But that romp in the underbelly of Vietnam and Cambodia put us both in peril. Remember?"

"I don't mean that I'll become involved in rescuing anyone. I'm thinking we could be a sounding board for Lien — help her with ideas for getting the job done. She might appreciate having family nearby while she's in a big strange city. Other than her nightmare in Cambodia, she's never been outside Vietnam."

"You might be right about that. Given all she went through in Svay Pak, she's probably still pretty fragile."

"And I'm her grandfather. Who else does she have to worry about her? Neither Ngoc or her grandmother are in any position to travel. Besides, a little escape to Singapore might be fun for us. I've never had a Singapore Sling at Raffles and that's on my bucket list."

They resumed walking toward the north meadow, the former Fort Lawton firing range, and Catherine grew silent. Trutch's discovery of a Vietnamese granddaughter had created turbulence in their marriage. They'd been married for over forty years when he'd received the letter from Ngoc, and it had exposed his affair with Ngoc's mother during his second tour of duty in Vietnam. "Dream," she had called herself.

"Singapore, huh?" Catherine finally said. "Well, I suppose I could get into some mischief in those upscale malls on Orchard Road. And the food in the night markets is supposed to be out of this world."

CHAPTER FOUR — PETE TRUTCH

Trutch considered his plate, which contained two runny soft-boiled eggs swimming in a pond of soy sauce, dotted with flakes of dried chili pepper. "I see why they call it a 'slap up.' It looks like it's been slapped silly and then drowned."

"Grandfather," Lien said. "This is the most famous breakfast, Singapore style. You put jam on the toast, and then dip it into the eggs and soy. It tastes wonderful."

The two of them sat on round, white stools at an unadorned table in Ya Kun Kaya Toast, an iconic eatery in Singapore — one of six in the chain — boasting a clean retro ambiance reflecting its origins in 1944 wartime Malaysia. This one was located in an upscale residential neighborhood of low-rise condos just off Cross Street, near Chinatown, and a few blocks from the hotel in which Trutch and Catherine stayed.

When Lien had met Trutch and Catherine at the airport the night before, she had been accompanied, to Trutch's relief, by a more mature male member of Green Gecko Children's Foundation, and they had all ridden downtown in the taxi to the New Majestic Hotel. Claiming a desire for quiet and a need to recover from jet lag, Catherine had begged off the early morning breakfast meeting, but Trutch was eager to learn the details of his granddaughter's assignment in Singapore. Mostly he wanted assurance that she was safe.

He slathered his already heavily buttered square of white toast with orange marmalade, and then plunged it into the pool of eggs and soy sauce imagining, as he swooshed the toast around the viscous egg mixture, that it would taste like something from a petri dish. To his amazement, the combination of textures and flavors — the salt, sugar, gluten, butter and eggs — pleased him despite its soupy look. "Wow. That's delicious. Who would have thought it?"

"I told you it's good. I still prefer a bowl of *mỳ quảng* or some *bánh bèo,* but many Singapore business people come here for a good breakfast. And I thought you would like it."

"I do. But the real treat is being with you here in Singapore. How's the case going?" As a retired army officer and business executive, he was accustomed to mining deep for information in order to arrive at sound conclusions and decisions, so he really wanted to ask, "What is the plan or strategy for finding this young woman and what have you done already?" But his experience in Vietnam and Cambodia during the rescue of Lien taught him that one couldn't bulldoze one's way to answers in the Asian culture. Catherine had helped him understand that aggressive or dominant male behavior wasn't tolerated in the West either.

"You met Bryan last night at the airport. He's Green Gecko's representative here. They have a small office near the National University of Singapore. He's a Singapore citizen of Malaysian ancestors, and he supervises me. My job is to show pictures of Pha to people in the Geylang Road District. It's about eight stops from downtown by MRT. I go there every day for six days and show the picture. No one knows her."

He gobbled more bites of the eggy stew and asked, "Do you think Pha may be controlled by someone else and kept imprisoned when she's not working?"

"I don't know, Grandfather. We only know that she and her mother lived alone in the fishing village of Cua Dai. Her father, a fisherman, drowned several years ago in a bad storm off the Cham Islands. Pha and her mother were having a difficult time. They were — how do you say? — dirty poor."

"Dirt poor," Trutch corrected. He searched the table for a napkin to wipe a rivulet of yolk off his chin. Unable to find one, he used his neatly folded handkerchief.

Lien giggled. "Yes. Dirt poor. According to the mother, a matchmaker for poor girls and rich Singapore businessmen spoke to Pha. He promised to fly her first class to Singapore. A driver would pick her up and take her to a nice hotel. She would stay there two nights before meeting with her husband."

The proprietor, having seen Trutch use his handkerchief, arrived at the table with a stack of brown paper napkins.

Trutch nodded his thanks. "Why would she be put up in a hotel if there's a husband waiting?"

"Bryan said the husband would have a doctor check that she is ..." she flushed and averted her eyes, "... uh, a virgin, before he makes a final decision."

Lien drank from her cooling coffee cup and then regained eye contact. "The mother also told us that they promised Pha money to send home."

"Typical. Catherine and I would like to help you if we can."

"Grandfather, you're old already. You have lots of wisdom, but I don't think you should try to help."

"I don't want to be physically involved. I may be able to help with ideas. And let me guess. No money ever arrived."

"Yes. I mean no. No money ever came. She made only one phone call, after she had been gone for a month. She told her mother that her husband was not treating her well. He beat her whenever she didn't please him. Another week passed before Pha's mother's friend, a hotel housekeeper who speaks English, called the Singaporean businessman. That's when she learned that they were no longer together."

"How did she know how to reach this businessman, and does she know his name?"

"She doesn't know his name. Pha wasn't allowed to call home, but one time when her husband was napping, she took his cell phone and called her mother. So the mother called back to that number."

"If Green Gecko can get that number from the mother, you should be able to figure out who the businessman is. He might know where Pha could be."

"That's one of the problems. The mother lost her cell phone in the Thu Bon river while she was on the ferry from Hoi An to Cam Kim Island."

"That's a tough break."

"Nothing is broken. Just missing."

"Just an expression, Lien. It means, that's too bad. But why is Green Gecko focusing on Geylang Road? Aren't there other red light districts in Singapore? How do you know that Pha is even in the sex trade? Why are you concentrating on that?"

"That's too many questions, Grandfather. But the Singapore Police have told Green Gecko that there are many, many cases of imported young brides being dumped after a month or two. The typical scenario is that the girls have no money, no phone, no ticket home and nowhere to go. They come to the

Geylang Road area and become hookers or to Joo Chiat Road, nearby. Joo Chiat Road is called Little Vietnam, because many Vietnamese men, here as guest workers, go there to find fun at night in Vietnamese restaurants and bars and hotels with hourly rates. Pimps control the women and keep them poor by taking most of their earnings. It's true that most of them are locked in their rooms when they're not working."

"That's typical in many parts of the world," Trutch said. "In some North American cities included. I've read, though, that prostitution is regulated in Singapore. Don't the police keep an eye on them?"

"But most of the girls working the streets and bars in Geylang are foreigners with no papers. Many are from Vietnam and China, a few from Korea and Japan and some from the Philippines who came in to Singapore to find jobs as domestics. As illegal immigrants they have no human rights, no legal representation …" Her tongue tripped over the pronunciation. "And no social advocates. Bryan said that sometimes the police arrest the ones working openly, but most of the time they can't be bothered."

"What time of day do you usually go to Geylang Road?"

"Always in the morning. Bryan wants me to make my rounds early in the day so I'm not there after dark. That's when the — Bryan calls them "miscreants" — show up and the lights come on in the karaoke bars."

"I think Bryan's being sensible. But it's possible no one recognizes the picture you show because the morning people aren't there later when Pha's on the street."

"Yes. We thought of that. And I appreciate your help. But I must go now. I need to catch the MRT to Geylang in twenty minutes."

"Okay. Listen, could I meet with you and Bryan later this afternoon or tomorrow? Maybe I can offer some ideas." He really meant, I'd like to keep my eye on you, precious Lien.

She looked skeptical, but said, "Come to our office at about five tomorrow. Here's Bryan's card." She rose from her chair and placed her arm on his shoulder and gave him an affectionate pat. "Keep your seat and finish your coffee, Grandfather."

***

"I hope that's you." Catherine's voice rang out over the noise of the shower as Trutch entered their mini-suite. "How's our lovely Lien? Did you have a good meeting?

"Yes. But it's about eighty-five degrees outside already. I'm sweaty just from the short walk back to the hotel. Mind if I jump in that shower with you?"

The shower went off.

"Ha. No time for hanky-panky this morning, Colonel. I'm heading off to Orchard Road. I want to see what all the excitement is about and mingle with the fashionistas." She emerged from the bathroom swathed in a deep-pile terrycloth towel and pecked him on the cheek on her way to the dressing table, where she turned on the blow dryer.

"Hmm. I guess I know where I stand. Just as well, though — I've got some homework to do on the telephone."

"I knew you wouldn't be able to resist plunging in. I'm glad you'll be busy, though. You'd just be an encumbrance if you chose to go with me."

"Be careful out there. This is Southeast Asia after all."

"Oh phooey. This is Singapore. You're still locked into your negative experiences in Vietnam and Cambodia."

Was he? True, during his two tours of duty during the Vietnam War in the 60s and 70s he had experienced some ugly events that left him with nightmares for years. And much of that trauma resurfaced during his search for Lien, as he confronted not only his ghosts of four decades earlier, but contemporary evil in the form of pimps, traffickers and crooked cops. Was he now tarring Singapore, and the whole of Southeast Asia, with the same negative brush?

Trutch shook off the questions and ordered a pot of coffee from room service. Before it arrived, he booted up the internet to search for some local phone numbers.

His first call was to an office in Building 7-4 inside the Port of Singapore Authority complex at Sembawang on the far north side of the city-state. Someone answered on the second ring. "Navy Region Center, Singapore. How may I direct your call?"

"Yes. Can you connect me with the NCIS field office, please?" Trutch knew no one, other than Lien, in the Republic of Singapore, but his web research had informed him that there was a small U.S. military presence on the island, including a detachment of the Navy Criminal Investigation Service (NCIS). He hoped to play the military brotherhood card to facilitate a meeting with the local constabulary, the Singapore Police Force.

This time the phone was picked up on the first ring. "Criminal Investigation Service, Agent Sweeney speaking."

Trutch introduced himself as a retired U.S. Army lieutenant colonel. He explained the purpose of his call and asked if someone would be able to pave the way for him to speak to an intelligence officer in the SPF.

"We'll try to help, sir. Can you give me a day or so? I'm juggling several balls at the moment, and as usual, we're understaffed and overworked. But I'll put an agent on it and ask him to start with the SFP's International Cooperation Department, that's the office with which we normally coordinate matters of mutual interest."

"Thank you. That sounds like the place to start."

Trutch pictured Agent Sweeney sitting behind a grey metal desk in a drab government office. The "Agent" title was just a form of address to avoid his military rank being revealed. He would probably be a chief petty officer or maybe a warrant officer, likely wearing a cheap suit that had "government employee" written all over it, or, more likely, given the climate, a pair of linen slacks and a guayabera shirt worn outside the trousers.

"The ICD may be able to introduce you to someone in the Intelligence Department who can help," Sweeney continued. "They work out of the head office on Irrawaddy Road, but it may take some rooting around to find the right person. The Singapore Police Force is a complex bureaucracy of thirty-eight thousand people."

"I appreciate that."

"Can you give me a mobile number where someone can reach you?"

***

Trutch's next call was to the Green Gecko Children's Foundation office in Hoi An. He identified himself and asked to speak to Stewy Fitzsimmons, the founding director. He was promptly connected.

"Mr. Trutch. This is Stewy. It's good to hear from you. Lien has told me about you. The hero who rescued her from the jaws of depravity." The resonant voice spoke with an Aussie accent. Trutch remembered reading on the foundation's website that it was founded by an Australian schoolteacher.

"I'm not so sure I was a hero. I had a lot of assistance, and I'm just an old, retired soldier. One who only recently learned the power of love. A previously unknown granddaughter in peril has a way of facilitating that."

"Nevertheless, I hear that you're headed up this way when you leave Singapore. I'm keen to meet you. I'll fill you in on the trafficking problem in and around Hoi An."

"I'm eager to know about it. Since Lien's abduction, I've been outraged by this vile problem. Just briefly, if you can tell me, what's the scope of the problem in Central Vietnam?"

"An active ring of traffickers operates mostly in the villages surrounding Hoi An and Da Nang. They prey mostly on girls from poor families. I refer to the entity as the *Pied Piper*, only this is no fairy tale. This is real life."

"Listen, that's why I'm calling. I understand the missing girl, Pha, used her husband's cell phone to call her mother but that the mother subsequently lost her own cell phone in the river."

"That's right."

"Maybe you've already thought of this, but could you ask the mother for her cell number? Then request the record of incoming calls be searched for one from Singapore? Once you have the number in Singapore, it should be easy to locate the guy who cast Pha out onto the street."

"We're onto that angle, Mr. Trutch. Believe it or not, we know what we're doing."

Trutch laughed at his forthrightness. "I didn't mean to imply otherwise. Forgive me for poking my nose in your business, but Lien's my granddaughter. I want to see her succeed."

"So do we. But obtaining cell phone records is easier said than done. There happens to be six mobile phone network providers in this country, all very rigorously regulated by the Communist government. The networks guard their call records closely, but we do enjoy a good relationship with the anti-trafficking police and the Ministry of Public Security. Our Vietnamese lawyers are seeking help from the police in obtaining the records, but in this country things take time. Everything is a tea dance. 'Okay' doesn't mean 'yes' and 'yes' doesn't mean 'Okay,' if you know what I mean."

"I do. I have first hand experience with what I like to call Vietnamese bureaucratic inertia."

Stewy chuckled. "That's a good description. I'll have to remember it. To complicate the issue even further, in this country of 90 million, there are 134 million mobile phone subscribers. Frankly, cell phones provide most of our leads to missing girls. Often, the girls manage to get hold of one somehow and call home, just as Pha did. Hopefully, in her case, we'll make some progress with the police in the next few days."

"I should've known you'd be on top of this. Green Gecko's reputation for success is truly astounding. By the way, if it's not too impertinent to ask, is Stewy your real name? It's not a name I've heard before."

"Ha ha, no. It's Steve actually. But, several years ago I was asked to spell my name over the phone before attending a dinner party. When I arrived at the party, I found a place card with my name spelled S T E U E. I've been Stewy ever since."

"Ah. I would treasure that nickname. I hope to see you in Hoi An soon."

***

An hour later, Trutch sipped a cup of hot tea in the hotel's leafy lobby and contemplated the legend of the Pied Piper of Hamelin. His mind conjured up an image of a fairy-tale caricature wearing red tights, pointed shoes, a vest and alpine hat marching down a cobblestoned Bavarian street playing the flute. But instead of rats, he was followed by a long stream of Vietnamese teen-age girls, all wearing traditional peasant garb, huge innocent smiles on their faces.

His mobile phone interrupted this thought. "Peter Trutch here," he said.

"This is Sergeant Chee, with the SFP Intelligence Department, Mr. Trutch. How can I be of service?"

"That was quick," Trutch said. "Thank you for your call." He explained the situation with the missing girl, Pha, and the specific type of assistance he was seeking. "It's not really for me. I'm just making the request on the part of the Green Gecko Children's Foundation. My granddaughter works for them."

"I see, Mr. Trutch." His English was impeccable, with only a trace of a Chinese accent. "Still, I don't have the authority to assist you with that kind of request. I'll have to run it up the flagpole. I doubt you'll get much help of that sort. I'll get back to you within a day."

Trutch silently fumed at the wait, but said only, "Thanks. You're very kind. I'll await your call."

As he finished settling his bill, it occurred to him that he hadn't heard from Catherine though she'd been gone for several hours. This was unlike her. The two of them had gotten in the habit of checking in with each other when apart, particularly if anything took longer than expected. He hoped she was already back in their room admiring her purchases, trying to determine how she'd make them fit into her luggage.

But he arrived to find their room empty but recently made up by housekeeping. He tried to call her mobile phone but heard ten or twelve ring tones with no answer. Maybe she'd let her battery run down. But that was out of character for the efficient and thorough Catherine. He suppressed a twinge of anxiety. She was an experienced world traveler who knew how to take care of herself.

He thought about looking for her, but unless she hadn't yet left the shopping district, where would he start in this city of millions? Instead he occupied himself by studying Google Earth and MapQuest images of the Geylang Road district, not certain what he was looking for — a hint, any kind of clue that would provide some substance for deeper investigation. By 3:30 pm, emotional alarms were ringing. Something was wrong. Catherine certainly would have checked in by now. His mind sped through the possibilities. Accident? Kidnapping? Taken ill?

When his phone jangled, he startled and didn't recognize the eight-digit number. "Trutch here."

"It's me."

A wave of relief passed over him.

"Sorry I couldn't call sooner. My purse was snatched. They took my cell, my wallet, my credit cards. I'm just …"

Adrenaline shot through him. "Where are you? Are you hurt?"

"No. No. I'm okay Pete. I'm just outside the Plaza Singapura shopping mall on Orchard Road, sitting in the back seat of a police car. Two very polite policemen are taking my report, but they're not optimistic about apprehending the culprit."

"I'm relieved that you're okay. How will you get back to the hotel?"

"The police will drive me. I've got a lot of work to do, going online and reporting stolen credit cards and so forth. First they'd like me to go to their headquarters to look at some photos of known street gang members. I'll give that a go, but it happened so fast, I didn't get much of a look at the perp."

"How about your passport? Was that in the purse?"

"Fortunately, no. It's in the hotel safe."

"Whew. Hurry back. I'll help you with your creditors." They had agreed years earlier to manage their money and their various accounts separately, so at least they could manage with one account while her cards were in limbo.

He heard a subdued echo in memory, Catherine's voice saying, "Singapore is safe."

CHAPTER FIVE — PHA

Thank God he was leaving now, Pha thought. She had endured his pounding as he grunted and groaned over her for the better part of an hour. As always, she numbed her mind and body to the shame he visited upon her.

He ordered her to stay naked and on the bed while he got dressed, then flipped two bills, an American fifty and a twenty, onto her buttocks. "The twenty's just a tip. Buy something for yourself, like a decent hair-do." He was about fifty, corpulent and bald with gray stubble on his face and a thick mat of hair on his chest and ample stomach. "It's been fun, but I gotta run," he said, and lumbered out the door.

Pha pulled on her underwear, then, with the money in her palm, stepped from her tiny bedroom into the grimy front room and placed the fifty dollars under an overflowing glass ashtray on a battered table. That, she would dutifully hand over to Chester. With the rest, she strode purposefully to the kitchen and plucked a nail file from its resting spot beside her compact on the counter. She fumbled for a few seconds as she coaxed the blade, too large for the job, into the slot on a screw holding the cover plate to a wall-mounted light switch. With damp fingers, she loosened the screw sufficiently that she could remove it with her hand. Now using the file as a lever, she removed three tightly rolled green banknotes hidden in the metal electrical box. Painstakingly she unrolled each of them, one twenty- and two ten-dollar bills. She added the twenty her customer had tipped her to the unfurled wad, then rerolled it and stuffed it back into the box. Sixty dollars, total. That was nearly half of the $131 she needed for the budget flight from Singapore to Da Nang on Jetstar Airways, something she'd learned from a secret foray to a nearby internet café while Chester snored drunkenly in her bed. Once in Da Nang, she'd hop on the back of a motorbike for the trip to her home near Hoi An.

Pha plunked herself into a straight-backed chair and swiped at a bead of sweat on her forehead. The slowly revolving overhead fan did little to quell the sultry August heat. From a drawer in the table she removed the stub of a well-chewed pencil and a small square of buff-colored newsprint. She erased the few scratches on the paper with what was left of the worn eraser then jotted down a couple of figures. If she could squeeze out five or ten dollars in tips from about twelve to fifteen customers over the next few weeks, she should be able to make her break. A hundred and fifty dollars would cover the airfare and leave a little extra for meals. She would also need about five dollars, or the equivalent in Vietnamese dong, for the motorbike ride home.

If the tips worked out as she had calculated, she could leave Singapore by September 30. The budget flight left Changi Airport at 9:30 nightly. During the six-hour layover in Saigon, she could sleep on a lounge chair in the airport. She'd get into Da Nang by 8:30 the next morning and be home by ten. To accomplish all this, she'd need to leave for the airport by 7:00 pm. She could ride the MRT to the airport from the station two blocks from her flat. Planning the details gave rise to the fantasy of her return home and made it seem more real.

She pictured her mother's wide smile. How happy their reunion would be. Mom would be surprised to see her at first, but she'd squeal with joy as they embraced. Mother would make moon cakes, a sweet glutinous rice and mung bean paste mixture, one of her country's most popular celebratory foods. The neighbors would all gather for tea and sweets to celebrate Pha's return. Her uncles, cousins and aunties would come for dinner, each bringing a small gift: flowers, nuts, rice cakes. Rice wine would be served with the dinner and some of her uncles would drink a bit too much. Later, over tea and more wine, someone would start singing a sweet ballad. Other voices would join in and soon her young cousins, nieces and nephews would giggle and dance on the cold concrete pad outside her house.

She was jarred back to the present by a flaw in her plan. How could she leave Singapore without her Vietnamese passport? Her husband had taken it and locked it up, and he hadn't returned it. Could she sneak away from Geylang a couple of weeks before her planned departure to visit the Vietnamese embassy? The embassy wouldn't foot the bill to repatriate a young women in her situation, but would they at least provide her with some kind of temporary travel document?

28

But Chester kept her under lock and key when she wasn't working, and the embassy would surely be closed by the time she started her beat. She dressed and rushed to get back on the street to turn a couple more tricks before she incurred Chester's wrath. The last time she had pissed him off he'd beaten her so severely she couldn't hit the street for two nights.

He would be near her station on the street, sitting astride his Kawasaki Ninja motorcycle, his pride and joy. Or he'd be in one of the coffee shops, watching his girls as they solicited, ready to pounce if one of them slouched on the job, ready to go to her room and drag her out if she lingered too long after her John had finished with her.

Her situation was bleak but not hopeless. The stash of money tucked away in the electrical junction box gave her hope, a small glimmer on the horizon.

CHAPTER SIX — PETE TRUTCH, CATHERINE TRUTCH

At 5:30 p.m., Trutch sat in the hotel lobby across from a young, well-dressed woman, a low coffee table between them. Thirty minutes earlier Chee had called to explain that the police were unable to act on Trutch's request for assistance, but as a courtesy, a young woman from "another government agency" would come to his hotel to explain.

"Mr. Trutch," she said now, "let me explain something. While it's true that Singapore is a surveillance state, the purpose of our technical capability is to serve our homeland security apparatus. We take the threat of terrorism seriously and our ability to use technology to keep our eye on things is unparalleled anywhere in the world."

"I'll bet," Trutch said, observing that her unfortunate choice of hairstyle, stylishly bobbed into a pageboy and slightly puffy at the sides, only made her pinched oval face look like an olive.

"Our absolute priority is to protect our citizens, our way of life and our economy from the ever-increasing global threat of radicalism. We cannot, and will not, devote any of our resources to looking for a single prostitute. I empathize with your granddaughter's dilemma and I take pity on the many young women who have been duped into sexual exploitation. But this issue must be addressed by means other than diverting national security resources."

"All I'm asking for is perhaps a few hours of computer run time, using facial recognition software to pinpoint the location of this Pha. Would that erode your security posture?"

"We cannot give Green Gecko access to any official closed circuit surveillance videos. Period. It would be setting a precedent that could easily lead to further requests. You might, however, approach private security companies. I've brought a list of several who provide the security cameras to businesses in the Geylang road district."

"Hmm. I'd hoped for more from the government of Southeast Asia's beacon of progress."

"I think I detect a note of sarcasm there, Mr. Trutch. We are *not* progressive in the sense that many Western governments are. It may interest you to know that we still employ corporal punishment, in the form of caning across the bare buttocks for some offenses."

"I suppose that includes chewing gum, or flatulence on the streets. I'll try to stay out of trouble." He was beginning to dislike this arrogant olive.

"You're correct. Chewing gum in public is illegal. The latter is discouraged. I suggest you take my list. It's the most help I can offer."

"All right. I'll pass this on to the Green Gecko office here. I appreciate you driving over to explain your policy to me personally."

"Okay. Now I'd like to change the subject. I want you to know a little more about the girls who work the streets and karaoke parlors in Singapore. And, if you're open to it, I can offer you some advice."

"I'm listening."

"I'm afraid Singapore's reputation as squeaky clean is a bit sullied by what goes on in the dimly lit streets of our red light district. It's reasonably well hidden from tourists, except for sex tourists and visiting businessmen. Nobody knows for sure how many foreign prostitutes are on the streets. Many of them came on social-visit visas and overextended their stays. Others are rejected brides, such as the girl your granddaughter seeks. But they are largely ignored by the police as long as they are controlled by their pimps and brothel owners."

"Because prostitution is legal here?"

"In part. It's true that prostitution is legal, but promoting prostitution, such as pimping and brothel owning, are *not* legal. Nor is solicitation on the part of the hooker herself. Obviously pimping is rampant and the girls openly solicit after dark in Geylang."

"Are the police profiting from the practice? Is that why they ignore it?"

"Absolutely not. The Singapore Police Force is one of the most efficient and professional in the world. And they're well paid, so corruption is seldom a temptation. The attitude is that as long as the illegal practices are contained within certain boundaries, there is no public harm done."

"But what about the exploitation and abuse of the women themselves? Are the police concerned about that?"

"Not really. These are foreign nobodies. They are here illegally, so they're not entitled to any rights. A couple of social service agencies, UNIFEM Singapore, for example, sometimes lobbies for the legal and physical protection of the prostitutes, but we tend to ignore them."

She paused while a steward refilled her teacup. "Mr. Trutch, I'm telling you this because once Green Gecko has found this girl, assuming they do, the best way to get her home is to take her to the police. Have her confess to being an illegal immigrant, one who engages in solicitation. The policy, when a girl escapes and goes to the police, is to immediately place her under arrest. Then we will expeditiously process her for repatriation to her home country. Few girls realize this. They're afraid of the police."

***

The Division E police headquarters occupied a modern three-story building between Orchard Road and the Botanical Gardens in a leafy neighborhood of dense high-rise residences. Inside the foyer, Catherine sat on a hard bench waiting to look at digitized mug shots. Sobs drew her attention to a young woman sitting opposite her on the other side of the airy room. The girl, about seventeen, Catherine thought, swiped at her tears with a tattered piece of tissue. Catherine rose, and glancing at the constable sitting behind a side desk reading a newspaper, approached the girl.

"Hello. Can I help you? You seem very sad."

She looked up at Catherine, almond-shaped eyes wide with anxiety. "I don't think you can help. I am arrested. I'm waiting for go to jail."

Catherine sat down next to her. "Where are you from?"

The cop acknowledged her with a frown. "Don't touch her or give her anything. You can talk to her though. She's not going to jail. She's just being processed."

Catherine nodded.

"I live Vietnam. But live here in Singapore for one year."

"I'm Catherine. What's your name?"

"My name Phuong." She wiped her runny nose on the sleeve of her hoodie.

Catherine wished she could offer her a tissue. "But, why are you under arrest, Phuong?"

"I take hairspray and lip gloss. Police say I shoplift. I just want go home to Vietnam like other girls here to be brides. We come here to get married. Then husbands not like us anymore. Put us on the street like rubbish."

"But how do you live?" Catherine whispered. She knew the answer.

Phuong dropped her eyelids. "I'm too ashamed to say."

Catherine looked anxiously toward the policeman, then asked softly, "Are there many other girls from Vietnam you know that were brides here in Singapore?"

Phuong was silent.

"Phuong, do you know another Vietnamese girl named Pha? She was also a bride who was … uh, rejected by her husband after a month."

Phuong raised her head and looked straight ahead. "I don't know. I know lots of girls from Vietnam live here and work near me in Geylang. Several name Pha."

"I can show you a picture." She reached for her missing purse. "Oh damn. No I can't. My purse was stolen." Maybe after finishing here she could get another copy from Pete and find Phuong. But who knew how long it would take to "process" her or where she would be taken after that?

Catherine reached to touch Phuong on the shoulder, and then, glancing at the cop, drew her hand back. "Listen, Phuong. The Pha we're trying to find lived near Hoi An, Vietnam, in a fishing village called Cua Dai. Do you know anyone like that?"

Phuong looked down and studied her hands. She was silent for almost a minute. Then, "If I tell you, can you help me get back to Vietnam?" Now she looked Catherine straight in the eye.

"I can't promise that, Phuong. But we could ask a group of people called Green Gecko if they can help. Their job is to help Vietnamese girls get home."

The policeman interrupted again. "Actually madam, that's why she's being processed. We're deporting her back to Vietnam tomorrow."

Why on earth hadn't they told Phuong that sooner, Catherine wondered, instead of letting her sit here stewing? "Did you hear that, Phuong? The police are sending you home tomorrow."

Phuong's face brightened. "I hope the policeman tells the truth. No one in this place cares about us." She sat quietly staring at her hands again. Then, "I think the girl you looking for works in front of 7-11, Geylang and Lorong 12."

Catherine wanted to hug her. She looked beseechingly toward the young policeman, who gave her the hint of a nod then faced the other way.

CHAPTER SEVEN — LIEN

Nights were the part I hated. I was in bed in my hotel room. 3:00 am, my bedside lamp burning. I couldn't be alone in the dark. That was when the flashbacks came, in the blackness of the night. I'd be transported back to the brothel and the horrible nights and days would all blur together. I tried reading a book on my iPhone, *Three Moons in Vietnam*, but I couldn't concentrate. In my mind's eye my ancestors scolded me from the long shadows in the room. I couldn't hear their voices, but they were there, taunting me. *Broken girl. Broken girl. Whore.*

I hadn't visited my hometown since my rescue in Cambodia, but in my mind I saw the judging looks on my villagers' faces. I heard their gossip about my story.

On my face I felt the hot foul breath of the men who had violated me, and I jumped when one of them touched me *down there*. I wanted to sleep. I needed to sleep. I thought we would find Pha tomorrow. I wanted to believe that if I could help other girls like me, my soul would be cleansed. But the mocking spirits haunted me like hungry ghosts and the presence of the men who raped me denied me the sanctuary of rest.

On trembling legs I rose from the bed and walked to the sofa, then I opened my diary and started writing, the words arriving slowly at first as I glanced fearfully around the shadows of the hotel room. Then my mind kicked into gear and I scribbled furiously, as though this would expunge the demons.

Everyone says that I'm doing so well. They say that after three years of rehab I am confident and poised. They say there is no fear in my eyes. They say I am well adjusted. But that is what people see on the outside, people who don't know me from before. On the inside, where no one visits except me, I'm still not okay.

In Vietnam, family members honor one another. Children are taught to honor their parents, their grandparents and their aunts and uncles. I have shamed my family. I have stained our honor and deeply injured my ancestors. Because of what happened in Svay Pak, I think I am đứa con bất hiếu — I lack filial piety.

I know my father loves me. He moved to Saigon to be near me when I was in the rehabilitation center. Every second day he wheeled himself through the city's clotted streets to visit me. But although he hugged me and called me Peach Blossom, he hardly looked me in the eye. I hung my head in shame but I could still see the sadness in his eyes. His daughter's innocence was stolen, and with it the family's honor.

One of Grandmother Quy's proverbs was, "If near light you will shine. If near ink you will be black." This is true for me now. During the day, and when I am around other people, I can breathe. But at night I drown in an ocean of loneliness. I long for a deep and caring relationship like other young women have. But I will never know intimate love. In the countryside of Vietnam a girl must preserve her purity until she marries. How can a decent man want me when I have serviced over a hundred men, and have dishonored my ancestors? Who would marry such a woman?

I lifted the pen and fingered the jade Buddha on a chain around my neck. I hoped it would protect me from my demons as they swirled about the room. I still felt their jabs and heard their barbs. *Whore. Whore. Whore.* They chanted faster and faster. Their voices echoed and the words went round and round in my head. They became louder and bounced around the room.

I screamed. Then silence. Utter silence. I rose from the bed, my heart wild, and dashed to the other side of the room to turn on the other two lamps, reducing the gloom, and with it the now muted phantoms.

I breathed deeply to calm my pounding heart. I concentrated on the breaths and counted the inhalations … one … two …three … four … five. … keep breathing … in … and out … in … and out … in …

I gave up on sleep. With the lights on, I focused on the tasks of the next day. I needed to be prepared. In the morning I would view videos from the 7-11. We would find Pha.

***

The taxi delivered me to a modern, warehouse-like building on Ubi Link Avenue, twelve blocks north of Geylang Road. The building appeared to be three or four floors tall, but it was hard to tell because there were few windows. Against walls of white concrete, or maybe white-painted cinder blocks, a narrow strip of grass grew between the façade and the sidewalk. I entered the glass front door into a small lobby with a tiled floor. On one of the light blue walls hung framed logos of the four commercial tenants: a self-storage facility, a wholesale jewelry company, a distributor of industrial pumps and a company called SSSL. My eyes fixed on the bright, red block letters of Singapore Security Systems Limited. The letters were 3-D and leaned to the right, with horizontal streaks on the left side, like the letters were racing toward the future, jet propelled.

A building directory on the opposite wall showed that SSSL resided on the fourth floor. I pressed an intercom button to the right of the panel and waited. My arrival had already been detected as I entered the lobby, where high on the wall directly in front of me, a small smoky-colored glass dome concealed a surveillance camera. I wouldn't have noticed a month before, but Bryan had taught me to be alert for clues.

Soon a cheerful male voice resounded from the intercom panel, "Step in the elevator, Miss Lien. It will bring you up to the fourth floor." Under the security camera, an elevator door opened. Conscious that I was still being watched, I stepped in and tried not to move a muscle.

The elevator rose without seeming to move. Before I knew it, the door opened again. A handsome young man in a white shirt and blue and red necktie greeted me, so different from those filthy men in Svay Pak. Good energy emanated from him and I felt safe.

He held the elevator door for me. "I'm Rick," he said. "Let's see if we can find an image of this person you're looking for."

I felt a strange twinge in my chest as he spoke. He was so good-looking and polite. All the same, when he swung his arm over to reach for the "close" button on the elevator, I flinched, over-defensive. *Just breathe and act normal,* I told myself.

We walked through a long, well-lit room housing a wall of monitors above a long desk with half a dozen swivel chairs. Four of them were occupied, two by young men and two by women. Air conditioning hummed through overhead vents. Two of the people turned and smiled at me as we passed their stations. Rick sat at the end of the desk and pulled a chair up next to him. "Have a seat, Lien. I'll call up footage from the 7-11 on Geylang over the past four evenings, and we'll look at images from 6:00 p.m. to 10:00 p.m. or so."

I took my seat, my head spinning from so much technology.

"Would you like tea or a bottle of water before we get started?"

"Yes, please," I said, aware now of a faint scent of man, strong yet pleasant, unlike the stench of the brothel men. A cool tingle crept across the back of my neck, but I swiped at it with my hand.

"Which?"

"Oh. Water, please."

We fast forwarded through the first night's footage. My black and white photo of Pha sat on the desk beneath the monitor screen. The screen moved fast, but the lighting in front of the store and the camera resolution were good and I could catch the details of people coming and going in jerky movements. The camera must have been across the street, because the storefront, sidewalk, curb and people on the sidewalk could all be seen.

I felt Rick's nearness, but I concentrated on the screen and tried to ignore the curious feeling. I spotted a few fleeting frames of a girl or woman in front of the store wiggling her bare leg at passers-by. "Rick, go back. Can you slow it down?"

He tapped his keyboard and the images rolled back and then slowed to real time. I leaned forward and peered at the screen, holding the photo just below the monitor. The girl was shorter than most of the other passers-by in the scene. Wearing a miniskirt, she lifted her right leg and jounced it up and down to entice drivers of motor vehicles. But it was not Pha. Pha would be taller, with much longer hair. Stifling a sigh of disappointment, I asked Rick to go back to fast forward.

***

Friday night was hot, as was usual in September, and rain pounded on the roof of our rental vehicle so violently I thought the drops might come right through like steel spikes. The smell was as if someone had just taken the lid off a pot of steamed rice. Bryan and I parked at the curb about two hundred meters from the 7-11 on Geylang Road, on the opposite side of the street. He left the engine running with the wipers set on intermittent. We could see the lights in the 7-11 for only a few seconds before they blurred into a red blot.

Bryan slumped behind the steering wheel on the right side. "It's almost six o'clock," he said. "I don't understand why we haven't seen her yet." Two hookers stood in front of the convenience store. "Are you sure that's not her?"

I glanced down at the picture in my hands. "I don't think so. But it's hard to tell. In my picture, she's not wearing any makeup. And her hair could be different now."

"What time did she show up in the videos you watched at SSSL?"

"Just after six — if it was really her I saw. The height and face looked right, but she would look different than in a school picture. She has a little scar on her cheek in the picture and I couldn't see that on the video screen. Again, makeup might cover it."

I watched two hookers across the street. They tried to act bold and sexy when young men approached, but I knew the fear and loathing in their hearts. My hands trembled. I wanted to get away from there. Why had I agreed to the stakeout?

Bryan turned to face me. "Are you okay?"

"I ... uh. Yes. No." I swiped my hand across my forehead. "I will be." I put my face in my hands and lowered my head until Bryan tapped my shoulder.

"Here, drink some water," he said gently. He held out his plastic bottle. "Shall we get out of here? I can take you home and come back tomorrow night by myself."

I took several deep breaths and reached for the water bottle. "No. I'll be all right. I just ... I don't know, it takes me back to Cambodia."

"I think I'd better take you back to your hotel."

"No. I'll be okay." The thought of being alone in the hotel room tonight was even worse than the reality of what was going on out the window. "Look!" Another girl had walked up to stand in front of the 7-11. "She looks like the girl I spotted in the video. I'm sure it's Pha." I sat forward, my mind clear and focused.

CHAPTER EIGHT — PHA

Pha teetered her way on stiletto heels to her usual spot in front of the 7-11, her cheap umbrella little protection against the rain splattering her bare shoulders, dimpled with cold. In her lime green halter top and tight shorts, she had too much skin exposed for this monsoon weather, but with luck she'd soon have a customer and could get out of the downpour. The last three evenings had been quiet, so Chester was not pleased that she had brought home only thirty dollars one night and fifty for each of the other two. It seemed busier tonight. Hopefully, they weren't just looky-loos, and two of the other regular girls weren't in sight. Maybe they were already turning their first tricks.

Two middle-aged Asian men, slightly tipsy, walked up and grinned. Maybe Japanese businessmen. Plenty of those in Singapore, and many found their way to the red light neighborhoods. They appeared dignified even while sheltered under outlandish golfers' umbrellas. Gentlemen, for a change. "Are you looking for a date?" she asked in English.

The shorter of the two, balding, wearing conservative dress slacks and a short leather jacket, bowed slightly, the umbrella ludicrously bobbing with him, and said, "I like take you to my hotel. We have a drink and dinner, get to know each other."

She glanced at the other one then back to leather jacket, "How about your friend? I don't like to go with two men."

"No. He's looking for his own girl to treat to dinner. You have a friend might want to meet him?"

The other one was taller and looked distinguished in a charcoal business suit and open- collared blue shirt. He also offered her a shallow bow as she looked him over, appraising his character with a practiced eye. "I think he can find his own friend. No problem. He's very handsome. Plenty girls here on this street."

"Yes. Thank you very much." Another bob of the head and neck. "My car is there." He pointed to a black limo idling across the street. "Take you to my hotel. Marina Bay Sands — very nice."

Pha glanced at Chester sitting astride his motorcycle, wearing a DOT safety helmet and a yellow rubberized foul-weather suit, a poor disguise. He stared straight at her, raised his index finger and twirled it, his signal for her to hurry up, close the deal and get to work!

She eyed the expensive gold watch. A generous tip from this gentleman, added to the stash in the electrical box, might be enough to get home to Vietnam. She looped her arm through his and turned toward the limousine.

CHAPTER NINE — LIEN

To see clearly through the downpour, Bryan put our car into gear and edged closer to where the girl stood. We watched her flirt with two Asian men carrying umbrellas. "Japanese businessmen," said Bryan. "They have that look. You'd think they'd use expensive call girls instead of coming to this district. Do you still think that's her?"

I peeked at the picture in my hand and then back at her. "I'm almost sure. Look, she's turning to go with that shorter man. Do we follow them?" My heart was beating fast now, blood pounding in my ears.

Bryan eased the car forward another fifty meters. He slid into a parking spot and we peered through the sheets of rain as Pha and the Japanese man crossed Geylang Road. Bryan said, "If we can approach her someplace where she's alone, and can persuade her to get in the car with us, we can explain that the police will repatriate her if she'll allow us to take her to them."

"But how do we get her alone?"

"Maybe her client is taking her to a hotel room and when they're finished she'll come out by herself."

I pictured her in a room with this businessman. I saw him peeling off her clothes, his beady eyes gleaming with hunger, eager hands pawing her. My mouth filled with the sour taste of bile. Involuntarily, I clenched my pelvic muscles as I pictured his hand probing her crotch. "Bryan, let's get her now," I said. "Don't let her go with him."

"I … Wait, look, they're getting into that limo. Damn. We'll lose her now."

"Can we follow them? Try to grab her when they get out? Maybe he'll be distracted."

"I'll try. But I need to keep my distance."

The limo drove east. Bryan kept it in sight while he hung back a few cars. We almost lost them at one traffic light, but Bryan said, "Hope there's no police around," and gunned through on the yellow light.

We were speeding to keep up with the limo and the road was slick with rain. Bryan swerved back and forth between lanes and other drivers honked at us as we crossed the Geylang River on a low bridge. Past the bridge the limo made a sharp left turn and we followed onto a broad boulevard, edged by wide sidewalks and palm trees bending wildly in the deluge. Down the center, a toupee of lawn divided the northbound and southbound lanes. We sped into a curve where the boulevard bent ninety degrees to the right. After five more minutes of this thrill ride, our vehicle now only one car behind the limo, Bryan slowed. "Looks like he's heading for Gardens by the Bay," said Bryan. "They might be going to the Marina Bay Sands Resort. A pricey joint. These Japanese businessmen have big expense accounts."

We slowed across another low bridge. "The famous Helix Bridge," said Bryan.

I'd never seen the Marina Bay Sands up close before and as it loomed before us, its three showy towers came into view, connected across their tops by the Skypark, a one-hectare roof terrace. The complex had a ghostly appearance, with the window lights in the three towers flickering like a thousand lanterns through the torrents of rain and gloom of the night.

The limo abruptly pulled into the portico of the Marina Bay Sands. "We're hooped," Bryan said. "We've lost them for now, and I can't stop here. Have to keep rolling on Bayfront Avenue."

CHAPTER TEN — PHA

Pha stepped from the Tower-1 elevator into the ostentatious lobby of the Marina Bay Sands, somewhat lightheaded after a fifty-four-story descent. Two nights in a deluxe suite of the five-billion-dollar, attention-grabbing hotel had been a heady experience for a girl from a poor Vietnamese village. But even a dip in the world's longest rooftop infinity pool, in a bikini purchased by her Japanese John from one of the hotel gift shops, followed by an alfresco gourmet breakfast, had not caused her to lose focus of her objective — get out of Singapore and get home to Cua Dai.

Now with seven American fifty-dollar bills tucked into her bra, that objective was easily within reach. She'd dutifully hand over two hundred dollars to Chester and keep the rest. Her nest egg had grown overnight to a more than adequate sum to get home, if only she could surmount the problem of getting travel documents. But perhaps with the surplus funds she could find someone in one of the dimly lit back streets of the Geylang district to produce a passable facsimile of a Vietnamese passport. She'd ask some of the more experienced girls about that.

Through the five-hundred-foot length of the glitzy lobby she strode, past the bars, restaurants and high-end retail shops, feeling every pair of eyes upon her provocative attire. A uniformed security guard fell in beside her and walked apace. "We must ask you to leave the hotel, Miss."

She cast a sidelong glance at him. "Where you think I'm going? Taxi stand over there." The staff was not nearly as vigilant two nights ago when her john had slipped the doormen, desk clerk and various lobby attendants wads of Singapore dollars as they made their way to the suite.

During the ride back to her flat in Geylang, she considered which of her meager possessions she would take with her and which she would leave behind, conducting a mental inventory as the cab inched westward through the morning

44

rush hour. She would have no further need for sexy clothing, so she'd take only her cosmetics and the clothes she had worn when she arrived from Vietnam several months ago.

It might take several days to locate someone who could supply the necessary travel document. Meanwhile she would have to continue working. Chester would accept no excuses for her not to be earning — not even illness or injury. She would miss several of the other girls when she left. Not that she had established close friendships with any of them, but the common anxiety and horror they shared had created a bond. "Misery loves company," she had heard several English-speaking girls say.

As she trudged up the last few steps to the fourth floor, she noticed that the door to her flat was ajar, and a chill gripped her heart. Chester. She inched the door open. He sat at the table smoking, an open bottle of beer at his elbow. "You were gone two nights. You must have done well."

Eyes wide with fear, she nodded but said nothing.

He snapped, "Let's have it."

The plastic switch plate rested on the table next to his pocket knife, with the screwdriver blade open. The two short screws lay at right angles to each other. The greenbacks that she had squirreled away in the electrical box lay folded in half under the base of his beer bottle, as though they were a coaster, wet with condensation.

Chester slammed his fist on the table, causing the bottle to jump, and then stood abruptly, fury wrinkling his face. He started for her.

"No, Chester, please," she shrieked.

He grabbed the neckline of her halter top and pulled her, screaming, toward him, ripping the top. He jabbed his hand into her cleavage and grabbed the wad of fifty-dollar bills. "So, bitch, you've been holding out on me." He drew his hand back, forming a fist.

"Please, Chester. I'm sorry. I'm sorry …"

His fist smashed into her cheek with a meaty thump and she crumpled to the floor. He lifted the beer bottle and scooped up the rest of the money, shoving it into his pocket along with the $350 from the previous two nights. With Pha on the floor sobbing, he poured the remnants of the beer on her face. As he strode toward the doorway, he said, "Don't even think about leaving this flat today. I'll be back tonight."

She remained on the floor, whimpering, as a metallic taste filled her mouth. When she coughed, a red mist spewed out. Tentatively, she explored her cheek where he had hit her. It was warm to the touch and already swelling. She pushed herself up off the floor and spit a glob of blood into her open hand.

Moving cautiously, leaning first on the table and then against the wall, she opened the half-size refrigerator and placed the entire tray of ice cubes against her throbbing cheek. She then made her way through the bedroom and into the bathroom, where she sat on the commode, supporting her weight against the toilet tank as she turned the shower handle. Typical in Asian houses, no curtain or shower enclosure hindered her movements. The shower jutted out of the wall and sprayed directly onto the tile floor, the water eventually snaking its way to a drain across the room. The overhead pipe creaked and groaned with effort as the water spurted out in a ragged pattern of starts and stops. She forced herself to her feet and stepped under the water, leaning against the wall as she peeled off her shorts and slid out of the shredded halter top. Her mouth filled and she spat another bead of blood onto the tile floor, watching as it dissolved into threads and coursed toward the drain.

Dizzy, Pha reached up to grip the horizontal shower pipe to steady herself, the long stretch sending another jolt of pain to her injured jaw. When she allowed the pipe to take her full weight, it protested with another groan, but held. She stood under the patchy spray another five minutes, alternating hands to support herself on the pipe.

Chester was on to her. He'd found what she thought was the only secure hiding place in the tiny apartment. Now he'd be even more vigilant and if she were caught again the physical punishment would be much worse than a swollen cheek. As nothing but a plaything for rough men with tobacco-stained teeth and whiskey breath, how much longer could she bear the humiliation?

Her life was a dark tunnel, hopeless. With that thought, she ended the shower and lay on her bed blubbering. The pain of knowing that her ticket to freedom had vaporized was greater than the pain in her jaw.

CHAPTER ELEVEN — LIEN

For the second night in a row, Bryan and I waited across from the 7-11 with no sign of Pha. Another girl struck a deal with a middle-aged Caucasian man as we watched, and as she teased him with a light stroke of his crotch, nausea and disgust ripped through me again. Maybe this wasn't the right job for me, with its daily reminders of my nightmare in the brothel at Svay Pak.

"I don't think she's going to show tonight," Bryan said.

"Do you think the Japanese man harmed her?'

"No. More likely it turned into a longer gig, or she made a lot of money and is taking the night off. Let's give it another hour. If she hasn't shown by then, I'll take you home and we'll try again tomorrow night."

I was not eager to return to my hotel room, where I knew terror would visit me. If I did manage to sleep, my dreams would be filled with the shame of my own defiled virginity. I would hear my family's taunts again. I would smell the spoor of lustful men. The previous night, I had dreamt of Nakry, the mama-san in the brothel; she had wielded an electric cattle prod, threatening to use it on my private parts if I didn't please the men she forced me to service. The thought of another night like that left me in a state of near panic.

As if sensing my distress, Bryan filled our time waiting with success stories about the many young women Green Gecko had rescued. Most had finished high school and some had gone to college. Many of them were productive workers he said — seamstresses, tailors, cooks and day care workers. A number of them had married and were raising families.

Then, after another hour without sighting Pha, Bryan said, "Listen, Lien. I've got another idea. Let's see if we can find out where Pha lives and pay a visit to her house. See if she's there. Get down onto the floor in the back seat."

Wary, but curious, I complied, and Bryan started the engine and drove a short distance forward. He stopped and I heard the whir of the window being lowered. "Hi there," he said.

A feminine voice said, "Hey." I could smell her musky perfume as she leaned in the window and made a kissing noise. "You looking for a date, honey?"

"Yeah, babe. Why don't you get in the car with me?"

"Where you take me?"

"To my house. It's in a very nice neighborhood near Orchard Road."

"Fifty dollars, honey," she purred.

"Okay. Hop in."

For half a minute, I heard neither of their voices, until the left side door opened and she slid in, her cloying scent now filling the car.

The door closed and Bryan said, "Here's your fifty in advance. What's your name?"

"I'm called Jasmine."

"Okay, Jasmine. Look, I really don't want to have sex with you, but you can keep the fifty if you'll show us where the girl named Pha lives."

"Who's us?"

"My partner and me. Don't worry, we're not the police. Show yourself, Lien."

I sat up and the hooker looked over her shoulder at me. "Oh, wow. This is a trip. Which Pha you look for? I know several Phas."

I said, "Pha who works in front of this 7-11. She's from a village called Cua Dai in Vietnam."

"I still don't know."

"Look, here's her picture." I showed her the grainy photo.

"Okay." Her eyes held a glint of recognition. "Make a U-turn, then drive to Lorong 18 and turn right."

After the turn onto Lorong 18, we stopped half way down the block. "There on the right. Fourth floor, third door." She pointed to a plain concrete-faced building of about six stories. Open-walled walkways ran the width of the building on each floor and the apartments, about eight per floor, each had a door and a single window facing the front. "I'll go up with you."

"Not necessary," Bryan said.

"I want to see what you're going to do to her."

"We're not doing anything to her. We just want to speak with her. Look, here's another thirty dollars for you, Jasmine. Off you go please."

She pouted but snatched the money and clattered up the street toward Geylang Road, hips swinging, a syrupy scent wafting in her wake.

The lights were burned out between two of the landings, so we treaded carefully in the murky stairwell. On the fourth floor, sweaty and a little out of breath, we knocked on the third door. No one answered. Bryan knocked again and shouted, "Pha, we're here to help you. We just want to talk to you."

Still no answer, so Bryan twisted the door handle and pushed. The door opened but stopped abruptly after a few inches, with a chain lock across the gap. Bryan put his face to the crack and shouted, "Pha? Pha? Are you okay? My name is Bryan. A Vietnamese girl named Lien is with me. We're here to help you."

I shouted in Vietnamese, "*Pha oi*, don't to be afraid. Your mother sent us to help you."

A shuffling noise came from the back of the flat, a thump and the scraping of furniture on the floor.

"Pha! Let us in. We want to help you."

"Maybe she's with a ... customer," I stuttered, feeling squeamish at the thought.

"I don't think those are the sounds of sex. I'm putting my shoulder to it." He smacked the door heavily with his right shoulder and upper arm. It would bruise later. The door didn't give, so he took a step back and flew at it again. This time the chain broke and he stumbled in. I followed him as he regained his footing and shouted again, "Pha!"

We looked hastily around the front room. The blinds were broken and sagging, the cord ripped out. The only furniture was a battered table and two chairs. Atop the table was a paring knife and an electric switch cover with its two screws lying nearby. The sink had a slowly dripping tap beneath which was a large rust spot. Orange peelings littered the counter top next to the sink.

Bryan lurched through the open doorway and into the back room. I followed into a room devoid of any furniture, save a rumpled bed and a cardboard chest. I spotted the open door into a bathroom.

"Oh my God."

Pha stood on a chair beneath the shower head, a thin cord tied tightly around her neck. The other end of the cord was tied to a couple of colored scarves, which in turn were tied around the shower pipe sticking out from the wall. A foot of slack remained in the cord, draped loosely on her chest. Pha stared straight ahead.

"God Almighty. No!" shouted Bryan as he pushed past me. He threw his arms around Pha's waist to hold her steady and prevent her from stepping off the chair. "Get her down. Go get that knife on the table. Cut the rope."

The knife was dull, so I dragged the blade back and forth over the blue scarf until finally the threads parted. Two more swipes and it was free. Bryan lifted Pha off the chair and stood her on the floor, still supporting her.

She blinked and moved her eyes from Bryan to me.

"*Em an toàn rồi. Bọn chị sẽ đưa em về Pha ạ.* You are safe," I said. "We're taking you home, Pha."

When she wept, I wept too.

***

I had been on an airplane only once before. Something about flying at ten thousand meters above the sea puts my mind and heart in a different space, almost like meditating, which I have done only a few times. Maybe it was the humming noise of the engines, I don't know, but I escaped my demons while up there. The thing was, I felt deeply relaxed without being asleep. Sleep was when ghosts found me.

Pha sat in the window seat next to me. She hadn't said anything since we left Singapore, and she hadn't looked out the window either. Occasionally she glanced at the flight attendants as they moved up and down the aisle, but mostly she just sat there, her downcast eyes shifting left and right. An hour into the flight, she spoke for the first time. "I couldn't wait to get out of my village and go to the big city. Now I just want to be back in the village of Cua Dai. Singapore was like a terrible dream." I patted her hand, "I know what you mean. Just a couple more hours and you'll be home. We've notified your mother that you're coming home today. You'll probably have a nice welcome at the Da Nang airport."

Grandmother Quy used to say, "A fish doesn't know that it swims in water." I didn't know what that meant until after my own experience in Cambodia. The fish is surrounded by water so does not know it until it is removed from the water, then it squirms and wiggles and flops and tries to get back into it.

I could not have known that life anywhere else was different than it was in my village of Tuy Phuoc until I was taken to Saigon and then to Cambodia.

50

Then I not only saw it, but also really felt it.

Now I wondered if I could continue to see these girls whose innocence had been stolen, whose virginity had been pilfered at a tender age by vile men. Could I help them when just seeing them on the street being pawed by animals made me feel dirty? By helping other girls would I be able to wash away my own defilement and shame?

I thought I must. I must do this to make my life mean something to *me*, if to no one else. I needed to rise above my self-pity and my self-loathing, and find my way back to the water. Without this work as a focus I could see no hope for my future.

I considered myself lucky to be working with Green Gecko. The Hoi An office had about twenty staff members, and several of the other young women were former trafficking victims who had also been forced into prostitution. We lived together in a house that Stewy had rented for us, just off Hai Ba Trung Street. We were like a support group, sisters trying to forget, to heal, and when I woke from nightmares, at least I wasn't alone. I understood that my sisters and I had been victims. We each needed to find the girl inside who had never left despite our torture.

I heard a chime and the captain announced our descent to Da Nang International Airport. I patted Pha's hand again.

She looked scared. She turned her head toward me and said, "I don't know what it will be like to be home. I feel ashamed. I have disgraced my mother and my aunties and uncles. I don't know if they will love me."

"I know Pha. I went through the same thing." I didn't tell her that I hadn't been home to Tuy Phuoc since my rehabilitation. My father lived in Saigon in his own apartment with a live-in caregiver and Grandmother Quy was in a care center in Saigon. I had no relatives in Tuy Phuoc anymore, so I had no reason to go back. And I didn't want to anyway. I couldn't face my former neighbors and schoolteachers. In rehab, the counselors always told me that I wasn't to blame for what happened to me and that I still have worth as a human being. But I really wondered about that. I still felt that I was broken, contaminated. If Pha was feeling these same things, she would not be comfortable in her village. She wouldn't want to show her face.

BOOK TWO

CHAPTER TWELVE — COLONEL KHLOT

Colonel Khlot gazed out the window at the carved prangs and stupas of the Royal Palace as it shimmered in afternoon sunlight, his eyes narrowed and chin resting in the junction of his thumb and forefinger. His uniform was crisp and neatly ironed; five broad gold stripes blazed across each of his epaulettes. The teak and marble appointments of his office reflected his privileged status in the Cambodian National Police.

He was fifty-five and would soon retire. It was time.

What would be left after his long, lucrative career had run its course?

He turned from the window and picked up a framed photo of his family. His home life, although comfortable, was less than scintillating. His two boys were now in university, leaving only him, his wife of thirty years and their fourteen-year-old, adopted daughter, Chaya, to ramble around the large, penthouse condo in Phnom Penh's trendy Tonle Bassac district. Although a handsome and stately woman who carried herself well, Kalliyan, his wife, bored him with her endless prattle about art and music. She had been a good woman and a loyal mate for three decades but the spark had drifted out of their sex life years before. He much preferred taking his pleasure from teen-aged girls in the brothels of Svay Pak, where the mama-sans accorded him special privileges for making his men look the other way.

What would he do to stay active and stimulated after retirement? Khlot replaced the picture and turned to admire his wall full of plaques and certificates. Golf at one of Cambodia's chic new golf clubs didn't appeal to him, nor did the prospect of playing cards over a long morning coffee klatch with other retired men. He could afford to travel. Maybe see some of the world beyond Southeast Asia. Australia? New Zealand? North America? Europe? But he didn't fancy traveling, or doing anything, for that matter, without indulging in the company of the opposite sex. And Kalliyan wouldn't be much fun. Nor did he think he'd like other women who traveled. He much preferred the company of naïve young women, or girls.

The phone on his desk rang. "Khlot here." He listened for a moment.

"When?" … "Is Internal Affairs on it?" … "Well damn it. Get them on it. And keep it out of the damned media." He hung up.

Imbeciles. Why, as a senior officer, did he have to spend eighty-five percent of his time on personnel issues? What had become of the good old days when police work meant doing police work — not wiping runny noses?

He gazed out the window again. Maybe there would be an opportunity for him to get in on the ground floor of Phnom Penh's burgeoning nightlife business. He had quite a pile of American dollars salted away, even a couple hundred thousand dollars worth of gold discretely stored in safe deposit boxes in Hong Kong and Singapore. Investing in a few of the clubs, bars or cafes that were springing up all over Phnom Penh might be a perfect way for him to stay busy, make some cash, and, more enticingly, stay close to nubile flesh.

His iPhone's jarring ring tone interrupted his thoughts, and recognizing his home phone number on the screen, he touched the answer icon. "Yes, what is it?" he said irritably.

Kalliyan spoke breathlessly, "Chaya's gone! I found a note!"

"Calm down. What do you mean she's gone? Gone where?"

"The note says she's gone to China with her boyfriend in his car."

"I didn't know she had a boyfriend."

"You don't pay enough attention to know. I'm worried. This boy is ten years older than Chaya."

"I'll alert the police at the border crossings into Laos and Thailand. Do you know what he was driving?"

"I saw his car once in front of our building. It's gray I think."

"Gray? That's not much to go on, Kalliyan," he said sharply. "What's her boyfriend's name?"

"Kosal. That's all I know. He's tall for a Khmer and has black hair."

"Well, that narrows it down to about nine hundred thousand young Cambodian men in their twenties."

He hung up and stared out the window again. Stupid girl, he thought. Her head was always full of boys and music and that damned phone. Spoiled brat.

She hadn't learned a thing about the real world in that pricey private school he spent his money on.

A gray car. Black hair. No help at all. He picked up the phone and pushed two buttons. "Captain, come in here."

An hour later, his conscience satisfied that he had taken the necessary action to find Chaya, he dialed the proprietor of the Pussycat Bar on Street 136. This woman owed him some huge favors.

CHAPTER THIRTEEN — PETE TRUTCH

A day after he and Catherine departed Singapore, Pete Trutch sat on a rattan settee, his sandaled feet on the bamboo coffee table at *Hai Cua*, an open-air, thatch-roofed bistro on An Bang Beach. The popular eatery and watering hole, cooled by the gentle trade winds off the South China Sea, was a favorite among Western expats living and working in Hoi An. During the daytime, young families parked themselves on the beachfront lounge chairs, the children playing at the edge of the surf under the watchful eyes of their parents. Evenings, the place morphed into a singles joint. Twenty and thirty-somethings came to drink, flirt, talk and smoke tobacco and weed.

Earlier, Lien had called, excited to tell him about Pha's rescue and that she would be bringing her back to Hoi An. Now Trutch could unwind. He and Catherine would relax for a month in Hoi An, known as a foodie haven. Catherine would do some serious yoga. Trutch would visit Green Gecko and familiarize himself with their work.

A twenty-two-year military career, followed by another successful career in business had shaped his values and attitudes into a decidedly conservative mold. But five years ago, as he sought to find Lien, he had become sensitized to the hardships of many Southeast Asia residents, and to the lack of social justice. It had surprised him to conclude that he had become more of a feeler, a humanist. When the search for Lien reached its successful conclusion, he liked himself better. And Catherine liked him better. He had even written a novel exposing the scourge of trafficking in Southeast Asia. Could it be there was another book in this?

A friendly male voice brought him back to the present. "Excuse me. Are you Lien's grandfather?" A young Buddhist monk in deep rust-colored robes hovered over him, his shaved head glistening.

Trutch bolted upright. "Yes. Is something wrong? Has something happened to her?"

"No. No. No. I'm so sorry," the monk said. "I didn't mean to alarm you. It's only that I knew Lien's grandfather had come to Hoi An. You looked like a possible fit."

Trutch blinked a couple of times at this monk with such perfect English. He glanced at his watch. "And how is it you speak English so well?"

The fresh-faced monk laughed. "I'm actually a Viet Kieu from San Diego. I'm trying this monk gig for a six-month trial. Hoping to buy some karma I guess. I come to the beach every day after morning meditation. My name is Paul Pham." He offered Trutch his right hand and smiled warmly.

"It doesn't sound like a terribly ascetic life."

"No. It's almost like a spiritual vacation." He waved a robed arm toward the beach. "I eat, sleep, meditate and attend classes in the pagoda. I have six hours free each day, so I try to get out and soak up as much of my ancestral culture as I can. And I try to come here to An Bang Beach about three mornings a week. The beach, the bikinis, the music, the rich coffee and beer — they remind me of home. San Diego, I mean. I can't indulge in any of those pleasures, other than to just watch, but they feel familiar."

Trutch, still suspicious, asked, "How do you know Lien? And me?"

"I do some work for Green Gecko. I met Lien there. She's a cute kid."

Trutch rankled at "cute kid" and stared. Who was this punk monk?

"My job is to keep my eyes and ears open. Mostly for information about the people who prey on poor girls in the outlying villages, then lure them to Singapore. There's no better cover than being a monk. I meet with Stewy Fitzsimmons regularly. He told me that Lien is in Singapore, and that you were here, staying in a villa in An Bang Beach."

Trutch felt a sense of déjà vu. The young man reminded him of Andrew Quang. Also a Viet Kieu, Andrew had been an Australian graduate student working temporarily in Vietnam. He had become Trutch's assistant and confidant in the initial stages of the search for Lien when she had been abducted. In a few short weeks, they had become a team, Andrew's youthful vigor and cultural awareness a complement to Trutch's experience in solving problems and making decisions.

Trutch motioned to a chair, still unsure of the monk's motives, but willing to feel him out a bit. "Do you have time for a coffee?"

"I'm not supposed to drink coffee, but I'll have a tea. Can you let me know when it's a quarter to ten? I need to be on time for a meeting."

Their drinks were served by a tall, slender man in his late thirties who spoke English with a French accent and appeared to be part Vietnamese. Paul introduced him as Alexandre, the owner of the bistro.

"Welcome to Hai Cua," Alexandre said. His handshake was firm, his smile genuine and warm. "How long will you be in Hoi An?"

"About a month, I think. My granddaughter works here." He purposely avoided saying where. "My wife and I are here to visit her as well as to get some Hoi An R&R."

"Excellent. You're welcome to hang out here all you'd like. Most of my expat patrons consider this their home away from home." He smiled again, and bowed slightly as he backed away.

"Nice guy," said Trutch.

"Yes. He's been here all his life. His mother is French and his father Vietnamese." Then he veered abruptly back to Lien. "When Lien has finished up in Singapore, do you know what her next assignment will be?"

Now even more wary, Trutch said only, "Don't know. Sounds like you may know more than I do."

"Ahh, I think you question my motive in asking, Mr. Trutch. I don't blame you. I ask because I worry about Lien a little. Green Gecko has a good record when it comes to rescuing kids who've been taken into China. More recently they've expanded their work to Singapore, where the market is mostly for brides, and Cambodia where the demand is for prostitutes."

Somewhat impatiently, Trutch said, "And something about this causes you concern for my granddaughter?"

"Typically, the traffickers aren't fazed when kids are rescued. They've already made their profit and are out of the picture. But over the past year, GG — Green Gecko — has expanded its mandate into prevention as well as rescue. This threatens the traffickers' supply chain. They don't like it. Reducing their supply of kids is like cutting off the cocaine supply to a drug dealer. So GG has had some threatening phone calls and Stewy Fitzsimmons found a dead pig at his doorstep recently."

"The dead pig was a warning of some kind from the traffickers?"

"That's what the police think."

"I'm not pleased to hear that." Trutch looked over his shoulder to Catherine's yoga group, all standing on one leg, arms over their heads, with the sole of the opposite foot rested against the thigh of the rigid leg. The tree pose, thought Trutch; they'll be finished soon. He looked back at Paul, "What specifically is GG doing in the prevention area?"

"They've developed educational materials, using pictures and graphics so that the message can be understood by the marginally literate, even illiterate people. GG has recruited about a hundred young Vietnamese volunteers to visit poor villages and rural communities. The volunteers use these materials to promote awareness of the trafficking threat and to show villagers how to identify potential traffickers. These young people, mostly university and college graduates, are socially conscious and zealous. They're targeting policemen, teachers and village officials as well as parents and relatives. Based on feedback from local police units, it seems to be making a difference. Of course, with limited resources they can't cover a lot of ground. They're focusing on Quang Nam province and the highlands villages west of Da Nang."

"Has any harm come to any of these volunteers?"

"No, but that's why I brought it up. I thought you should be aware of the situation. Stewy is concerned about the security of all of his staff. There's a uniformed security guard at the GG office and he's recently budgeted for nighttime security guards at the homes of his staff, including the group home where Lien stays."

Trutch glanced at Catherine finishing her yoga. "My wife and I are meeting with Stewy Fitzsimmons tomorrow morning. I appreciate the information." So much for relaxing on the beach, he thought.

CHAPTER FOURTEEN — COLONEL KHLOT

"Are you absolutely certain?"

"Yes, Colonel Khlot," a nervous voice croaked over the telephone line. "I've been telling you for four straight days, there have been no sightings of anyone resembling your daughter, in the company of a young man leaving our country through any of the crossings along the Lao or Thai borders. And it's the same story today. No sightings. I'm sorry. Have you tried calling her on her cell phone, Colonel?"

"You imbecile," Khlot snapped. "My wife and I have tried her every hour."

Khlot slammed the cordless phone down. He stared at the female police captain sitting rigidly in a rattan chair on the other side of his mammoth teak desk. "Any luck ID-ing this young Kosal stud?" he asked.

"Not really, sir." She glanced at the legal pad in her lap. "The R&I Department can find only three males with the name Kosal in our database. None is of the right age. Two of the three are in prison and the other has no known address, but he's over fifty anyway."

"And my brilliant wife who didn't even know what make of car he was driving?"

"Negative. She's been on the third floor all day looking at digital mug shots and hasn't recognized any of them. She's really quite distraught, sir. Maybe you should go down there and sit with her for a while."

Colonel Khlot massaged his temples with his fingertips. He tapped a cigarette from the package of Winstons, then offered the package to the captain.

"No thanks, Colonel. I don't smoke," she said with a shake of her head.

Khlot watched her luxuriant ponytail waggle then dropped his eyes to her pert breasts.

She stiffened in her chair and crossed her legs. The khaki material of her slacks clung enticingly, and no doubt had the opposite effect on him than she had intended.

He put the cigarette to his lips and snatched the sterling silver table lighter off his desk. He thumbed its spark wheel several times with no results. "Damn. Flint's gone." He threw the lighter across the room and crushed his unlit cigarette in the crystal ashtray. "Go find me a goddamn light from someone, will you?" He shook out another cigarette.

When she returned with a disposable lighter he was staring out the window. "I suppose it's possible they crossed into Vietnam instead of Laos or Thailand. I'd ruled that out. Vietnam is tough on human traffickers. I assumed this Kosal guy would head for China by way of Laos or Thailand because they're more lax."

"But Colonel, the note indicated she was going of her own free will. Is that illegal?"

"She's only fourteen, damn it. And he's taking her across an international frontier. That's trafficking!" His voice had risen to a roar, so he took a breath and lowered it. "Hell, they could have left the country by air. Have someone find out if any of the airlines checked them in. Get Chaya's picture and the best description possible of Kosal to them. And tell my wife to take a break from the mug shots and come up here."

Moments later Kalliyan entered the office looking apprehensive and weary. She slumped in the rattan chair. "I've been looking at pictures for five hours. No luck."

"I want you to go home now. I'll send a policeman with you. I know you've searched Chaya's room, but I want you and the policeman to really ransack it. Look at the underside of drawers, the underside of her study table, under the legs of her furniture, inside the light fixtures, inside folded clothing, everywhere. Search her bathroom too, even inside the toilet tank."

"What am I looking for?"

"Anything that might be a clue. Notes from this Kosal fellow, mementos of their dates, diary pages. And I know you've looked through her iPad for a picture of Kosal, but I want you to give it to the policeman to bring into the station. We'll have our technicians get into the hard drive to recover anything useful that may have been deleted."

Kalliyan's eyes were wet. "Do you think we'll find our baby?"

"I don't know. When you met this Kosal, how was he dressed? Did he look like he had money?"

"He was neatly dressed in slacks and a dress shirt. I suspect he has a good job."

"Did you notice any hint of a foreign accent? Another dialect?"

"No. He spoke perfect Khmer. Listen, one of your policemen on the third floor told me there's a group of people in Hoi An that rescue children abducted to China. They're called Green Gecko."

"Let's not get ahead of ourselves. Green Gecko wouldn't be of any help unless we know where Chaya is. Plenty of those do-good foundations exist in Southeast Asia. They beg money from churches and ask for government grants and donations from individuals. They're a nuisance to police departments, coming around with what they think is evidence and insisting that homes and businesses be raided."

"But I've been to their website. They've rescued dozens of children."

"I've been to their website too. They can't rescue a child unless they know where the child is. We don't even know for sure that she's in China, do we?"

"I guess not." Kalliyan's voice quaked. She bowed her head, the years of his dominance heavy on her sagging shoulders.

"Go home," he barked. "See if you can dig up a clue or two. Something useful for a change."

CHAPTER FIFTEEN — CHAYA

Five days is a long time to be cooped up in a small Russian-made car traveling on poorly maintained secondary roads. The eighteen-hundred-kilometer trip from Phnom Penh had been hot and dusty for the first half, wet, windy and winding for the second, largely mountainous, half. The northeast monsoon season was just getting cranked up and its early sputters smacked Northern Vietnam with intermittent thunderstorms and vicious windstorms. Now as they neared the small city of Mong Cai in Vietnam's extreme northeast corner, Chaya could hardly contain her excitement. This was the biggest adventure she'd had in her fourteen years. Five days and nights with the handsome Kosal had been a magical fairy tale. Too bad the pea-green Vaz 2101 had bucket seats in the front. She longed to slide to the left and snuggle against him. She reached across the space between them and playfully brushed back a lock of black hair that hung over his right eye.

"Careful," he admonished. "You don't want to distract the driver." He placed his right hand between her thighs and applied light pressure.

"But it's okay for you to distract the passenger?" She giggled.

"Of course. It's my duty to keep you entertained." He put his hand back on the wheel and expertly steered them through a series of S turns as the mountainous road gradually descended onto the coastal plain. "We'll be in Mong Cai in about twenty minutes. But I think we'll push on another ten kilometers to Tra Co Beach, a nice resort town. We can get a room in a four-star hotel. Then we'll come back into Mong Cai tomorrow to make the crossing into China."

Chaya hadn't minded the backpacker hotels they'd been staying in for the past five nights, but a night at the beach would be a treat. What a turn her life had taken in the past weeks. Although she found it easy do her assignments and get good grades, school bored her, as did her home life. Compared to most

Cambodian teenagers she lived a life of privilege. But most of the other kids her age were too simple, and her adoptive parents were … well, parents. She hardly saw her dad. He was too busy being Colonel Khlot, the supercop. And while her mother clearly adored her, all the fussing to make the house perfect for her dad, and all those starchy ladies' committee meetings for the arts drove her nuts. Kosal, twenty-four years old and worldly, had swept her from those monotonous realities.

She'd first noticed him in the gleaming new Starbucks on Sothearos Boulevard, in downtown Phnom Penh, where she and two classmates liked to stop after school. At first she'd felt conspicuous and foolish entering burdened with books, and in the brown plaid jumper of her school uniform. But the smiling, green-aproned baristas and servers welcomed her and her friends.

When Kosal introduced himself, the chrome and glass shop was teeming with young professionals, mostly business people and government workers, and all the seats were in use. Tall and slender, dressed in crisply pressed slacks and an open-collar shirt, he flashed a dazzling smile as he offered Chaya his seat. Probably a technology worker, she thought. She returned his smile and slid into the seat.

He complimented her on her hair as his sparkling eyes drank in the rest of her body. Within minutes their conversation flowed easily and she soon forgot about her two friends.

Within a week, he'd charmed her into bed, but carefully avoided penetration. Totally smitten, she trusted him completely. Confused, she had asked, "Don't you want to go all the way with me?"

"I want to save your purity for marriage."

"Do you want to marry me, Kosal?"

"Any man would be proud to have you as his bride."

Soon they would have even more adventures together, once they crossed the border into China, Kosal had promised. He had several days' worth of business in the city of Nanning, something to do with buying antiquities for resale to international customers on eBay, then they'd be off to Hong Kong and Macau, playgrounds, he said, for affluent citizens of the world. She'd have glamorous new clothing, stay in fancy hotels, eat in fine restaurants and see opulent gambling casinos, all at the side of handsome Kosal.

The Sao Bien Hotel in Tra Co Beach was, to Chaya, luxurious

accommodation, though Kosal complained that it was tired and outmoded. Their room was a garishly decorated mini-suite, the pièce de résistance a pair of luxuriant bath towels folded and twisted into the shape of two swans, their head and necks curled into a valentine heart, ensconced atop the vivid red bed runner. The top corners of the bedding had been turned down to reveal heart-shaped, foil-wrapped chocolates nested on the pillows. A silver bucket with a bottle of chilled champagne sat on a pedestal next to the window.

Chaya's eyes were wide. She didn't know what to say.

"Let's have a glass of that bubbly, then we'll order dinner in the room," said Kosal, oozing charm as he deftly lifted the bottle from its burrow of ice.

Chaya said, "I've never had champagne before."

"No problem. You'll love it. It's like the nectar of the gods." He eased up the edges of the stopper until it popped, launched upward and ricocheted off the ceiling.

"Oh my," she squealed, and took a tentative sip from the flute Kosal handed her, and then a large gulp.

By the time dinner arrived, a single filet of fish, richly garnished with cilantro, onions and greens and presented on a bed of rice, Chaya's limbs were loose. "I love you, Kosal," she slurred. "Can we get in bed right after dinner?"

"Of course. I love you too."

***

The city of Mong Cai, when they returned to it the next morning, was dusty, the buildings ramshackle and many of the streets potholed. When they saw the sign indicating that the Chinese border was one kilometer distant, Chaya tensed and gnawed on a fingernail.

Kosal said softly, "All our papers are in order, and I've been through this border crossing many times. It's quite easy." Two days earlier, they had stopped at the Chinese consulate in Hanoi and had obtained Chinese visas in their Cambodian passports. Kosal had paid an extra $30 U.S. for rush service.

"My father may have alerted the border police to watch for us. He will not have been happy when they found my note."

"That's why I chose a crossing point from Vietnam instead of Thailand or Laos. I doubt that the Vietnamese or the Chinese border police will be watching for you."

Chaya remained taut, with tension creasing her eyes as they drove through the Vietnamese checkpoint, with barely a glance from the guards, and onto the bridge across the Ka Long River. Her stomach felt leaden when they stopped, as instructed by signage on the Chinese end of the bridge, and a border guard stepped up to the driver's window of the Vaz.

After a short exchange in Chinese, Kosal handed over their passports, open to the picture page.

The man in the green uniform officiously leafed through the pages of her passport, found the Chinese visa, then continued thumbing through the document. When he looked up, she felt his stare bore right through her. She whimpered slightly when he directed a statement at her in a harsh, flinty monotone.

"He'd like you to remove your sunglasses," Kosal said.

The officer took a few seconds too long to compare her face to the picture on her passport. But Kosal slid his hand over the window ledge and surreptitiously placed an envelope into the official's palm. With a barely perceptible nod, the officer stepped back from the window, did a cursory walk around the entire car, then signaled Kosal to proceed.

As the vehicle pulled away from the crossing, Chaya sat back in her seat and expelled her breath. She glanced back to the border. Assured that no one was in pursuit of them, she said to Kosal, "I thought he was going to get me."

"He was concerned about your age and the fact that we're not related. Don't worry. I made it okay. They won't bother you."

Now Chaya recalled that Kosal had also shoved an envelope into the hand of the immigration officer in the Chinese embassy in Hanoi. "Can we get in trouble for that? The money?"

"Nah. We're safely inside China now. Don't worry. Just think of how much fun we'll have in Hong Kong and Macau."

***

Everything looked so green and clean as they left the expressway and drove into Nanning proper. "I didn't think there'd be so many parks and trees ... and tall buildings too." She turned her head left and right and hung out the passenger-side window to gaze up at the skyscrapers, topped with blue sky and cumulous clouds.

"Nanning's very prosperous, situated to send masses of goods into the markets of Vietnam, Laos and Cambodia." They crossed a graceful bridge over a wide, sluggish river then turned into a narrow street flanked by office buildings of modern architectural design and fashionable storefronts. "We're going to check into our hotel. It's another nice one. We'll have a short rest then go to dinner."

For dinner, they strolled through the Zhongsham Lu night market with its smorgasbord of vendors' stalls, each with hawkers shouting, steam tables and woks hissing and bubbling, rich, spicy aromas wafting about and mixing together. They found a table with two vacant stools and ate crispy noodles with barbecued duck and steamed bok choy. Kosal opened a plastic bottle of water for Chaya and popped the top of a chilled bottle of Tsing Tao beer for himself.

"I have to do business for about half a day tomorrow, but I'll have a big surprise for you in the afternoon," he said, as he belted down a swallow of beer.

"What surprise? Can you tell me now?"

"It wouldn't be a surprise if I told you now. You'll have to wait until tomorrow."

"You sound like my father, the colonel," she pouted. "I want you to be my boyfriend and someday my husband, not my father."

"You'll like the surprise if you can wait until tomorrow. I promise."

CHAPTER SIXTEEN — PETE TRUTCH

Located on Tran Hung Dao Street near Hoi An's post office, the Green Gecko office occupied a two-story building set back in a serene nest of Areca palms and bougainvillea, away from the chaotic traffic. Stewy Fitzsimmons showed Trutch and Catherine into an air-conditioned lounge furnished with rattan furniture, upholstered in floral patterned silk. Luscious green houseplants added a cool ambiance.

"I'd like you to meet Dr. Jacqueline Hartzog," Stewy said. "Jackie is a clinical psychologist with offices in both Brisbane and Da Nang. She's on contract with us. She does psychological assessments of the victims we bring here and of staff members. Then she follows up with counseling and therapy when needed."

A tall woman in her late fifties stood and offered her hand to both Trutch and Catherine. She wore a blue floral print dress, held in at her slender waist with a silver chain belt, and accented with a navy blue and white silk scarf. Her silver hair was short and stylish. "I'm pleased to meet both of you," she said. "I've had a chance to meet with Lien. She's a lovely girl. And she very much loves the two of you."

"Thank you," Trutch said. "It's a pleasure to meet you."

"We're looking forward to this discussion," Catherine said.

Stewy poured them each a cup of tea. "I know you'd like to talk about the threats that we've received at Green Gecko and I'll get to that in a few minutes. I take them very seriously, but first I'd like to talk about Lien, if you don't mind." He sat easily on the armchair with one leg casually crossed over the other, his Ivy League mien projecting cordiality.

Catherine spoke from where she and Trutch sat on a love seat. "We're concerned about Lien's vulnerability."

"There's nothing terribly worrisome," said Jacqueline. "Considering all she's been through, she's remarkably strong. But I have done an assessment, as we do with all of the staff and volunteers. I have the results here and Lien has given permission for you to see them." She handed Catherine a copy of a two-page document.

As Catherine scanned the first page, Trutch said, "Can you just tell us the highlights?"

"Okay. I asked Lien to respond to a couple of assessment instruments, questionnaires with either open-ended or fixed alternative responses, the Wechsler and the Beck Anxiety Inventory, or BAI. Are you familiar with either of those?"

"I believe the Wechsler is a form of IQ examination," Catherine said. "And the anxiety indicator must be just that."

"Yes. The full name of the former is the Wechsler Adult Intelligence Scale. Lien scored 37, which puts her in the 98th percentile. That translates to an IQ of between 132 and 135. She's of well above average intelligence."

"We assumed that," Trutch grumbled.

"Yes. Well her score on the BAI was 29. That number indicates moderate depressive or anxiety symptoms. Again, that's not surprising given all that she's been through."

Trutch agreed. The first time he'd seen Lien she had stood quaking, confused and distraught. Her eyes had that thousand-yard stare, the look of a soldier who's seen too much combat.

"But it says here," Catherine said, reading from the report, "that Lien described her mood as 'mostly good but subject to negative alternations including sadness, depression, anxiety and apprehension, particularly when alone at night or confronted with situations that remind her of trauma during and immediately after her confinement in sexual slavery. She suffers from sleep deprivation and has frequent flashbacks and nightmares.' Doesn't that mean she may have trouble doing the kind of work that Green Gecko has for her?"

"Not necessarily. It's complex. But my interviews do tend to reinforce the BAI results."

"Can we cut to the chase here?" Trutch asked. "Is she fit for this work or not?"

Jacqueline blinked at Trutch and then said evenly, "Well, let me give you my diagnostic impression. Lien's symptoms and behaviors are consistent with a DSM-V diagnosis of post-traumatic stress disorder …"

"Oh for God's sake," Trutch said. "Of course she has PTSD. It doesn't take a DS … whatever you said, to see that."

Catherine put her hand on his knee.

Trutch took a deep breath and addressed the psychologist in a more civil tone. "I'm sorry Jacqueline. Please forgive my impatience. Are you recommending she continue to work with Green Gecko or not? I mean she's already been hired and has already been on one rescue mission to Singapore where she acquitted herself very well."

As if to stem his questions, she raised her hand. "My report also states that Lien is convinced she will never have a normal loving relationship with a man because she's *damaged* and would be *unwanted*. She reports feelings of self-blame for what happened to her and guilt that she has dishonored her family. In order to recover she will need the help of a nurturing support group and you, Mr. and Mrs. Trutch, are part of it."

"But Jacqueline," Catherine started.

"Please, call me Jackie."

"Jackie, you seem to be evading our question. The report clearly says that Lien tries to avoid anything that reminds her of her own forced prostitution. Surely in working for Green Gecko she'll be embroiled in the pain and anguish of the other girls — so like her own experience. How can that be healing? And for that matter, how can Green Gecko be confident that her avoidance won't affect her performance? How will she hang in when the investigations get too … too graphic?"

"Those are good questions," Stewy said. "It's a gamble on both our parts, Green Gecko's and Lien's. But there are enough case histories, even published accounts like that of Somaly Mam …"

"Who?" Trutch said.

"She's a well known Cambodian trafficking victim-cum-crusader for anti-trafficking," Jacqueline clarified.

"The accounts suggest," Stewy said, "that if a former victim is strong enough, helping to rescue others is therapeutic. As they say, 'by helping others we help ourselves.' We believe Lien has that strength and determination." He divided his attention equally between them. "If she faltered, we'd pull her immediately from whatever case she's working on."

"You'll see in my conclusion," Jacqueline added, "that I believe conditional employment with the Green Gecko Children's Foundation would likely be beneficial. It would meet her expressed need to help other victims of sexual slavery. It would also give her focus." She glanced down at her report again. "During the interview her thought process was linear and organized. Her thought content was topical to questioning. There was no evidence of suicidal or homicidal ideation. She had good insight and judgment and was alert and oriented. In short her anxiety and depression does not consume her."

Lien had been poised and confident when she met Trutch for breakfast in Singapore, and she had competently participated in the rescue of Pha, so he weighed in. "I think she'll be strong enough to do this work."

"Actually Mr. Trutch," Jacqueline looked up from her notes, "I also believe that if structured carefully and monitored by a qualified mental health professional, the work may serve as a desensitization therapy. I'm recommending she continue counseling therapy with a qualified professional provider on a once-a-week basis. At this point, I don't think she needs any meds."

"Well, thank you for this, Dr. Hartzog. And Stewy, I'm glad you hired Lien. I agree that this is an opportunity for her to heal."

"I'm confident you won't give her any assignments that put her in harm's way," Catherine said.

***

After a quick break, Stewy introduced a Vietnamese woman who'd entered to offer them more tea. Young and barefooted, she wore jeans and a white tunic. She beamed at them over the ceramic pot.

"This is Mai," said Stewy. "She's my right arm around here."

"That's not that much of a compliment given that Stewy's left handed," Mai said with an engaging laugh.

Stewy chuckled. "She's one of the main ingredients in our recipe for success. She performs liaison with the police and with parents of victims and potential victims, supervises the volunteers, finds shelter and emotional support for rescued children. And ..." he smiled, "she serves as an interpreter when my marginally fluent Vietnamese fails me."

"That's an impressive resume," Catherine said.

"As though that's not enough, she's one of three staffers who go into China to rescue girls when we get leads as to where they are. She's fluent in Mandarin and Cantonese as well as Vietnamese."

"I grew up in Hanoi and went to university there," Mai said. "I joined Green Gecko when their office was still there. When they moved here, I couldn't resist the opportunity to follow. I've met your granddaughter, Mr. Trutch. I'm looking forward to working with her on a case."

"If I may ask, what motivated you to do this kind of work?" Catherine asked.

"My sister was trafficked to China to become a forced bride when she was seventeen — a student at Hanoi Open University. A boyfriend duped her into going to China with him for a 'vacation.' The boyfriend returned to Hanoi a week later. He claimed that my sister fell in love with a Chinese man while there and would not come back. That was three years ago. We don't know where she is or how to reach her. I came to work for GG with the notion that one day I would rescue my sister. I still hope for that."

Catherine resisted an urge to reach out to her. "Not knowing must be very difficult for your family, Mai."

"The pain never goes away. But my father says it's better to keep feeling the pain than to forget. And it makes me sad that even in and around this beautiful town, someone is persuading gullible girls to leave their villages to become brides. Most of them are wide-eyed with hope at the possibility. They don't have any idea that they'll be used up and then discarded. If they go to China, they have little chance of seeing their homes or families again. If they go to Singapore there's a faint hope that they'll get home, as in Pha's case. She was very lucky."

"It was lucky alright. Or maybe it was fate," Catherine offered. "As if I lost my purse to a mugger so I could end up in that police station. Predestined."

"That's the way we Vietnamese think," Mai said. "The Confucian influence. Maybe you've spent too much time in Vietnam, Catherine."

Stewy said to Mai, "I was just about to discuss with Mr. and Mrs. Trutch the threats we've received. I'd like you to stay for this conversation." Then to Trutch and Catherine, "As I said earlier, I won't play down the threats. It's a worry. But we're taking precautions. We have twenty-four-hour security here at the office and nighttime security at the group home where Lien is staying."

"Who do you think is behind the threats?" Trutch asked.

"Maybe traffickers or thugs who see our awareness education as a threat, or it could be just crackpots. Hoi An isn't known for violence or serious crime, so it's unusual, and the police aren't terribly concerned about it. Still, I take it seriously."

"I wouldn't think a city like Hoi An would be the epicenter of trafficking. I'd guess Saigon, Hanoi and the border cities would be more likely places for these predators to lurk," said Trutch.

"Actually, Saigon, Hanoi and the remote border regions have been the main source areas of trafficking victims. But about two years ago girls from this province started to be lured away, some to Cambodia to work in brothels, some to China and some to Singapore, as was the case that Lien just helped with. As I told you on the phone, we've dubbed the culprit the Pied Piper, although we don't know if it's a man, a woman or a syndicate. Most likely it's a small gang.

"Ahh. That explains the staffer in Singapore. From reviewing your website, Catherine and I had the impression that most of your rescue work was in China."

"It is. Girls from all over Vietnam, Cambodia and Laos are in high demand as brides in China. Many are lured across the border by boyfriends and others are outright kidnapped and smuggled through the frontier. The customer demographic is much different in China than it is in Singapore though. In Singapore it's well-off businessmen. The typical Chinese client is a poor rural farmer or laborer in a city who's probably taken out a loan to buy his bride."

"And the Chinese demand has something to do with China's one-child policy?" Catherine asked.

"Exactly. Rural China has a huge surplus of bachelors, owing to the one-child policy coupled with the strong preference for boy children. The attitude was, 'What good is a girl doing farm work?' Consequently the country is short of gender balance by 35 million females. Traffickers and matchmakers come to the rescue by providing brides to rural farmers for $5,000 or more, even as high as $10,000.

"Do you or the police have any suspicions about local predators?"

"No one. The local police aren't interested until a crime is committed, and duping a girl into leaving Hoi An willingly isn't necessarily a crime. Only if it can be demonstrated that the people who persuaded her received payment for their service, or if the girl is under eighteen. Usually the girl and whoever takes her away are both long gone before the parents report anything amiss."

Trutch took a sip of the hot tea. "Doesn't the Vietnamese National Police have a unit that specializes in anti-trafficking?"

"Department C-45, and they work closely with us when it's clear that *trafficking* has actually occurred. In the case of Pha — she's only the second girl that we know of who has returned from Singapore — we've asked them to get involved in her case. She's only seventeen and we believe that the perpetrators received money for duping her. Under the law, that's trafficking. One of their officers is coming down from Da Nang the day after tomorrow to interview Lien and Pha and her mom."

"We've noticed a lot of young people socializing in coffee shops. Is that where these young women meet this Pied Piper or his or her cronies?"

"The young folks who frequent the coffee shops tend to be urbane and educated. Most of the victims of the Pied Piper are poor, marginally educated and unsophisticated. They're not sitting around drinking a beverage that would cost them half of what their parents earn in a day. The Piper who's tweedling girls away probably finds them selling trinkets or lottery tickets on the street. That said, we don't know if the Piper is white, Asian, male or female, or all of the above."

A door chime rang. Mai excused herself and left the room. Moments later she returned with a brown plastic envelope, which she handed to Stewy. He opened it and withdrew a single sheet of foolscap. He handed it to Mai. "It's in Vietnamese. Help me with this, please."

The corners of her mouth tightened as she read. She glanced at Catherine and Pete, and then leveled a look at Stewy. When he gave a subtle nod, she said, "It says they'll firebomb one of your staffer's homes if you continue the education program in outlying villages."

CHAPTER SEVENTEEN — CHAYA

Kosal piloted the Vaz down a wide Nanning boulevard lined with palm trees. The four-lane divided roadway teemed with trucks, busses and passenger cars, with few of the motorbikes or tuk tuks that clotted the streets of Phnom Penh. The buildings rising just beyond the street-side palm trees were contemporary and stylish, glittering with glass and polished metal. Ahead, Chaya saw a familiar landmark looming — Colonel Harlan Sanders peered down from the red and white KFC sign in his signature white suit and string tie.

At a corner, Kosal made a quick right turn and the texture of the city changed abruptly. In an instant the glitzy and energetic district, hustling and bustling beneath a brilliant blue sky, was transformed into a drab and fatigued neighborhood, the narrow street dark in the shadows of tenement buildings on either side.

A five-story apartment building a block long was peppered randomly with graffiti and mold, blotting out all but a few defiant patches of the original yellow paint. Sagging balconies held a potpourri of household junk and were garnished with limply hanging laundry. Scrawny potted plants fought for scarce sunlight and fresh air. On the other side of the street, a row of dingy storefronts displayed various wares ranging from bicycle tires to used appliances. Among the shops, a musical instrument store and a coffin shop stood side by side; the latter exhibited its products in a variety of colors and materials through two wide-open bay doors. Chaya raised her window against the stench of garbage and rancid cooking oil. "What just happened to the city?"

"Ignore this mess. We're heading for a nice beauty parlor."

"A hair stylist?"

"Yep. And more. That's the surprise. Three Chinese lovelies are going to give you the pampering of your life. They take great pride in their work and in their salon. It's one of the nicest in this region of China."

"What kind of pampering?"

"Manicure, pedicure, a shampoo and a beautiful new hairstyle. You'll be even more stunning than you are already. I've asked them to start with a relaxing massage."

Chaya's feeling of optimism returned as she flirted with Kosal. "I've never had a massage. Will it feel as good as what you do to me with your hands?"

"Ha. It will be one of the most relaxing experiences of your life. I guarantee that you'll want to do this every week for the rest of your life. And in several hours, after they've finished with you, we'll go shopping to get you some new clothes for Hong Kong and Macau."

When they arrived at the salon a few minutes later, there was no street-side parking available, so Kosal stopped in the traffic lane, set the brake, and left the engine running. Chaya studied the storefront as Kosal opened the door for her. As shabby as any of the other narrow shops they had passed, this one was identifiable by a huge plywood sign just over the open doorway. The top two rows of signage were in unfathomable Chinese characters. The English subtext read *New China Beauty Salon No. 15.*

"Kosal?"

"Don't let the outside fool you. The inside is like a crystal palace. It's beautiful and luxurious." He took her hand. "Come on. I'll introduce you to Miss Wong."

He led her through the door and released her hand. As she absorbed her surroundings, Kosal left.

She stood just inside the doorway alone in the narrow room, about three, maybe five meters long. Overhead, fluorescent lights flickered and cast only desultory light. On one side, two plastic treatment chairs, both empty, forlornly faced the wall, which was dominated by a long mirror, smudgy and cracked. Beneath the mirror a ledge jutted out, home to dozens of tired bottles, spritzers, tubes, combs and a pair of blow dryers. Chipped porcelain sinks were set into the ledge behind each chair. On the other side of the room, a droopy love seat leaned against the wall, its orange and white vinyl upholstery cracked and faded.

When a woman in an ill-fitting red sheath appeared, Chaya asked in English, "Where's Kosal gone?"

The woman had a businesslike manner. "I'm Miss Wong. Come with me. Kosal will be back for you later." She led Chaya by the upper arm toward the rear of the room.

But Chaya planted her feet and resisted. "We should wait. He must be parking. He wouldn't just leave me here." She surveyed the room again with deliberate contempt.

Miss Wong raised her voice, as if using more volume would coerce Chaya into compliance. "He'll be back. Come with me now. We'll get you some tea."

Panic laced Chaya's quivering voice. "This is no beauty shop. I won't go with you. Let me go. I want Kosal here, now." She tugged violently and jerked her arm free of the woman's vice-like grip.

Miss Wong shouted something in Chinese over her shoulder and grabbed Chaya again, this time by the wrist. She twisted and pulled, shoving the girl onto the broken love seat.

A beaded curtain parted at the rear of the salon and a beefy man, sporting a Fu Manchu moustache took hold of Chaya by the shoulders, yanked her up and pushed her through the curtain into the back room.

Twisting and writhing, she screamed a stream of words in Khmer.

With the strength of an ox and a ferocious face, the brute pinioned Chaya to a straight chair while Miss Wong tied her arms to the rungs at the back with leather thongs.

Chaya kicked her feet straight out, connecting with the lout's crotch.

His eyes bulged as he let out a groan and bent over at the waist clutching his groin.

Legs still free, Chaya continued to kick and wriggle with superhuman strength, moving the chair around the room with scrapes and creaks while she yelled and cursed. The chair toppled over onto its side and she with it, her arms secured behind her back. Her thrashing feet made contact again, this time with a flimsy stand holding a cheap colored television, which crashed to the floor, its screen shattering. She felt a dead weight fall upon her legs as Miss Wong immobilized them with her own body.

Miss Wong shouted something at the still moaning lummox. In obvious pain, he moved to where the two of them lay, then took over the job of pinioning Chaya while Miss Wong retrieved another length of leather and thoroughly secured Chaya to the chair and righted it. Chaya's tantrum subsided into sobbing, until she slowly recovered her breath. "I'm supposed to have a massage and hair style. Kosal is taking me shopping this afternoon. Please phone his cell. This is wrong, but he'll fix it. I know he will."

Miss Wong held a smudgy glass in front of Chaya's lips. "This is hot tea. Drink this. You'll feel better. Then we'll talk. I'll explain everything."

Her energy expended, Chaya succumbed and allowed the woman to tip the glass to her lips. She took a swallow. Its warmth felt good on her raw throat, and in no time her head fell forward.

***

Gossamer light penetrated the darkness, and as ethereal consciousness crept over her, Chaya had no idea where she was or how she had got there. When she tried to stretch her cramped body, constraints prevented her. Attempting to call out, she emitted only a hoarse croak. She felt no pain, but a foul taste tickled the back of her throat, and her tongue felt fuzzy. She moved her fingers and then understood that they were behind her back.

She tried to concentrate, to remember why she was here — wherever *here* was. Something teased the back of her mind, but she lacked the energy to bring it to life, to give it clarity. An image of a filthy street flashed before her. She was in a moving car and Kosal was driving. How long had she been like this and where was Kosal? What had happened?

A bright light blinded her then. She closed her eyes and recoiled from it and from the stern female voice that accompanied it.

"Chaya wake up. Snap out of it. It's time to talk."

Ice cold water slapped her in the face with a rousing jolt. She flinched and yelped. The chair moved as hands shook her shoulders. That voice, it was familiar. She opened her eyes and recognized Miss Wong. Everything flooded back, cutting through the fog in her mind. This woman … and a big man with long strings of hair hanging off the corners of his mouth … they had tied her to the chair. What did they want? Where was Kosal?

"I'm going to untie your legs, Chaya. If you stay still and listen to me for a few minutes, maybe I'll untie your arms."

The chair under her felt wet, and she smelled urine. She'd peed herself. Mortified and desperately thirsty, she croaked, "How long have I been here?"

"You've been here for about fifteen hours. It's six o'clock in the morning."

Sobs rose in her chest again. "Where's Kosal? When will he come for me?"

"Listen to me carefully, Chaya. Kosal will not be coming back for you today. As soon as I untie your hands, I want you to drink some water and use the bathroom. It's right over there." She pointed to a door in the corner of the room.

Chaya glanced at the beaded curtain in the doorway. She saw no other exit from the room. "But when *will* Kosal come?"

"After you've cleaned yourself up a bit, you can change into clean underwear and clothes. Kosal left your suitcase for you. Then, we'll bring you some noodle soup. Later this morning, a few men will come to meet you. One of them will probably decide he wants to marry you and you will go off with him to his village."

"No!" she shouted. "I'm marrying Kosal. You can't do this. My dad's a police colonel. He'll get you."

"Kosal is not coming back. You are in China now. This is how …"

"Noooooo." A deep guttural noise rose from Chaya's belly. She shook her head back and forth. "No no no no no no."

"Alright, Chaya. I'm leaving you tied and you can sit in your puddle of piss until you calm down." Miss Wong strode to the curtain, pushed it aside and went into the front of the shop.

An hour later, Chaya was out of tears but still numb with shock. She felt a bout of diarrhea coming on. Barely able to find her voice, she directed it toward the curtain, "Please. I'm thirsty and I need a toilet. I'm stiff and sore. Please untie me."

Miss Wong brushed back through the curtain, followed by the lummox with the droopy moustache. She freed Chaya's bonds and marched her to the tiny bathroom in the corner and shoved her through the door. "Clean yourself up and throw your clothes in the trash bin under the sink. Then step back out here. I'll give you something fresh to wear. You'll find bottles of drinking water in there."

A few minutes later, clad in the single thin towel provided, Chaya stepped cautiously out of the bathroom. The ugly brute of a man still stood with Miss Wong. Instinctively, Chaya wrapped her arms tighter across her chest. Miss Wong thrust a bundle of clothing towards her crossed arms and allowed Chaya to flee back to the bathroom.

***

Dressed now in black silk trousers below a pink silk top with a mandarin collar and frog buttons, Chaya cowered in one of the plastic salon chairs while Miss Wong rounded out her appearance with lip gloss and eye makeup. She still half expected Kosal to return at any moment. Another part of her recognized that she had been duped, but she couldn't summon the spirit to fight. The big Fu Manchu sat on the love seat watching everything.

The door from the street opened just as Miss Wong finished with her, and Chaya turned with a start as two men and an older woman entered. One of the men looked like a peasant farmer, with a simple face and blue work shirt buttoned to the top. He wore a dirt-stained Mao cap and had wispy chin whiskers. The other man, although somewhat more sophisticated in khaki slacks and an open-collared white shirt, appeared menacing, with the swagger and cocky expression of some of the policemen who worked for her father. As she watched in the mirror from the salon chair, the cocky one spoke with Miss Wong in Chinese. Instinctively, the hairs on her arms bristled.

***

Highway G325, a two-lane ribbon of patchy and potholed asphalt, meandered aimlessly through the rugged country south of Nanning. Scattered houses and a few villages sat perched on land too inhospitable for rice farming but suitable for small family garden plots, a few scrawny chickens and freely wandering pigs. Scarcely aware of the landscape outside the rusty old car, Chaya sat numbly in the back seat, her mind already saturated with fear and sorrow. The driver, the man with the chin whiskers, had paid Miss Wong a lot of money, and then he had taken her gently by the arm and led her outside to the old grey coupe. She guessed that the female passenger in front, perhaps twenty years older than the driver, was possibly his mother.

When the vehicle made a turn onto a rutted dirt road and from there into a shabby village consisting mostly of mud dwellings with clay tile roofs, Chaya sensed that their destination was near and became more alert. A few buildings were constructed of concrete or cinder block, and many had been only partially completed. The car stopped in front of a shanty made of rattan panels with a corrugated tin roof. With the car doors opened, the stench reminded her of open sewage canals in the poor districts of Phnom Penh.

The man who had paid Miss Wong urged her out of the car and guided her by the elbow to the open doorway of the shack.

"Where am I? What's happening?" she asked in Khmer.

The man let loose an unintelligible torrent of Chinese.

Chaya tried English, "Where am I?"

Again, a tide of Mandarin.

Now villagers gathered to gawk at Chaya. Children in tattered shorts and unkempt hair giggled and pointed. One wizened old woman with a pipe clenched between her sparse teeth poked the driver and made some sort of lewd joke.

"Hong Li," the villagers called. "Hong Li."

Hong Li led Chaya through the opening that served as a doorway and into the hovel, with the older woman following. Truck tires rose in stacks everywhere, and the room smelled of burnt rubber. Tools and rusty equipment, likely having something to do with repairing or mounting tires, filled the rest of the space. A piece of plywood, serving as a table, rested atop two short stacks of metal tire rims, flanked by three red plastic stools. Gripping her elbow, Hong Li steered her to a platform bed behind a large smelly air compressor, among debris of tire chunks and tools. Gently, he sat her on the edge of the bed, and then busied himself pouring water from a large jug into a battered teakettle, which he placed on the one-burner gas cooker off in one corner.

Chaya twisted a knot of her pants fabric between agitated fingers as she looked around the room. Curious villagers, mostly children, surrounded the shack and stared in at her between the wall slats. She received an urgent call from her bladder and shouted her need to Hong Li in Khmer. When he didn't respond, she tried English, "*Toilet, toilet.*"

The older woman rose from where she sat smoking on a truck tire and beckoned for Chaya to follow. They threaded their way through the curious onlookers and started up a muddy path behind the tire shop. A tall square of concrete with a tin roof loomed ahead. The woman gestured toward the structure, "Toilet."

With no way to ignore the stench, Chaya squatted over the hole in the concrete floor. There was no toilet paper, only a pail of stagnant water with a plastic dipper. She stood and raised her pants, leaned her forehead against the outhouse wall and wept openly. Why had Kosal done this to her?

Outside, the woman had gone and Chaya swept her eyes aloft to the jagged terrain enveloping the hamlet. Low gray mist cloaked the surrounding hills, with tendrils reaching down into valleys, clawing their way up and over ridges. Higher up, angry black clouds blanketed the peaks. From somewhere behind her she heard a steady drone of highway traffic.

In the village, buildings were strewn about without any discernible pattern, like toys dumped from a box. A cone-shaped loudspeaker sat atop a weathered pole, and a few older cars and one or two ancient tractors sat parked in the village. Five lorries waited in a cluster around the tire shop, where a crowd of curious villagers still encircled the walls. Some spoke with Hong Li through gaps in the rattan panels.

A feeling of utter hopelessness washed over her as she realized she was lost and utterly alone. Now she thought not of Kosal but of her father, Colonel Khlot. Would he come for her?

CHAPTER EIGHTEEN — LIEN

On Tuesday morning, I accompanied Nga, from the anti-trafficking police, to gather information from Pha about the man or men who had lured her to Singapore to become a bride. Anticipating the visit, the previous night had been another episode of nightmares upon nightmares for me. I dreamt of the windowless sleeping room of the brothel. The body of one of the other girls was being carried out of the room in a rice sack. The rest of us keened and wailed, lamenting the loss of our friend, terrified that any one of us could be next.

Then someone shook me. "Wake up, Lien. Wake up." But I awoke to find myself still in the brothel bedroom, where the other girls had become demons, with piercing red eyes and wild hair, all of them pointing at me and laughing, taunting me about being broken. I cried so loudly that I woke for real, from a dream within a dream, bathed in sweat, clasping the tiny jade Buddha I wore around my neck.

This small gem, while it brought me good thoughts of my grandmother and our happy times in the village, sometimes also reminded me of those last terrifying hours before I was freed from my captors on the Cambodian-Thai border. Luong, one of the three men who had held me in a house in Poipet, had ripped a same-same image from around my neck and tossed it onto the dusty floor. "No cheap trinkets!" he had shouted. But how could an image of Lord Buddha be seen as a cheap trinket?

Now I touched its replacement, a gift from *Bà* Catherine, my step-grandmother, and swore to myself that I would do my job and maintain my composure, whatever emotions arose as Pha told her story.

The policewoman, Nga, had navigated our way to Pha's mother's house by motorbike through narrow, garbage-strewn lanes. The house had only two rooms, built of bricks and mortar, with a corrugated tin roof. The outdoor toilet sat dangerously close to the neighbors' fence, but everything in the house was immaculate, and we sat on the edge of the pallet bed in the main room. Her mother sat on a red plastic stool, with Pha standing awkwardly at her side, facing Nga.

Nga was about thirty with clear skin and high cheekbones, striking, with an aquiline nose, full lips and a waist-length ponytail. She wore a crisp uniform — a short-sleeved, shamrock-green shirt with red epaulettes and collar tabs, paired with trim slacks — and the buttons on her tunic were brass, like the nameplate over her right breast. She wore no other adornments. With a trace of a smile, she asked the first question, "You are Pha?"

Pha's eyes, wide with apprehension, also gleamed with admiration for the policewoman. "Yes," she said.

"I want to ask about what happened to you in Singapore." Nga spoke gently. "Did you go to Singapore to marry a wealthy businessman?"

"Yes."

"How old are you?"

"I'm seventeen."

"Did you go to Singapore of your own free will?"

Tears pooled in Pha's eyes. "I was fooled. They told me a rich man would love me and take care of me, but he was mean, and after one month he threw me away." She raised her voice, her fists clenched. "Like garbage. One year ago, when another girl from my village went to Singapore, she was so excited and happy before she left. Nobody heard from her for a whole year, so we thought she must be very happy in her new life."

"But you weren't forced to go to Singapore," Nga asked. "You went because you wanted to?"

Tears streamed down Pha's cheeks. "They said I would be happy in Singapore. But I wasn't. I brought shame on my family by selling my body. Those men lied to me. It's their fault."

Nga reached out and enfolded one of Pha's hands into both of her own. "Okay, Pha. Now tell me what men. How many were there?"

Pha wiped away her tears on her sleeve. "They were young. Different men talked to me at different times, three altogether."

"How did you meet these men?"

Pha's mother listened and watched, silently twisting a piece of tissue paper between her hands until it was in shreds.

"I was on the beach trying to sell postcards and sunglasses to tourists. The one with a little moustache walked up to me. He had a nice smile. He offered to buy me a tea. When I went with him to the coffee and tea vendor, he showed me a picture of an older man in a suit and tie. He said, this man is very rich and he is looking for a young Vietnamese wife."

"Was the man with the moustache Vietnamese?"

"Yes. But I had never seen him before, and he talked like someone from the north."

"Did the man with the moustache tell you his name, or the name of the businessman?"

Pha shook her head. Her tears faded and Nga released her hand. "He only told me to keep the picture and that another young man would be in touch to see if I wanted to go. In Singapore, my husband, the businessman, was named Wang. At least that's what he told me."

"What else did the man with the moustache say?" Nga looked toward me and made a gesture that I should take notes. I pulled a little notebook and a pencil from my bag.

"Nothing. Only that I should think about it. It would be an opportunity to improve my life. Then he left."

"Did he ever ask your name or where you live?"

"No, but two days later the second man came to me on the beach. He also sounded like he was from somewhere in the north. He just walked up and asked if I had thought about going to Singapore. I told him that I showed the picture of the businessman to two of my friends, and they both thought I should go, but I hadn't decided yet."

I asked, "Pha, do you know if any other girls from Cua Dai have been approached recently with this same suggestion?"

"Not recently."

"What else did the second man say to you," Nga asked. "Did he convince you to go?"

"He took me for tea to the same stand and showed me pictures of other Vietnamese girls who had gone to become brides. Some were dressed in their bride gowns, standing next to handsome men in suits. They were all smiling and looked very happy. One couple had a fancy car — a BMW I think. So I told him I would think about it some more. The pictures made me think it might be wonderful."

"And then?"

"The man said he'd come on Sunday with a car and driver, and that if I was ready, we'd go to the airport in Da Nang and he'd buy me a first-class ticket to Singapore. If I wanted to go, I should pack a light suitcase or backpack. I shouldn't bring much because I could have everything I needed once I got to Singapore." Now Pha began to weep again. "Oh yeah, he had a tattoo on the back of his hand."

"What was the tattoo of?"

"It holds a boat in place. I think you call it an anchor."

"Which hand was it on?"

"Um, I think his right hand. It was the hand he used to drink his tea."

"When did you decide to go, Pha?"

"I went home that night and told my mother about it."

Pha's mother looked into her lap and brushed the shreds of tissue onto the concrete floor.

"At first she didn't want me to do it. But when I told her I could probably send money home, she softened and said maybe I should go."

Pha's mother held her head high and defiant. She avoided eye contact.

"And so?" Nga asked.

"On Sunday I went to the tea stand with my backpack and the man was there with a car."

"You said there were three men involved but so far we've heard of only two."

"The third was the driver. He and the second man were standing by the car when I walked up to them. When they saw me they smiled at each other and bumped their fists together."

"So you got in the car and went to Da Nang International Airport?"

"Yes. It was a stupid mistake. I ruined my life and shamed my mother."

The mother's insolent expression dissolved. She turned and embraced her daughter.

"Do you have a passport? How did you get on the plane to Singapore?" asked Nga.

"When we changed planes in Ho Chi Minh another man came and handed me a passport. It had my name and my school picture. I don't know how he did that. I didn't have a passport."

"Can you describe the third man?"

"He was sort of tall. That's all I remember."

"Was he Vietnamese too?"

"Maybe partly Vietnamese and partly a Westerner. But he spoke Vietnamese."

"Is there anything else you remember about him?"

"Only that he was tall."

"Alright, Pha," Nga said. "We'll take a break. Then you can tell us what happened after you got to Singapore."

While the mother rose to put a kettle on the cooker, and Pha headed for the outhouse out back, Nga and I walked to the motorbike and drank water from plastic bottles. The tiny lane had become crowded with pedestrians and bicycles that had slowed or stopped to admire Nga's shiny police motorbike. Some of the neighbors clustered in their tiny yards to watch us.

When we continued after the break, Pha told Nga that she had been met at the Singapore airport by a woman of about thirty, named Chen, who took her in a limousine to a hotel called the Intercontinental, the tallest and nicest building Pha had ever seen. Their room had two bedrooms, one for each of them, and was so high that just looking out the window made her feel queasy.

"How long did you stay at the hotel, Pha?"

"Two nights. Our meals came to the room on a little cart with wheels, pushed by a man in a blue and red uniform. On the second day, a doctor came to the room ..." Pha looked down at her sandaled feet. "He came to check my ... to see if I was a ... I can't say it."

"Did he come to see if you were a virgin?" Nga asked.

"Yes." She told how the doctor had put his fingers inside her while Chen watched.

"The next day, after breakfast, the limousine came again and took us to a nice house, part of a row of skinny houses all hooked together on a curvy street. Inside the house, Chen introduced me to Wang, the man whose picture I had seen in Cua Dai. He was not as handsome as in the picture and he was a little bit short. Chen told me that I was now his wife. But I don't think we were really married. Later, on Geylang Road, a girl told me that to be married in Singapore you have to go to an office to sign papers, then wait fifteen days. Still, Wang made me go with him to a bedroom and he ... you know." She looked down at her feet again.

"Okay, I think we get the picture," Nga said. "I'm sorry you went through that, Pha. Tell us about your daily life in that house. Did you ever get out? To go to the market, or for walks?"

As Nga guided her through a series of further questions Pha described how she had been holed up in the house, cooking, cleaning and servicing Wang at his pleasure — a portrait of enslavement that I knew all too well. In sudden pain, I held back tears until I could take a deep breath and recover.

For a month Pha was unable to leave the house. Chen stayed to watch her, except when Wang came around, usually once a day for about two hours, and never at night. Pha said she found the house comfortable, and that she had enough food, but it soon became clear to her that she was no more than a piece of tender meat to Wang. After thirty-one days, Chen said, "You have to leave this house now. Wang doesn't want to be married to you anymore. Pack your things."

Terrified, Pha wandered aimlessly for several hours. Then a smiling young man on a motorbike offered to take her to a "shelter." That was Chester Lim, a pimp, and her story now turned to her life as a hooker on Geylang Road.

So many bad memories rose for me then, along with pain, fear, repulsion. I focused on my little Buddha to keep the tears inside.

***

As we rode back to Hoi An on Nga's police motorbike, I leaned forward and said over her shoulder. "That wasn't really very useful, was it? All we learned is that there were three men involved in luring her away and one might be a Vietnamese-speaking Caucasian."

She turned her head slightly to the right, moved her helmet-mounted microphone boom away from her mouth, and said, "It may be helpful, if my unit can piece this information together with some of the bits we've obtained from other villages."

She negotiated a tricky intersection where there was no traffic control, and then shouted over the traffic. "Pha is one of only two girls in this province who've returned from Singapore. There may be a network of several young men who make initial contacts with vulnerable girls. These men are probably recruited by a ringleader with clients in Singapore. We think this same gang is also selling girls to Cambodian pimps."

Nga skillfully drove the motorbike west on Tran Hung Dao, and turned right onto Hai Ba Trung Street. As she turned past the Yamaha motorbike dealer, I realized that something was horribly wrong.

The red and blue strobe lights of two fire trucks shimmered in the mid-morning humidity. Tangled canvas hoses crisscrossed the street, and at least five police motorbikes rested on their kickstands, blue lights flashing. The air was bitter, smoky. The stucco façade of the house I had left earlier was blackened around the door and a shattered front window. The door hung by a single hinge, the tiled stoop littered with debris. My roommates, five young girls in blue jeans and high heels, two in ao dais, stood in front of the house, staring. My GG coworkers.

CHAPTER NINETEEN — CHAYA

Chaya plodded uncertainly from the toilet back to the tire shop. An ancient woman clad in peasant pajamas stood in the front of the shop and met her. With a snaggle-toothed smile, the crone beckoned for Chaya to follow her down the side of the shack. Hong Li and his mother stood aside nodding and smiling encouragement for Chaya to follow the woman. Incapable of imagining an option, Chaya cautiously went along with the old woman. A boy followed them, lugging her suitcase, until the muddy path terminated at a small concrete house with a terra cotta-tiled roof.

The main living area of the dwelling was considerably more substantial than the tire shop. Near the table, a middle-aged woman and a girl of about twelve stood waiting. They smiled at Chaya as she entered. The girl spoke kindly in Chinese and took Chaya's hand. With gestures she invited Chaya to look around the house, and then led her through an inner doorway to a windowless bedroom. Overhead a single fluorescent tube illuminated the small room, which contained two platform beds separated by a red plastic stool between them.

Was she supposed to wait here until Hong Li came for her?

The boy placed Chaya's suitcase on one of the beds and left. The girl gabbled away in Chinese until Chaya realized that by pointing first at herself, then at Chaya and then at the two beds, the girl aimed to explain that they would sleep here.

"But why? Where is the man who will be my husband?" Chaya asked uselessly. More questions raced apprehensively through her mind. What did these people want of her?

The middle-aged woman appeared in the doorway. She spoke a single sentence and signaled that both Chaya and the girl should return to the main room and sit on stools at the table. There, with a few words augmented with gestures and body language, she made it known that her name was Ju and that the girl, her daughter, was Lan. The crone remained silent and poured tea for the three of them.

Ju left the table for a moment and returned with two worn and tattered magazines with missing covers. She turned pages rapidly, resuming her soliloquy while she looked for something. Soon, Lan joined in and the two of them jabbered excitedly while Ju continued turning pages.

Chaya felt as though they were all fowl in a mixed flock, the other two clucking like hens while she could only quack, their only communication through movement and eye contact.

At last Ju found what she was looking for. She pointed to a glossy but well-worn picture of a white bridal gown in one of the magazines, then pointed at Chaya. She twisted sideways on her stool, pointed through the open door and up the muddy path. "Hong Li," she said. "Hong Li." Then pointed back to the bridal gown picture and to Chaya.

The full meaning struck Chaya like a slap across the face. She jerked backward with an electric shock of repulsion, her skin suddenly on fire.

Lan now pointed to a picture in another magazine, of a wizened old Chinese man with a long wispy white beard, wearing a white robe covered with mystical symbols and Chinese characters. Ju nodded and leapt off the stool to stand before a large paper wall calendar. She pointed to the box and number signifying the next day, then with her opposite index finger indicated each of the three of them: herself, Lan and Chaya. Then she pointed to the picture of the wizened old man, then back to the calendar.

Did she mean that they would all go to see this strange wizard tomorrow? Would he come to them? It occurred to her that he might be a fortune-teller. She had read in one of her school textbooks that rural Chinese people could be superstitious. Or, could it be that he performed weddings and that she was meant to marry Hong Li tomorrow?

When the crone offered Chaya a tin plate of watery rice, accompanied by bits of chicken and stir-fried bok choy, Chaya stared dully at the plate. She ate a few pieces of bok choy and pushed the rest back and forth with her chopsticks.

After dinner, she crawled under the thin blanket on her pallet bed and wept silently as images of Kosal swam through her head. She had loved him so much. Why had he done this to her?

***

Chaya woke, disoriented, unaware of her whereabouts, to a choir of roosters proclaiming their sovereignty. From multiple directions, they squawked in surround sound. The windowless room allowed no other hint of light or time. Within seconds, her predicament crystallized. She wept silently.

From the other bed, Lan whispered a few syllables in Mandarin, unintelligible to Chaya.

"Huh?"

Lan repeated the utterance. It sounded like "*jai quich u an ga*" but was still meaningless to Chaya.

Stirring and low voices came from the main room as Ju and the crone moved about. Chaya squeezed her eyes shut and tried to wish herself somewhere else — with Kosal in his car, or home in Phnom Penh, safe in her bedroom. No good. The roosters continued to boast of their dominance. Soon the sounds of village activities penetrated the walls. Then kitchen noises drifted into the darkened room and cooking smells wafted under the door.

A moment later, the rattle of tinny, static-riddled martial music came from outside, no doubt from the pole-mounted loud speakers she'd noticed the day before. A woman's amplified, scratchy voice soon replaced the music, and Chaya instantly recognized it as the morning propaganda pitch, which Kosal had explained when they heard it in Nanning. There would be another one in the evening, each exhorting the villagers to do something — wake, work hard, remain true to Communist principles.

In the dark, Chaya slid her legs to the floor and sat on the edge of the bed. Less than a meter away Lan rustled her thin blanket, cleared her throat, and, from the sound of it, scratched at her head. Chaya groped for the light switch. Finding it near the end of her bed, she flicked it on.

Lan, also sitting on the edge of her bed, chirped a little "Oh," then smiled at Chaya while she dragged her fingernails through her long shaggy hair, vigorously scraping at her scalp.

Chaya felt the focus of determination. Today she would learn where she was and what plans these people had for her. She'd search her mind for a solution. She came from a family of achievers, educated people. She may be only fourteen, but she was not stupid. Surely she could find a way out of this mess.

Her captors were poorly educated village peasants. She would find a way to thwart them. Everyone had mobile phones these days, even these peasants — if she could find one, she would call Kosal. Or her dad.

But Kosal didn't love her. He had tricked her, sold her for his own gain. This now seemed so obvious. Her father would be angry with her, but if she could tell him where she was, somehow he would rescue her.

The door from the main room opened and Ju appeared, beckoning for Chaya and Lan to come out of the bedroom. A new woman, someone Chaya had not seen before, sat on one of the plastic stools at the table. Dressed in jeans and a fashionable white tunic, she wore plastic-rimmed glasses and looked young and bright.

In her borrowed peasant pajamas, hair askew and her face still puckered from a semi-sleepless night, Chaya set her expression into a blank meant to hide her embarrassment.

"Hello, Chaya," the woman said in heavily accented English. "I am Biyu. I am a teacher in this village. I think you speak some English. I too have learned to speak some English. So I'm here to help translate for you."

"Oh … Yes. I'm learning … *was* learning English in school in Phnom Penh."

"Good. We have some tea. Then you get cleaned up. Put on some clothes from your suitcase and we talk."

After a breakfast of hot tea, boiled quail eggs and rice porridge, Lan handed Chaya a threadbare towel, a rough cake of homemade soap and a half-full hotel amenity bottle of shampoo. She led her to an outdoor shower behind a two-sided wall of corrugated fiberglass near the concrete backhouse.

To Chaya's surprise, the water was warmish, apparently heated by the same system of hot water pipes that provided scant heat for the inside of the house. After nearly two days without bathing, the shower lifted her spirits instantly, and lathering her hair with the shampoo felt like a rare luxury. She toweled off and dressed in a pair of jeans, Teva sandals and the same pink top with frog buttons that Miss Wong had dressed her in.

When she returned to the middle room, the four women — Ju, Lan, Biyu and Chaya — sat around the table drinking tea poured by the older woman. Biyu said, "Chaya, today we see the fortune teller. He will tell Hong Li and you when is best day for marry."

The corners of Chaya's mouth tightened. Without revealing any further emotion, she asked, "Where are we?"

"We are in Ju's house. After you are married you will move to Hong Li's house."

"Where is his house?"

"But you've been there. It's in his tire shop."

Chaya grimaced. "That's a horrible house. But, I meant what is this village?"

"Here in the village we call it Xing Xiang Tun. But, drink tea now. We must go to the fortune-teller and not be late."

Shing Sheang Ton, Chaya repeated to herself, Shing Sheang Ton, Shing Sheang Ton. She must remember that.

***

Chaya, Ju, Lan, Biyu and the crone walked down the path from the house to the main hard-packed dirt road that ran through the center of the village and connected it on both ends to the highway slightly uphill. They walked in the direction of drifting fog and mists.

Biyu pointed out several important highlights to Chaya. "Village chief's house." She indicated a mud and stucco structure only slightly larger, and perhaps a bit tidier, than the other houses in the village. The flag of China hung limply from a soffit, its red background and cluster of one large and four smaller gold stars soiled with dust and grime. "But he's not really the village boss. Party secretary has more power. He lives up the hill in a bigger house."

She waved her arm toward the largest building in the hamlet, constructed largely of wood but with brick and cinder block facades here and there. "Here is the village meeting house. You and Hong Li get married here."

Chaya cringed. Not if she could make a phone call to her dad, she thought. Once again, she silently repeated the name of the village she would tell him: *Shing Sheang Ton.*

Near the market, they passed the communal well where several women awaited their turn to draw water. All of them turned their heads to watch the procession and two or three laughed and shouted jocular comments to the group traipsing along the road. Ju and Lan waved and reciprocated with gibes of their own.

Biyu continued her monologue and pointed out the ancestor worship hall and the one house that also served as the only retail store in the village, selling cigarettes, soap, grain, sugar and cooking oil.

Chaya only half listened to Biyu's discourse as she took in all the details of the village. She wasn't certain exactly what she was looking for, anything that might give her a clue as to precisely where she was, or anyone who could help her in some way. In those houses that had television, the sets were on and running even when no one watched them.

As they carefully threaded their way through a portion of the road where corn had been spread, apparently to dry, Biyu pointed. "This is fortune teller's house just ahead."

The building looked pretty much like any other house along this main road. It shared walls with the houses on either side, had a stucco front with one door, which stood open, and one window. The ancient terra cotta-tiled roof extended out a couple of feet over the roadway. Two woven baskets containing corn rested near the doorway. A hen sat on the rim of one of the baskets, pecking at the cobs. This part of the village didn't smell as badly as the area around Hong Li's hovel and tire shop.

Ju put one foot in the door and chirped a greeting. A wrinkled old man with wispy white chin whiskers immediately appeared and beckoned the party of women inside. While he was not the same man as in the magazine picture, he bore some resemblance to him. He wore a loose-fitting black pullover shirt and a woolen toque. A pair of small, wire-rimmed glasses were perched on the bridge of his ample nose.

Inside, a red silk runner adorned a heavy rectangular wooden table that dominated the front room, an assortment of yellowed, dog-eared almanacs and gazetteers spread across its top. Astrological charts and posters covered the wall behind the table.

Hong Li sat in a dark corner behind the table. He wore grease-stained khaki work pants and a similarly filthy blue shirt, torn in several places. Instinctively, Chaya's nose wrinkled at his repugnant body odor.

The wizard took his seat at the back of the table, in the center, and left the five women standing. When he gestured for Chaya to come forward and stand opposite him, she advanced cautiously and cast furtive glances toward Hong Li.

Through a gap in his front teeth, the old man lisped several words and Biyu immediately translated.

"He wants to see the palm of your hand."

With painstaking attention to detail, he examined her palm, turning it this way and that, tracing lines with his index finger and probing with the eraser end of a stubby pencil. Finally, he raised his head and uttered a few more words, looking directly into Chaya's eyes. "Your birthday?" asked Biyu.

"Twenty-two January, 2002."

He leafed furiously through one of his almanacs, pages falling first to the right, then to the left and then to the right again until he slowed and stopped with a grunt of satisfaction. His index finger ran down the page, stopped, then moved horizontally to the left. He muttered something to himself then turned over his shoulder and asked something of Hong Li. He received a six-syllable response.

He again rustled vigorously through the pages of the big book, stopping at last near the back cover. He raised his head, removed his spectacles and rubbed his temples for several seconds, apparently deep in thought. He then opened a drawer, withdrew a calendar and placed his index finger against one of the cells. No elaboration was necessary.

Hong Li stared at the calendar for a second or two, then he stood and let out a little whoop. He pirouetted two or three times, his body odor wafting across the room.

Biyu placed her hand on Chaya's elbow. "Best time for marriage to Hong Li is in four days. Thirteenth day of tenth lunar month, year of dragon."

CHAPTER TWENTY — LIEN

My grandparents and I sat at one of the bamboo tables at Hai Cua waiting to order breakfast. This was the first meal we'd had together since they had arrived in Hoi An. The beachside bistro was less than half a kilometer from my grandparents' villa, and at seven in the morning we were the only people there. The night watchman, who sleeps there, had just left and a young village woman who worked mornings was warming up the cookers. My grandfather had ordered the English breakfast: fried eggs, bacon, baked beans and a buttered *bánh mỳ* — a short baguette, a legacy of the French who once colonized my country. Catherine just wanted hot tea and a baguette. I asked the young woman for *mỳ quảng* — a thick noodle soup popular in this part of Vietnam.

The sea was choppy and frothy, the morning windy and grey. Huge grey clouds swirled and skipped across the sky, with no line separating it from the sea. The before-work crowds of local bathers, who arrived in a swarm of motorbikes most mornings, were not around.

Catherine said, "This is exciting. I rather like storm watching from here. At least it's not bone chilling like Seattle would be." Then she asked me, "Lien, do you think you'd like to visit us in Seattle next summer? I think you'd love the Northwest in summertime. Maybe your father could come too."

My grandfather said, "Great idea. We'd love for you to visit us there. I'll talk to your dad about coming too."

"I don't know," I said. "If I can get away from work at GG, I would like to go, but I think it's difficult for my Dad to go on such a long airplane trip with his wheelchair."

"I think he might be fairly comfortable if we booked him into business class."

Catherine said, "But, Pete. It's twenty hours of flying in two segments. The longest leg from either Hong Kong or Taipei to Seattle is about eleven hours long. What about ... uh, toilet needs?"

"The airlines must have a way of accommodating special-needs passengers in this day and age. Let's investigate it."

I wondered if they only wanted to move my mind from the worries of the moment, but *Bà* Catherine's eyes danced and *Ông* Pete looked excited. They were sincere.

The night before, I had stayed on a camp cot at their rental villa in the village of An Bang. Although no one had been hurt in the fire and Stewy had already arranged for carpenters to repair the door and replace the window, the group home off Hai Ba Trung Street was still too smelly from smoke for anyone to sleep there.

But even safe with my grandparents, I hadn't slept at all. All night I kept seeing the front of the house with its broken door and window and all the blinking lights of the fire trucks and police motorbikes. Stewy had said that the black scorch marks would probably never scrub off, but *Bà* Catherine had held my hand and said that maybe the imagery of the bomb would replace my preoccupation with Svay Pak. That could be good.

My grandfather, *Ông* Pete, was not so calm about it. He said *he* had tossed and turned, fighting off nightmares, all evening. I knew he really worried about me. But I knew too that if I wanted to work for Green Gecko, he would support my decision.

Chó sủa là chó không cắn. This was another of the things Grandma Quy said. It means, "barking dogs seldom bite." This was how I chose to think of the firebombing of our house. The dog barked, but he didn't bite — this time.

Still, how could we know what the dog would do next time? Nga, from the anti-trafficking police unit in Da Nang, told me that this was a warning to Stewy from the traffickers. They wanted him to stop the education program in the poor villages. Nga planned to return to Hoi An later in the day to meet with Stewy and the local Hoi An police. I would be working in the office, so I hoped that I would learn what they wanted to do.

I didn't think Stewy would stop the visits and the training sessions. He had over a hundred trained and dedicated young volunteers out delivering information about suspicious behavior to teachers, local police and parents in the hamlets. The firebombing showed that this was doing some good. The traffickers were scared. So I pushed it all from my mind as much as possible and savored this occasion to be with Grandfather and *Bà* Catherine, whose company I enjoyed so much.

Then the young woman showed up at our table with the food for *Bà* Catherine and *Ông* Pete. "I'll be right back with your *my quang*," she told me in Vietnamese.

Soon after she returned, I heard a thump, and several bare light bulbs, suspended from the timbers supporting the thatched roof, went out.

"It's okay, we have a generator," the young woman shouted from the kitchen area. "I call Alexandre. He come, start generator."

It didn't make any difference to me. We had our food, cooked with propane. Yes it was a little dark, but why did we need lights when it was morning? I must have been thinking like a simple village girl because my grandfather said, "Yes. Please do. I want to use your WiFi to check email and news services."

Moments later Alexandre, the bistro owner, came buzzing up on his motorbike. As he climbed off his bike and lowered the kickstand, a black puppy came running out from the kitchen area, wiggling all over, his little pink tongue hanging out. He stood on his hind legs and tried to reach up to Alexandre.

The puppy looked so cute, I got up from the table to pet him. The young woman, seeing the huge grin on my face, smiled and said, "His name Lucky. He's lucky because he lives here at the bistro and the dog men can't get him to sell for lunch."

Then, just as I reached Lucky and Alexandre, Alexandre removed his helmet and I saw his face. Something like an icy fist squeezed my heart. I gasped and dashed back to Grandfather and Catherine, where I fell heavily into my chair.

"What was it, Lien?" Catherine asked. She placed her hand on top of mine.

I couldn't respond. Alexandre looked like one of the men who had come to have sex with me several times in the brothel. As though I had been socked in the gut, I lost my breath and for a moment was unable to inhale.

But when Alexandre spoke to the young woman, I realized he had a French accent, definitely not the voice of my tormenter. It wasn't him. Still, my trembling didn't stop. The shock wave that had washed over me would vibrate for some time. I lost my appetite for the *my quang* and pushed the bowl away.

Grandfather and *Bà* Catherine were both looking at me wide-eyed with concern, questions written all over their faces.

"It's okay," I said, finding my voice. "I thought he was someone I knew from before, but it's not him."

Catherine peered at me for a second and then her features softened. "I think we understand, dear. Shall we all leave and go back to the villa?"

Huge breakers thudded and thumped onto the beach behind us. "No. Finish your breakfast," I said. "I'll be okay." But inside, I thought that I would probably never be okay.

***

Tran Hung Dao Street was Hoi An's busiest roadway. As I walked toward GG's office, it seemed especially hectic. Heavy trucks and buses took up most of the room on the two-lane road, most of them blowing their loud horns. Cars and motorbikes competed for the rest of the space. At intersections, even the ones with traffic lights, everyone seemed to make up their own rules. The rough and broken sidewalks were almost as difficult to travel as the street. Many of the storefronts, cafés and coffee shops used some of the sidewalk space for displays or seating and walkers had to step into the crowded street to get around parked motorbikes. As one motorbike plowed through a puddle in the street it splashed me with muddy water. I felt grateful to be wearing jeans and not one of my pretty *ao dais*.

Near the elementary school, just two doors away from Green Gecko, traffic stopped me for several minutes as hundreds of motorbikes parked or moved in close quarters on both the road and the sidewalk. Children, all wearing identical white shirts with red scarves and blue trousers, sat behind their parents on the motorbikes, ready to hop off and troop into the school just before the 7:30 starting bell.

When I at last opened the gate at the Green Gecko office and walked across the small tiled courtyard, crowded with bougainvillea and small potted palms, Mai pulled the door handle open abruptly from the inside, yanking me into the entry. She greeted me, "Lien, come upstairs to the small rear office. I want you to meet someone."

Up the wooden staircase with its polished railings, we entered the back office and were greeted by a tall young man with a thick nest of curly black hair and black plastic-rimmed glasses. I hesitated at the doorway, afraid as always when I encountered a man I didn't know. He wasn't rough like the men in the brothel, but still my heart stuttered.

"This is Tam," Mai said. "He's the main man who goes into China to rescue trafficked children. He speaks both Vietnamese and Mandarin."

Tam took a step toward me and offered his hand. When he smiled, he had a mouth full of dental braces, making him look a little weird. My pulse slowed then. At some level, my mind must have decided that he was not a threat. I took the offered hand and stepped into the room.

We all took seats on the mismatched furniture that Stewy had found in second-hand stores, and Mai spoke again. "Lien, I asked you to meet with us because I know you want to go into China on rescue trips. Actually, I'm hoping that Tam and I can discourage you, as it can be dangerous, but I want you to have a chance to ask questions about it. Tam has been in about seven times and I've been on one rescue trip with him."

"Oh," I said. "I don't know what to ask. I guess I'd like to know how it usually works and why it's dangerous. And also, who are the victims usually?"

"Okay, let's start with the last question," Tam said. "Victims taken into China can come from anywhere in Asia. But here in Vietnam, they're mostly girls, and a few boys too, who live in poor villages and whose parents are not well educated. Ethnic minorities from villages close to the Chinese border are most vulnerable. Many tribal girls from the Sapa region become victims."

"Why Sapa when so many other villages are close to the border too?"

"In the Hmong culture, when a young man chooses who he wants to marry, he sometimes simply kidnaps her with the help of several of his friends. Because that happens so often, traffickers like Sapa. It's easier for them to grab a girl and take her across the border. But girls have been trafficked into China from bigger cities and towns too. Often a relative or boyfriend will fool an educated girl from a successful family into thinking she is being taken on a vacation to China. In fact, she will be sold to a brothel or as a bride."

"Can you tell me about the danger?"

"Of course," Tam said. "Once a victim has been sold to either a brothel or a husband, that new person thinks of him or herself as an 'owner' and doesn't want to lose what he now considers his property. Those individuals will resist and fight the rescuer. Even when the rescuer succeeds in getting the victim away, they must still get back across the border to Vietnam. The Chinese who bought the victim, whether it's a brothel or a village farmer, will have people looking for the rescuers. They'll want the victim back, even if that means using force. Often they'll contact the traffickers themselves to report that the young person has escaped. The traffickers are extremely motivated toward recapture. They're desperate people who will use force."

"But they've already collected their money. What do they care if the girl gets away?"

"The traffickers know that if she makes it back to her home country, they can be identified. If they can be identified, they can be caught. If they can be caught, they can go to jail for a very long time. When the traffickers deliver children to China, they're counting on those children never returning to their home country. They assume the victims will die in China, usually from AIDS in the case of those who go to brothels. It's a brutal business and they're evil people."

I heard myself saying, "I want to go on one of the rescue trips."

"I don't think it's a good idea," Tam said. "You're not ready yet."

"But I really want to. This is one of the reasons I joined Green Gecko."

As Tam shook his head vigorously, Mai said, "Lien, it could be too dangerous."

"Then I'll talk to Stewy," I said. "I need to go." I knew it was the only way I could repair my broken soul.

CHAPTER TWENTY-ONE — CHAYA

Over a breakfast of rice porridge on the thirteenth day of the tenth lunar month, Tuesday the eighth of November, 2016, Biyu told Chaya, "This morning a woman comes to dress your hair in the style of a bride and do your face makeup. Then we put you in red jacket, skirt and red shoes for the wedding. Hong Li and other men from the village will come to take you for marriage today."

Chaya looked into her untouched bowl of porridge and gagged. For four days she had had diarrhea and could scarcely eat or drink. Now, with the prospect of a forced marriage merely hours away, waves of nausea rolled over her. She rose from the table, and brought her hands to her mouth in an attempt to staunch the thin stream of escaping vomit. Dizzy and weak, she rushed out the door to the backhouse, her fingers still laced over her mouth. Just short of the outhouse she fell to her knees and retched.

She felt herself being guided up by the elbows. "It will be okay," Biyu said, in a soothing and mellifluous voice. "Come back inside and have some nice ginseng tea. We will clean you up before the hair lady comes."

Inside, Biyu continued to speak to Chaya in calm, reassuring tones as she gave her sips of tea. "The wedding ceremony is very simple and you will be beautiful. Everyone in the village will admire you. They will offer you much love and wish for you to have happiness."

The old crone then entered the room, no longer attired in peasant pajamas but dressed in a royal blue silk robe. She took up a position near the table and gave instructions to Ju and Lan.

"She is the good luck lady today and must supervise the bride preparations," Biyu explained.

Ju and Lan approached Chaya and, while Biyu continued to console her, they gently peeled off her pajamas and sponged her body with a warm solution of water infused with pomelo and essential oils.

The sponge bath and tea began to have their effect. Chaya felt mellow. The occasional tear still leaked down her cheek, but now they were tears of tranquil resignation, not panic. "Will I have to sleep with Hong Li after the ceremony?" she asked with a muted voice.

"That's what happens after a wedding, Chaya. But other women from the village will be with you. They will help you feel okay."

"I'm a pure girl. I want to save my honor for the man I want to marry."

"You will be married today, Chaya. So it's okay to lose your purity. Hong Li is a good man. Everyone in the village respects him."

"But I don't love Hong Li. I can't love him. And he smells like a pig. I can't let him touch me."

"He will bathe this morning. He will be clean, and he will smell good. Other village women will treat his body with oils. His mother and sister will make his bed with fresh clean linens. His whole house will be clean and filled with flowers."

Chaya sobbed and leaned her face into both hands. "I want to go home."

The makeup woman arrived, a grandmotherly type neatly attired in a black and gold housedress. A string of fake pearls and a pair of wire-rimmed spectacles subtly accented her pleasant face.

Chaya wept quietly, submissive as the woman applied pancake makeup and contoured her eyes. At the end of the session the woman piled her hair neatly on top of her head in several overlapping waves and topped them with a large bun-shaped hairpiece. Several ornate, sequined combs at the back held everything in place. The pièce de résistance was a classical Chinese wedding headdress, a coronet of gold filigree resembling a cluster of fifteen delicate flowers each with a brilliant red glass bead in the center. Six long gold tassels with red beads on the ends hung down on each side, framing her face like curtains. Finally, nearly two hours after she had begun, the woman applied lip gloss to Chaya's lips in the same shade of brilliant red as the beads on the tiara.

Then, under the old crone's intense supervision, Ju and Lan dressed her in a red skirt and a waist-length red silk jacket with a Mandarin collar and embroidered with gold thread. The jacket was a size or two too large and had a few telltale frays that suggested this wasn't the first time it had been worn, but Ju deftly took a couple of tucks at the rear and secured them on the inside with safety pins. She stood back to admire her work, "Aah." Finally, they slipped her feet into a pair of red pumps. The old good luck lady uttered something in Chinese. Biyu translated, "Red is a lucky color. You have lucky marriage."

Chaya sniffed sharply. Not so lucky, she thought.

Minutes later, firecrackers snapped outside, and the tinny notes and percussion of a small band moved toward the house. "This is the ceremony coming for you," Biyu said. "Come, we will wait in front."

With Biyu and Ju supporting her by the elbows, Chaya minced through the room and out the front door, her face a map of self-restraint and reticence. She allowed herself to look in the direction of the blaring music.

At the front of the procession a rank of four young women, clad in red pantsuits with yellow sashes, each used a cloth-covered mallet to beat a small conga drum suspended horizontally from her shoulders. Following them two ranks of young men, similarly attired, played a variety of wind instruments — trombones, trumpets, a sousaphone and a clarinet. Immediately behind them Hong Li, flanked by two other men, marched stiffly, looking awkward in a worn blue suit, white shirt and red tie. A crowd of men, women and children, all gleefully laughing and chattering, brought up the rear.

Chaya fiddled with the buttons of her jacket as she watched them approach.

The procession stopped about three meters from the front of the house and the music abruptly ceased. Hong Li, wearing an idiotic grin, stepped with the two men around the musicians and approached Chaya and her attendants.

"We walk with them now to the chief's house," said Biyu. She and Ju, still supporting Chaya's elbows, nudged her forward until she stood next to Hong Li, then released their holds. Hong Li clasped her upper arm and propelled her smoothly away from the house, toward the road. The crowd of villagers parted to allow room for the wedding party — Hong Li, Chaya and the four attendants — to pass through. The procession moved toward the center of the village with the wedding party in the lead, followed by the band, which had resumed playing, and, finally, the congregation of burghers.

Chaya allowed herself to be led along. With no good fix on where she was — only a name, Shing Sheang Ton — and no means of communicating with her parents, or anyone else who could help her, what option did she have?

The procession made a brief stop at the village chief's house, where Chaya and Hong Li signed the marriage papers — Hong Li enthusiastically, Chaya reticent but compliant. It's only paper, she thought. It doesn't mean anything.

But once they arrived at the village meeting hall, the inside of the wooden building now lavishly decorated with red and white tablecloths and colorful flowers on every table, the full impact of her situation hit her squarely. She stumbled, and Hong Li gripped her upper arm more tightly as they entered. At the head of the large room, a garishly decorated dais held mammoth sound amplifiers, and a young male emcee in a white suit and red tie stood in the middle of the platform. As Hong Li and Chaya entered, he initiated long applause, punctuated by whistles and whoops as the attendees stood to greet them.

The ritual was simple. Hong Li and Chaya stood on the dais bowing to the applauding audience while the master of ceremonies, doubling as a DJ, manipulated knobs and buttons that resulted in a deafening rendition of celebratory music blasting forth from the outsized amplifiers. Simultaneously, a phalanx of awkward teenagers, wearing the garb of waiters, delivered trays of food to the tables — boiled chicken, barbecued pork, heaping bowls of steamed rice, green and yellow vegetables. At the same time, a pyrotechnic display of silver, gold and red sparklers and Roman candles erupted over them. Hong Li grinned as Chaya flinched in response, and the crowd let out a roar of approval.

Then the tone of the roaring changed, and screams erupted as flames shot toward the ceiling. The pyrotechnics had ignited the bunting.

CHAPTER TWENTY-TWO — LIEN

It had begun to rain and I immediately regretted wearing an *ao dai* for my coffee date with *Bà* Catherine. Foolish decision, made out of nervousness because I didn't know why she had asked me out alone.

"Just you and me," she had said over the phone. "Girls only."

I wondered why she didn't want Grandfather Pete to come with us. They had spent time with Stewy and I suspected that they had been talking about me. I worried all the time about what they thought of me — what everybody thought of me. Half the time I didn't know what to think of myself — a country girl living in the city, educated in an international school, speaking English, wearing western clothes, yet carrying around painful memories of my life as a child prostitute. It was hard to feel clean and worthy. I could talk to Catherine about this more easily than I could talk to my Grandmother Quy, who I worried might be judging me for being a prostitute.

So, I had taken special care to dress nicely for my date — maybe if I dressed like a traditional pure Vietnamese girl in my best white *ao dai* I would feel like a "good girl" and Catherine would think the same. I even put on a little lipstick and brushed my hair one hundred times like *Bà* Quy had taught me. But by the time I had walked the three blocks to the coffee shop on Hai Ba Trung, the bottoms of my trousers were soaked from the puddles and splashes from passing motorbikes. I cringed, tarnished again.

Catherine was already seated in the coffee shop, her wavy red-grey hair perfectly done and with that big smile on her face. She rose and kissed both of my cheeks as she always did.

"*Xin chao,*" she said. "*Em khoẻ không?* How is my Vietnamese coming along? I'm so happy to see you. Thanks for coming."

I giggled at Catherine's incorrect usage. "*Bà* Catherine, as a grandmother you should call me *con* not *em*. I'm fine, but a little embarrassed. Look at the dirt on my trousers. Is that the right word, 'trousers'? In English you always have so many words for the same thing!"

"Yes, trousers, slacks, pants, even pantaloons," Catherine said, laughing. "You look lovely and no one will notice a few spots of water. Pop your feet under the table until you dry off."

Americans always look so relaxed to me, Australians too. I sometimes have trouble figuring out when they are joking, a real joke, and when they are making light of a more serious topic to put their companions at ease. I wanted to understand this woman who had become my grandmother. I wanted to understand Stewy, as well. Sometimes I almost made myself sick worrying about how to be what I thought they wanted me to be. "Self-loathing." That was a term that our counselors used at the rehab centre, to help us describe the disgust we felt about ourselves.

I smiled back at Catherine through my nervousness. A Westerner would have made a joke back, but I only managed a quiet, "So nice to see you. Thank you for asking me out for a coffee." I felt like a child, like a kid at school who wanted the teacher to praise my work and choose me to be her favorite. The more savvy girls in my house would be telling me to "get a grip."

"Shall we order? I would like a *café sữa đá*. Now did I say that right? Will I get sweet coffee on ice?"

I assured Catherine that yes, she would get iced coffee with condensed milk, and I ordered the same. I wanted to blurt out that I was agitated and curious as to what this meeting was all about, but I couldn't.

Catherine graciously began to talk. "I'm so glad that we're having this chat, Lien. Ever since Singapore, our meeting with Stewy, and the fire at your group home, Pete and I have been concerned for your welfare. Not only for your safety, but also about whether you're strong enough emotionally to do this work that you've set out to do."

Trời ơi. I wondered too. Could I really be of service to other girls when I was so far from being whole myself? I remained silent.

"I understand that working to prevent trafficking and to rescue and rehabilitate girls could be very restorative for you, but you've chosen something difficult." She paused. "I've become so fond of you. You're like a real granddaughter to me."

Catherine touched my hand and I felt the tears coming. Something deep within me remembered that I used to trust people, that some people are kind, but could I really tell her about my ghosts, my nightmares, my "self-loathing" without causing her to yank me from the program? How could she understand my agony, my shame and how hopeless I felt?

Nevertheless, I began to talk, hesitantly at first and then, in a torrent of words that all came pouring out. I told Catherine about my nightmares. I told her about the ghosts that visit me. I even told her about the fear I felt whenever a man stood too close or looked at me with desire or lust or simply just looked at me. I told her how dirty I felt. I told her how fearful I was that I would never be "normal" again, that no one, especially a good man, would be able to love me.

Catherine had been stroking my arm while I spoke. She looked at me with love and with tears in her eyes. Briefly I wondered if anyone in the restaurant was staring at me, a Vietnamese girl, weeping over my coffee, while a white woman comforted me.

"Oh sweetie, I knew that you were still suffering, but I had no idea how deeply wounded you still are. I'm almost at a loss for words. Nothing in my life has prepared me for hearing such anguish. But I do know how it feels to be betrayed, to lose faith, to wonder about one's own worth. I too have been deeply hurt, but my pain was so small compared to what you've just told me."

The way she held my eyes the whole time, I thought of the nun at the temple where I had felt safe, really safe from the clutches of my captors. Catherine was not a Buddhist, but she had the same aura.

"I'm afraid that I will never be whole," I blubbered.

"The human spirit is resilient, Lien. Like a flower, it just needs tending and nourishment, a little love and attention and it becomes whole again."

"I think I know that. My Grandmother Quy used to say, 'You must endure the darkness before you see the light.' But I wonder if I will ever see the light again."

"You know, just talking about it is a good start. When you're able to tell your story and be heard with empathy, when you know that you're accepted without judgment, you'll learn not to judge yourself so harshly. Now, how can I help? Pete and I will stand behind you all the way. I hope you know that."

I could hardly breathe. I had said the unthinkable to a woman whose love I cherished and would never want to lose. I worried that when she went home to think about what I had told her, she would think less of me. And yet, here she was holding my hand, unflinching. I looked into her hazel eyes and thought, here is an older woman whose beauty will not dissolve.

CHAPTER TWENTY-THREE — CHAYA

The screams of terror escalated as the pyrotechnic flames raced up the bunting and began to devour roof timbers with a roar. Chairs fell as they were knocked over, tables collapsed, waiters dropped their trays of food and scrambled toward the doorways. The DJ dropped his microphone and pushed Chaya aside to leap off the dais and scramble toward the rear exit. What had been a cheering but well-behaved crowd was now a frenzied mob of people scrambling and clawing their way toward the exits. Chaya felt the heat, heard the crackling and bolted from the platform to plunge into the stampede toward the doors, leaving Hong Li standing with a vacant expression on his face.

As Chaya rushed from the platform onto the chaotic floor of the hall, burning debris rained down from the ceiling in suitcase-size chunks. Fire shot across the beams and dry shingles in a furious rush of orange tongues and thunderous cracking. One woman's dress was afire, and she shrieked and pulled at her clothing.

"Drop to the floor!" Chaya screamed at the woman, but the fiery figure could not understand her and twirled in terror until she collapsed in flames. Horrified, Chaya ran through the pandemonium toward a side door, where she spotted a mobile phone on the floor. Instinctively, she bent to retrieve it but was knocked flat by the surging press of fleeing people. When she attempted to rise she was bumped onto her belly by another wave until a woman dressed in purple grabbed Chaya by the arm and half-pulled, half-lifted her to her feet, then disappeared into the mob.

Now choking on smoke, her carefully coifed hair a nest of strings and snarls, Chaya found her way to one of the side exits and stepped into the hazy air clutching the phone. The village's sole piece of fire-fighting equipment, a pickup truck laden with hoses and pumps, had just arrived, and its crew of volunteer fire fighters, some still in their party attire, frantically attempted to organize their apparatus.

Chaya coughed raggedly once or twice, then stumbled for several steps to escape the searing heat now at her back. She broke into a trot for another thirty yards before her coughing overcame her again. She collapsed onto the stoop of the village's retail store to clear her throat and lungs as screaming, terrorized villagers raced past her.

With sudden clarity, she looked at the possible instrument of freedom she held and tucked it into the waistband of her skirt. She wiped her runny nose with the sleeve of her tunic and then draped the hem of her smoke-smudged jacket over the phone.

"Chaya. Are you all right?" Biyu approached, her brows furrowed. "Are you hurt? Where is Hong Li, do you know?"

"I'm okay. I left Hong Li in the fire."

"I don't know if everyone got out," Biyu said. "This is terrible. Terrible for our village." She sat next to Chaya on the stoop and draped her arm around her. "Are you sure you're okay? You look sick."

"I'm just shook … shook up. But I will be better soon because now I don't have to marry Hong Li today."

"But Chaya, you're married already. That's what happened when you signed papers at the chief's house."

"No way," she blurted. But a second later said, "Then I'm glad if Hong Li burns up in the fire. I want to go home."

"Don't say that, Chaya. If Hong Li dies, you are a widow. And Hong Li is too young to have adult children you could live with."

"I'm not married to Hong Li. I don't want to live here. I just want to go home. Biyu, can you help me get back to Cambodia?"

Hong Li appeared then, sooty but alive, and he reached for Chaya's hand. He muttered something in Chinese.

Biyu translated, "Hong Li said you and he will go to his house now."

Using the vernacular of English-speaking teenagers in Phnom Penh, Chaya responded with a shrill, "Bullshit. This is crazy. People are running and screaming in panic, a building is on fire, people might die in there. He wants to take me to his bed? Bullshit!"

Unfazed, Hong Li tugged on her arm and yanked her to her feet. The old crone from Ju's house showed up, took hold of Chaya's other arm and joined in the tugging. Chaya dug the square heels of her red pumps into the dirt and pushed backwards with all her strength, but she was no match for the combined strength of Hong Li and the crone. They yanked her forward, causing her to lose one of the shoes, then dragged and pulled her along the roadway toward the tire shop. Biyu traipsed along behind the threesome offering reassurances.

They passed the charred and collapsing embers that had been the meeting hall, all but totally consumed in the vicious flames. Fire fighters were still wetting down the few standing components of the building, and others had re-entered the structure to look for casualties. Nearby, a makeshift first-aid station had been set up under the eave of another building, and two tarp-covered corpses lay on the dusty ground.

Soon the tire shop came into view and Hong Li pushed Chaya inside the hovel. Hong Li's mother, sister and the crone from Ju's house stroked her and cooed as they steered her toward the flower-laden nuptial bed. Hong Li, in his disheveled and sooty suit, stood by with a grin.

But Chaya's stomach recoiled. She gripped her abdomen with both hands and squealed "Toilet. Toilet," then broke free and fled out the door and up the path behind the shop. Inside with the flimsy door latched, she pulled the cell phone from her waistband and held it carefully in one hand while she lifted her skirt and squatted over the toilet drain set into the concrete floor.

With her bowels voided, she studied the cell phone. The keys were similar to the ones on her own phone, and she gingerly pressed the 8. The keyboard lit up and the numeral 8 appeared in the tiny window. She punched in the rest of the country code for Cambodia.

It took her a moment to remember the nine-digit number of her father's mobile phone but she hurriedly jabbed it in. The phone seemed to consider the number for a second or two. Then she heard a series of tones indicating that her call was being placed. She put the phone to her ear.

There was no ring tone, only the harsh recorded voice of a female operator spouting something in Mandarin. Chaya jerked the phone from her ear and stared incredulously as the metallic voice gabbled on. After a pause the voice switched to heavily accented English, "The number you are calling cannot be reached as dialed." There was another short pause then a series of beeps and tones before the phone went dead and the lighted keyboard switched off.

A gentle tap came from outside on the biffy door. Chaya held the power button and frantically scanned the interior of the outhouse for a nook where she could stash the phone. She jammed it into a tiny space between the wall and the ceiling. Had the person on the other side of the way heard the voice or the electronic beeps?

"Chaya, it is Biyu. You must come now," she said, her voice soft. "Hong Li is waiting for you. It will be okay. I promise."

CHAPTER TWENTY-FOUR — THE PIED PIPER

In a nondescript stucco and clay house near a temple in the village of Tra Que outside Hoi An, the ringleader of the local trafficking network, the man Stewy had dubbed the Pied Piper, met with two of his confederates, a young male and a female, both Vietnamese, in the early evening darkness. Torrential rains and heavy winds pummeled the corrugated tin roof causing its panels to flap up and down, creating a tinny rattling, not an uncommon occurrence in early November when the northeast monsoon gears up for its big annual show along Vietnam's central coast. The wicked east wind skated its way into the meeting room under the door and through the poorly sealed windows, causing papers to rustle and bare light bulbs suspended from the ceiling to wobble.

"One of the girls we recruited from Cua Dai has returned to her mother," said the woman.

She would recognize either of you, I'm sure. And probably Vang too. By the way, where is Vang tonight?"

"He flew to Saigon today with a new girl from Cam Chau. He'll put her on Singapore Airlines tomorrow."

She studied the swaying light bulb for a minute. "So, I suggest you avoid Cua Dai for a while and concentrate on the other outlying villages."

"How did she find her way home from Singapore?" asked the Piper.

"How do you think? She was rescued by Green Gecko."

"That Aussie and his band of teenage disciples is an annoyance. We sent them a very strong message a week or so ago. Do you think they'll back off?"

"I don't. They believe they occupy the moral high ground. And the local people's committee thinks they are doing the area a service. They have the support of the authorities. Unless you want the police looking hard for you, I'd avoid any further violence. Right now the only department concerned about the girls from this district is the C-45 unit in Da Nang — a small unit with limited people."

The other man spoke for the first time, "So, no more firebombs. But is there a more subtle way we can discourage Green Gecko's volunteers from doing their work in the outlying villages?"

"Maybe so." The Piper placed both hands on the tabletop and pushed his chair back. "It means hurting people. But we try to make it look like an accident."

***

Next door, in one of the outbuildings of the pagoda complex, Paul Pham lay on his back on a hard-as-rock pallet bed, eyes wide open and fixed on the space over his head. The meditation session an hour earlier had been wholly unsatisfactory. He'd not been able to suspend his preoccupation with Lien. Although he'd only seen her two or three times in Green Gecko's office and had barely spoken with her, thoughts of her swirled through his mind constantly. As a novice monk he was expected to practice *brahmacharya* — celibacy. Still, he rationalized, the practices of Mahayana Buddhism of Vietnam were liberal compared to its Theravada neighbors in Cambodia, Laos and Thailand, and he was only a part-time, temporary monk. In a few months he'd be back in San Diego flirting with bikini-clad women at Coronado. So what could be wrong with getting friendly with Lien? It wasn't like he was lying here thinking about having sex with her. Well, maybe it had crossed his mind — just fleetingly. He gave his penis a little pat. Tomorrow he'd broach this topic with his teacher, Brother Thao and seek his advice.

As if in response, the bamboo door of his cell-like room flew open and smacked against the wall. With it came a curtain of rain that lashed the concrete floor and the foot of his bed, followed by Cuong, another novice.

"Pham, come. The master wants us all in the Grand Hall for a lesson before the storm puts the lights out."

Paul raised himself off the bed and slipped into his sandals. Irreverently, he hoped it wouldn't be another boring lecture on the Noble Eightfold Path. They had already covered Right Understanding and Right Thought, and he didn't know if he could listen to the master drone on about advanced thinking on the principles of Right Speech, Right Livelihood and Right Action with such perfect timing, just when he'd been on the verge of justifying his thoughts of Lien.

He stepped through the doorway, opened his big orange umbrella and leaned into the pelting rain. As he made his way to the Grand Hall, the roar of several motorbikes just outside the pagoda grounds overpowered the sound of the wind, and he cast a glance in the direction of the noise. In a flash of lightning, he saw three mounted figures departing the small house just across the road from the pagoda gate. A second sheet of lightning illuminated the scene just enough that Paul thought the tallest of the three figures looked vaguely familiar. The third, her silhouette smaller than the other two, was clearly a woman.

The Grand Hall was anything but grand. Although the largest of three nearly identical meeting rooms across a courtyard from the central prayer hall, the hall was little more than a whitewashed room with sparse interior furnishings. With eleven other young novices, all sitting or kneeling on bamboo mats on the concrete floor, he listened as the master monk bleated a windy harangue on virtuosness. Likely because his audience members consisted wholly of adolescents and young men, he concentrated on the *Cunda Kammaraputta Sutta* — the prohibition of sexual misconduct. For the young monastics seated before him, this meant strict celibacy.

As he half-listened to the lesson, Paul fantasized about Lien until his stomach heaved. This was wrong. By thinking about Lien during this lecture on abstinence, he was committing a transgression against the universal moral code, an action which, through the karmic process, could bring disaster into his life.

But what was the harm in merely thinking about her? And he *was* listening to the master at the same time. Maybe rather than seriously bad karma, his thoughts would only bring inconvenient karma.

At sixteen, he had heard a ludicrous joke. A mother had caught her son masturbating and had chastised him, "If you continue that practice, God will strike you blind." The boy responded with, "It's okay Mom. I'll just do it until I need glasses."

Paul's mouth curled up and a little chuckle escaped his lips.

The master stopped his spiel mid-sentence. With lowered brows and narrowed eyes he stared at Paul, his hands curled at his hips like a gunfighter preparing to draw.

In an act he hoped was sufficiently contrite, Paul quickly cast his eyes downward.

The master resumed his blather and Paul returned to his thoughts. This time his mind wandered to the three motorbikes he had seen leaving the neighboring house a few minutes earlier. Something about the tallest one felt familiar — the set of his shoulders? His posture? What was it? From where did he know him? The answer, teasing just below the surface of his consciousness, wouldn't crystallize.

CHAPTER TWENTY-FIVE —
CHAYA

For a week after the wedding, Chaya was swept from despair to determination and back again. Spurts of energetic resolve to escape punctuated the suffocating troughs of her depression.

The night the marriage was consummated, she had been horrified by the blood trickling down her thighs, and had cried almost endlessly over her lost virginity. And what if she got pregnant? She'd kill herself before carrying Hong Li's child.

But just as quickly, the moping gave way to near-violent bursts of willfulness. She would *not* become pregnant. She would escape this living hell.

With no one to talk to, no one to confide in, Chaya's days were long and lonely. When Hong Li's mother and sister came to the shop, they tried to reassure Chaya with chatter and gestures. They showed her how to prepare the simple meals favored by Hong Li — steamed rice, vegetables and chicken — and made it clear through sign language that she had a responsibility to her husband to cook and clean.

She bolted through the door and up to the outhouse. *Cook?* Who the hell did these bitches think they were? She had never cooked. Her mother never cooked. They had servants for that. She snatched the phone from its hiding place and tried, once again, to get through to her father. She listened to the same frustrating message as before. She shoved the phone back into its hiding place and slammed her open palm against the thin metal door.

When she wasn't engaged in resisting the mother and sister, she either sat on a small stool, staring despondently at her folded hands, or retreated to the outhouse to be alone. Emptiness consumed her and she longed for the comfort of her parents' penthouse in Tonle Bassac.

Hong Li paid little attention to her during the day. He busied himself with his tire repair work and engaged in man talk with the customers who came in and out of the shop. At night he forced himself upon her. Without comment or gesture, he would seize her with his grimy hands and lead her toward the platform bed. She bit and scratched in her attempts to escape him, but in the end he always overpowered her and raped her.

Afterwards, she seldom slept but instead lay staring up into the darkness while, next to her, Hong Li snored and farted contentedly. When she did sleep, violent dreams woke her. It felt safer to stay awake.

***

Eight days after the wedding and fire, Chaya disdainfully watched Hong Li mount a truck tire onto a steel rim, still unable to believe that this disgusting, dirty little man had made himself her husband. With one side of the tire already under the lip of the rim, he forced the back of the top side under the lip with his gloved hand. Then, with an old Windex spritzer bottle, he sprayed what looked like a soap and water solution around the rest of the inside tire edge. As he stood on the portion already under the edge of the rim, he used a pry bar to force the remainder onto the rim. He then put the tire on its treads and rolled it toward his compressor and air hose.

From the street, Biyu's voice rose above the clattering of the air compressor, "Chaya, are you there? I've come to see you."

"Yes. I'm here. Come in." With a sense of anticipation, she lifted her tense and battered body. Someone to talk with at last.

Biyu smiled warmly at Chaya as she entered, and then turned and said something in Chinese to Hong Li just as he finished inflating the truck tire. She turned back to Chaya, "Let's go for a walk. Hong Li said it's okay."

On the village's main lane, they wandered past the chief's house, toward the charred ruins of the meeting hall. For the first time since Chaya had arrived, the sky was partially blue, and the sun strove to break through a diaphanous layer of altostratus camouflage.

"You don't look good," Biyu said. "I'm worried about you. Is he treating you badly?"

"He hasn't beaten me. But he's not kind. The only time he even looks at me is when he wants to take me to bed. Then he's very rough. He pulls me to the bed and rapes me. The last seven days have been hell. I don't look so good because I'm heartsick. I want out of this place. I want to go home to Phnom Penh."

"Do you get any comfort from his mother and sister?"

"They just come every day to show me how I should be a servant to that man. I refuse. I feel like I'm two people, one sad and lonely and one angry and full of fire."

"Give it some time. You will get used to Hong Li and the village."

"Ha! I will never get used to Hong Li. Just to say his name I can smell him and feel his filthy touch on my skin. And this is the first I've seen of the village since the day of the fire. I don't want to get used to it either. I hate everything about it — except you. I can talk to you."

They reached the pile of ash and burnt timbers where the meeting hall had stood. Chaya stared at it and became silent. She felt sadness that people had died. But she wished that Hong Li had been incinerated. For a second or two she envied the two people who *had* died in the fire. She'd be better off dead than stuck in a life of slavery in an unknown corner of China.

When they started walking again Biyu said, "Chaya when I came to the toilet to get you the other day, I think I heard a telephone. Do you have a mobile phone?"

"No! I … where would I get one? My iPhone was left in Kosal's car when he *dumped* me at the shop in Nanning." She put an emphatic inflection on *dumped.*

"I don't know, Chaya." Biyu stopped walking, took Chaya gently by the elbow and turned toward her. "I just think I heard a recorded voice and electric tones when I approached the outhouse. Two or three villagers lost their mobile phones in the meeting hall during the fire. Perhaps you picked one up."

"No." Her gaze darted around the village as she looked for something to divert this conversation. Biyu's gaze was resolute but not unkind, so she blurted, "Okay. Yes. I did find a phone. I've hidden it. I want to reach my parents. I want to leave this place, Biyu. Please help me." She reached out and touched Biyu's shoulder.

Biyu was silent for a moment but then asked, "You tried to call your parents?"

"Yes. But I did something wrong with the phone. I heard a recorded voice then some beeping noises."

"What numbers did you put in the phone?"

"What numbers? I put the Cambodia code, then my father's mobile number."

"Chaya, I shouldn't tell you this because Hong Li deserves to have a wife. But I can see how desperate you are. When dialing outside of China, you must first put in the international dial code. It's 00. I will not tell anyone that you have a phone."

***

That afternoon Chaya visited the biffy, took the phone from its hiding place and turned on the power. When the screen lit up, she listened for the sounds of anyone near or approaching the outhouse before she punched in all fourteen necessary digits to route the call outside China and on to Cambodia.

She held her breath and listened to the rhapsody of electronic tones as the call was placed. Chaya's pulse raced as the soft brrrr of ringing sounded in her ear. One ring … two … three. Her heart continued to pound. She felt a bead of sweat drip down from her temple. Four … five. No answer.

Her hand trembled. "Come on. Come on."

Six rings. Still no answer.

Panicky now, she terminated the call before it rolled over to voice mail. Her mind raced, "What now? Why had she killed the call? She *could* have left a voice mail. All she would have had to do is tell her father the name of the village she was in — Shing Sheang Ton, or something that sounded like that. He would take it from there.

But she wanted a better connection than just a voice mail. She decided to text him. She opened the text function, pulled the number off of recent calls, and attempted to control her sweaty and shaking fingers as she typed in the message:

Its Chaya Im in China at place called Shing Sheang ton Can u help me Im prisoner here Want 2 come home.

CHAPTER TWENTY-SIX — COLONEL KHLOT

Despite a brilliant sun that had hoisted itself up and shone dominantly over the city of Phnom Penh, the atmosphere in the Pussycat Bar on Street 136 remained dingy. The few bar girls hanging around at this quiet hour sat in desultory groups of two or three working on their nails or makeup. Two young women were taking selfies of their cleavage.

A squeal, like a boiling teakettle, erupted from a dark corner as Colonel Khlot swaggered through the front door and into the dimly lit lounge. A ripple of giggles followed as the other girls recognized one of their favorite patrons.

He acknowledged their flummery with a nod and a broad smile, then strutted directly to the corner table where Madame Sawatdee sat decorously, hovering over account books, a Montblanc pen daintily poised in her left hand.

She rose and gave him a perfunctory hug — okay here in the lounge since they weren't outside where passersby might be offended. "Well Colonel, business or pleasure today?"

"Strictly business." He dragged another chair out from the table with a scrape. "Have someone bring me some ginseng tea."

Madame Sawatdee looked over her shoulder toward one of the girls and snapped her fingers. "Ginseng tea for both of us. And some rolled banana cake." She turned back to Khlot, "Now Colonel, are we here to talk about the terms of a partnership in this enterprise?"

"How much time do you have? I doubt if we'll reach a final agreement today, but I came prepared to make you an offer for a fifty percent equity position. I think you'll find it attractive."

He studied her as he waited for a reaction. She was a beautiful woman of about forty, with a classic aristocratic Asian face, broad nose, high angular cheekbones and irises the color of faded denim. What genetic anomaly in her ancestry had given her those, he wondered. Or was there a Western forebear somewhere in her lineage?

"For you, I have all the time in the world, Colonel. I suspect you'll want to talk not only about monetary return on your investment, but about having a say in the management."

He shrugged noncommittally. "We can negotiate that."

"And you will wish to have a liberal menu of perks where the girls are concerned."

"We can talk about that too."

The tray arrived, loaded with a teapot, porcelain cups and a plate of *num ansom chek* — banana cake rolled in ti leaves. While Madame Sawatdee busied herself cutting the delicacy into bite-sized pieces, Khlot's eyes scanned the darkened space, eagerly taking in the tender flesh around the large room. These sensuous young women were like comfort food to him.

He picked up a piece of the cake with his fingers. "The figure I'm prepared to offer," he abruptly announced, "is one hundred thousand American dollars."

Her expression inscrutable, Madame Sawatdee said, "And what terms and arrangements were you thinking of?"

In quintessential Asian fashion, the tea dance began. For the next thirty minutes, they bantered to and fro and circled around each other, a pair of dogs sniffing each other out. They dissected, and then arranged and rearranged their thoughts, arguments and counter- arguments like tiles in a game of mahjong.

Khlot's phone chirped and then broke into the melodic chords of the standard iPhone ring. Too engaged in the discussion to tolerate an interruption now, he silenced the ringer. The caller could leave a voice mail.

By the end of the hour, they had agreed on the price for fifty percent of the enterprise, but little else. To both participants, this represented a satisfactory conclusion for now. They congratulated each other with a handshake and a hug. They had achieved an acceptable level of agreement in principle and shared purpose. They would meet again in one week.

Now in an ebullient mood, Khlot made his way around the bar teasing and flirting. A kiss on the cheek here, a pinch on the ass there, light suggestive banter and playful gestures, all well-received and reciprocated with profligate grins and seductive wiggles.

He stopped short of the door when his iPhone murmured the signal for an incoming text message. Better to read it in dim light rather than outside in the brilliant sunshine.

He glanced at the screen. The message had come in an hour ago, apparently right after the series of rings he had ignored. Khlot opened the message:

No Caller ID Its Chaya Im in China at place called Shing Sheang ton Can u help me Im prisoner here Want 2 come home

His lips tightened with a brief surge of anger. Then he typed a reply: *What province in China or near what city? Who's holding you?*

When he received no response, he strode to his Toyota SUV and tossed the phone on the passenger seat where he could get to it in a hurry. Was this a joke? Was she really in China? The stupid girl. Why hadn't Kalliyan keep closer tabs on her instead of being consumed by her busy-body social stuff?

During the thirty-minute drive back to Headquarters, he received several calls pertaining to routine police business, but he heard nothing further from Chaya.

***

Colonel Khlot stopped in his own office just long enough to check his in-basket and scan his desktop for those ubiquitous little pink telephone message slips. Satisfied that nothing required his urgent attention, he bypassed the elevator and took the stairs three at a time down to the Technical Services Division on the second floor.

"I need you to work your magic and get me some coordinates for the origin of this message," he barked to the attendant as he laid the iPhone on the counter, the screen with the text from Chaya illuminated.

"All I can do is try call return, sir." He pushed three buttons and looked at the screen. "No sir. No luck with that. There is an app called Trap Call, which is supposed to unmask No Caller ID calls. I have no experience with it, so I don't know how well it works. Maybe you should download it for future use."

"That's not going to help me with this call. Let me use one of your computers to check for something on Google Earth."

"Right over there, sir." The attendant handed the phone back.

In the search window of Google Earth, Khlot typed Shing Sheang Ton,

125

China. The software took him on a 3-D flight, in full polychromatic color, from a vantage point hundreds of kilometers above the surface of the Eastern Hemisphere to zoom in on China. Seconds later, a disappointing message appeared on the screen: *Location Not Found.*

"Damn." He opened MapQuest and tried the name of the village again.

A large-scale map of the southeast coast of China immediately appeared on the screen. Two map tacks glowed bright red. One hovered over Macau and read, *Sheng Kung Hui School.* The other, on the northwest corner of the island of Taiwan, announced that it had pinpointed *Shing Shang Shing Dim Sum Restaurant.*

"Shit." Obviously Chaya had misspelled the place name. Likely she had heard it verbally and had provided him with the best English phonetic facsimile she could imagine.

"Sergeant, do you have a software program that will take that village name and search for the correct spelling?"

The sergeant shrugged. "Afraid not, Colonel. You'd probably have to ask the CIA or the NSA. Are you on good terms with the Americans? It probably doesn't matter, I doubt if they could be bothered giving a third world nation that kind of assistance without a ton of bureaucratic red tape to justify it."

"Damn it." He rose from the computer so abruptly that the chair fell over. "Try and figure something out. I don't give a damn who you have to call. I'll be in my office."

At his desk, Colonel Khlot lit his thirtieth cigarette of the day and inhaled deeply. He expelled the smoke with a long sigh, then dialed his home. Kalliyan answered on the first ring.

"I've heard from Chaya. A text message. We can't locate the origin of the call on any maps. A village in China, but she spelled it wrong." He departed momentarily from his gruff telephone voice and said with feeling, "At least we know she's okay. I'll come home in a few minutes and we can talk about this."

He got on the intercom. "Captain. Put a call through for me to something called the Green Gecko Children's Foundation. It's in Vietnam, Da Nang or Hoi An, I think."

CHAPTER TWENTY-SEVEN — PETE TRUTCH

The Boutique Hoi An Resort, a property that occupies several acres of prime beachfront property, defies the definition of "boutique" as something small and exclusive. The gleaming white buildings reflect a plantation-style architecture situated around meticulously manicured grounds, shaded by palms. Chaise lounges and comfortable tables for four, sheltered by immense umbrellas, surround the infinity swimming pool at the center of the complex.

Trutch sat at one of the shady tables closest to the sea. From this vantage point, he could view the comings and goings of people moving on the grounds and around the pool, as well as those lounging under umbrellas on the beach below the seawall. He had selected this setting for a meeting with Stewy and Nga, the policewoman from the anti-trafficking unit, because although it was in the open, it afforded privacy from eavesdroppers and listening devices. He ordered hot herbal tea from the svelte, *ao dai*-clad waitress and settled back to wait for the others.

At Stewy's request, they were meeting so that Trutch could advise him on how to best secure his office, employees and their homes from the threat of intimidation and violence.

"Why me?" he had asked. "Surely there are Vietnamese firms or agencies that would be well qualified to consult with you on physical security."

"I've had consultations with two of them," Stewy said, "but frankly, I'm not sure they can be trusted, and I'd like to tap into your knowledge as a former military man. I'm prepared to pay you a consulting fee. We can't afford much, mind you, but it would compensate you for your time."

Trutch, citing his vested interest in the safety of Stewy's people, had asked for a day to pull some ideas together. Today, he had come prepared with a point-form list of some basic security measures Green Gecko could implement.

Nga arrived first. Conspicuous in her green uniform, she stood at the far end of the pool shading her eyes with one hand as she surveyed the tables and lounges. Trutch waited to see if she could single him out.

She did and approached him confidently. "You would be Mr. Trutch, the only unaccompanied man of grandfather age sitting near the pool."

In Vietnam, to call someone *grandfather* is to show him respect, and the Vietnamese in general have a cultural penchant for being direct about age, so Trutch silenced any objections to his "grandfatherliness." He stood. "Yes, please sit down. I'm pleased to meet you, Nga."

"I know your granddaughter," she said, and scooted her chair closer to the table. With a hand flip, she shook her ponytail back into position. "She's smart and as I believe you English speakers would say, 'sharp.' I also know that she is hurting. I feel sorry for her."

"Thanks. She is bright," Trutch said, responding to her sensitivity and caring.

Then Stewy joined them, and without preamble he said, "Pete, I asked Nga to help you and me get a picture of what we're up against in the way of a threat to our people and our purpose. So why don't you start, Nga?"

"Okay." She screwed up her face a little, as though conflicted about her answer. "I honestly think," she hedged, "that there is little physical threat to your people. There's little history in this country of the perps involved in child trafficking actually retaliating against NGOs or their people. I do think, however, that there is danger of psychological damage to your people from the intimidation and threats made by the traffickers."

"You're absolutely right, Constable," Trutch said emphatically. "Dead pigs and fire bombs are acts of terrorism. They're meant to intimidate and create fear. Fear, in turn, disrupts not only job performance, but produces psychological casualties. This is serious."

"Mr. Trutch, we actually have no such rank or title as constable. I am *Chiến sỹ bậc 1*. That means policeman first class. But please call me Nga. I'm concerned about the morale and welfare of these fine young people working for GG."

Before Trutch could speak, Stewy intervened. "Nga, what can you tell us about *who* this Pied Piper might be? And how many of his or her crew might be operating in and around Hoi An?"

Nga appeared confused. "Pied Piper? What's it mean?"

Stewy laughed. "It's from a nursery rhyme, a centuries old tale for children. The piper lured children away from their parents and families. But, again, have your people any idea who these people are?"

"We only know that there are at least three men. So far they have been approaching vulnerable girls from poor families. They concentrate on the villages. They're probably paid by a ring leader either in Saigon or Singapore."

"Okay. I think we've already determined as much. Pete, let's start going through your points on security."

"Okay, let's cover information security first. You must train your people to avoid letting plans and movements go beyond those who have a need to know."

He explained the principle of "loose lips sink ships." He discussed common sense precautions around telephone conversations, meetings, discussions in public, and how to protect written communications and files from compromise. He concluded by cautioning, "Of course, the protection of electronically developed and stored data is a whole different topic which can be very technical and would take hours, if not days, to cover."

"Our systems are already pretty bulletproof," said Stewy. "It's the human factor we need to beef up in terms of awareness and good practices. This is useful, Pete."

"It's all just common sense," Nga said. "But really, I don't think this Pied Piper is sophisticated enough to tap telephones. You don't need to worry about anyone listening in."

Stewy nodded. "Pete, let's hear what else you have to say."

"Apart from having security guards on your office and the group home, the most important single element of keeping your people safe — both staff and volunteers — is to teach them to avoid setting patterns. They need to vary their movements. Don't use the same route to and from work and don't travel at the same time everyday. I could invest a couple of days to do some training sessions on this with your people if you'd like."

Nga stood abruptly. "I have to go now, as I have another meeting, but if you do these training sessions, please be gentle, Mr. Trutch. It's okay to make them aware of the need to be cautious, but please don't put fear and panic in their heads."

Trutch and Stewy both rose. "That makes good sense, Nga," Stewy said. "Thanks for coming."

"I'm glad to. I really care about these young people. That's why I do this job."

***

Thirty minutes later Stewy stepped into the office on 1123 Tran Hung Dao just as Mai was answering a phone. She looked up as he came into the room.

"Stewy, it's for you," she said. She covered the mouthpiece with her hand. "A Colonel Khlot, with the Cambodian National Police, calling from Phnom Penh."

***

The Pied Piper met again with two subordinates in the small house near the pagoda. "What's new with Green Gecko? Are they backing off with their warnings in the villages?"

"No, they're continuing. And now they're training their people, volunteers included, on measures to keep themselves safe. I was just at a meeting with Stewy Fitzsimmons and a man named Trutch."

"Okay. Good work. We'll just brazen our way through this. We won't threaten GG or its full-time staff any more. It might invite attention we don't want. Instead we'll be more aggressive in the villages. If we encounter any of GG's volunteer zealots, we'll scare them."

CHAPTER TWENTY-EIGHT — LIEN

At Dingo Deli, Pha and I found an empty table near the window. I had invited her for coffee to talk about how she was doing now that she'd been home from Singapore for several weeks. I'd chosen Dingo Deli because of the young people that hung out there, mostly her age, and because the Vietnamese waiters were all enthusiastic and filled with self-esteem.

I waited until our server had taken our orders for tea and scones and then said, "Are you still selling things on the beach?"

"No. I'm too busy going to the cooking school that Green Gecko pays for. My mother and I are getting along on her income as a housekeeper at the Victoria Hotel."

"I'm happy to hear about school and your mother's job. I asked about the beach because if you went there, maybe you'd see the men who tricked you into going to Singapore. You could identify them for Green Gecko and the police."

Pha blanched. "I'm afraid to go to the beach. If they see me they might be angry that I've come home. They might hurt me if they think I can tell the police who they are."

"What if I, or someone else from Green Gecko, were to go to the beach with you? We could change your hair and give you glasses so you're not so easy to recognize."

"I still think it might be dangerous. I'm trying to forget those horrible months in Singapore. Looking for them might remind me too much of everything that happened there."

"But if we can protect you, don't you think identifying those men and putting them away might save other girls from being sold?" I wondered if logic and compassion would work, or whether I should mention spirits or karma.

Her mouth tightened as she sipped her tea. When she lowered her cup, she looked me squarely in the eye. "Okay. I'll do it. I don't want them to trick any other girls from Hoi An. But you, or someone from Green Gecko, will be with me?"

"Yes, we'll have your back," I said, using an English idiom I had just learned from my Grandfather Pete. "Can we go this weekend?"

Before she had a chance to reply, I spotted Paul Pham, the Vietnamese/American from San Diego, sitting alone at a table close to the cash station, conspicuous with his rust-colored robes and shaved head. "Excuse me Pha," I said. "I should say hello to that monk over there. I know him from work." Because he visited several times a week with Stewy, he no longer intimidated me.

His eyes lit up and a crooked little smile crossed his face as I approached. He stood to greet me, and then his face turned beetroot red. I had caught him eating a bacon cheeseburger — one of Dingo Deli's signature dishes. "Um … Paul," I said in English, "what would the master monk say about that? Or was it a vegetarian cheeseburger?"

His gaze shifted from me to the plate, then back to me, then toward the cash station. Then he found his self-confidence and said, "Actually, there's lots of latitude in Buddhist thought for interpreting the strictures for yourself. I've decided that the occasional hit of sodium, fat and carbohydrates might stimulate my spirituality."

Unconvinced, I laughed and said, "Why don't you join us over there? I'll introduce you to Pha, one of the Pied Piper's victims we rescued from Singapore."

"Okay." He fumbled to his feet, and when he snatched up his plate he spilled French fries on the floor.

I ignored his awkwardness and led him back to our table, where he warmly greeted Pha. "Nice to meet you," he said. "I hear that Lien was instrumental in your rescue from Singapore."

Pha asked me to clarify what he had just said to her. I told her in Vietnamese, and while she squirmed under his gaze, she smiled shyly. I understood her uneasiness, similar to mine when I met men for the first time.

But most of his attention was now focused on me. So focused that when he picked up his half-eaten cheeseburger to take another bite, a large drop of mustard oozed from the bun and splattered on his robe. His facial expression was that of a young boy who had just spilled his milk, eyes wide and mouth agape.

I giggled like a teenager as he sat there, his shaved head glistening, reflecting the ceiling lights, rubbing at the amoeba-shaped mustard stain on his crotch with a dampened napkin. Other people in the deli looked curiously toward us.

"What would the master monk say," I asked between snickers, "about you providing the entertainment in an expat restaurant?"

He chuckled sheepishly. "Oh man, that's probably the bad karma getting me for eating the cheeseburger in the first place."

Pha stood then and said, "Lien, we can meet another time. Call me on my mobile phone."

I rose and put my hand on her elbow. "Oh Pha, I'm sorry," I said as she glided toward the door with me at her elbow. "Maybe that was unfair. I shouldn't have invited Paul to intrude on our visit."

"Men make me nervous," she said and slipped out of my grasp.

"I know that. How foolish of me. Do you want to go to the beach on the weekend to look for the bad men?"

"Call me," she said. Then she turned and was gone.

I returned to the table where Paul was still working on the mustard stain, my feelings turbulent. How could I have been so insensitive to Pha's tenderness when I still harbored similar uneasiness around men? It's just that, as a monk, Paul seemed so nonthreatening. And he *was* cute.

"Sorry, Paul. To use one of your American expressions, I screwed up."

"With Pha? No, it's early in her healing, but the more natural we are around her the better. Listen, I have to get back to the pagoda in a few minutes, but do you want to have tea one of these days?"

"We'll see," I said.

CHAPTER TWENTY-NINE — LIEN

"We have a request to attempt to rescue a young Cambodian girl who's been kidnapped and taken to China," Stewy said.

Beside him, his assistant Mai considered a sheaf of paper. Along with Tam, the young man who had made several rescue trips into China, the four of us were meeting in the lounge at the Green Gecko office. My heart stuttered at the mention of Cambodia, but I willed myself to stay focused.

"We know that her name is Chaya," Stewy said, "and that she is being held against her will in a village with a name that sounds like Shing Sheang Ton. That name doesn't come up on any mapping software. She managed to get one text message to her father about a week ago but nothing has been heard since. She's only fourteen. Her father will be here in Hoi An later today to talk with us about rescuing her."

I felt instant empathy for this girl, and I knew she would be going through hell. Was that why Stewy had asked me to attend the meeting? Was this my chance to go into China?

Before I could ask, Tam said, "In Mandarin, the *sh* or *ch* sounds are spelled in the Arabic alphabet with *x*. I've searched for villages spelled Xing Xiang Tun and still come up with nothing. But that could be explained by the fact that many places in China have both official names and colloquial place names. The colloquial version would usually not appear on a map."

"We'll keep looking," Stewy said. Then, perhaps reading the question in my eyes, he added, "Lien, I've included you in this so you can better understand how we work, or attempt to work, at rescuing children from China. I know you want to go on a rescue mission, and I don't know when, or even *if*, you might be ready for that but if you wish, I will keep you informed on this case. We're meeting with Chaya's father later today."

Yes, I thought. Yes. More than anything, I wanted to help free this girl.

***

I recognized him instantly. Still, my mind refused to accept what I saw as I looked straight into the eyes of the first man who had raped me in Svay Pak, the man who paid to take my purity. I teetered and grabbed the edge of the doorway to keep from falling.

He looked at me without recognition, as though he didn't see me. He just sat in the lounge at GG's office, smoking a cigarette, no doubt wondering who I was.

Stewy looked up from the papers he was writing on. "I'd like you to meet Colonel ..." He stood. "Lien, is something wrong?" He walked to me and took my arm. "Are you okay?"

Colonel Khlot cocked his head to one side and stared at me, his eyes narrowing. His mouth fell partly open, and he grunted, but he said nothing. He sat like that, with his mouth ajar, his eyes darting rapidly between Stewy and me, as if he was searching for something to say.

My head was spinning. Everything — my entire experience in the brothel in Svay Pak — came rushing back. The daily rapes, the smelly customers, the torture from Nakry and Mau, the dingy quarters, the lonely days and horrific nights, until shock swerved into volcanic anger. I found my voice, "*Thằng khốn nạn.*" Then in English, "You ... You ... *Bastard!*"

The fury in my tone and my volume jolted them both. Stewy released my arm and looked at me with eyes wide. Colonel Khlot closed his mouth. His Adam's apple bobbed up and down a couple of times in his throat. For sure, he recognized me now.

"Why are you here?" I shrieked. My trembling hands formed fists at my sides.

"What's come over you, Lien?" Stewy's voice registered disbelief. "This is Colonel Khlot from the Cambodian National Police. He's here because ..."

"I know who he is. Believe me, I know this bastard."

"You know him from Svay Pak? Listen ... listen to me, Lien. Colonel Khlot is here because it's his daughter, Chaya, who has been kidnapped and taken to

China. He wants GG's help in rescuing her."

"This is the man who took my innocence. He's a big shot, an important man, so he got the privilege to break my virginity. He raped me." I looked directly at Colonel Khlot. "Yes. It's me — Lien. I was Lotus to you then, the lovely young water lily that you deflowered. Now your daughter is in my situation back then. Poor her. You brought her bad karma."

He still stared, mouth open again.

The fire in my soul had no limits as tears raced down my cheeks. I spewed steam and white-hot lava. "Do you know what it's like for her if she's in a brothel? Every day your daughter is forced to have rough sex with dirty, cruel men. She's raped five or six, maybe ten or twenty, times a day. Men with grimy hands handle her body and push their nicotine-stained fingers and all sorts of other things into her vagina. Sometimes they take pictures of her. They force her to play with herself and take videos with their cell phones. They bite her nipples, causing them to bleed."

Khlot paled, sweating now. He squirmed in his chair.

"I'm sorry, Lien. I didn't know," said Stewy. He took my arm gently.

I pulled away. I wanted Colonel Khlot to suffer. I wanted him to squirm. "Imagine your daughter being forced to suck on the penises of men like you, your age, older. Imagine her bleeding from down there because men like you like to screw her in the ass." I swiped at my tears and stopped. Not because my fury was spent but because I was out of words. I turned down the corners of my mouth and glared at him with a hatred he could not mistake.

A dark stain appeared, and then grew, in the crotch of his tan slacks. He had peed himself.

CHAPTER THIRTY — CHAYA

Fingers of chimney smoke curled their way upward from the village houses as Chaya shuffled toward the outhouse. The sky was the color of oyster shells and a steady drizzle soaked the already saturated footpath. She slid twice on the muddy surface, her footwear slick-soled sandals made from old tires. She grasped the wooden handle on the decrepit sheet-metal door and gave it a yank. The door was stuck, locked from inside. The raspy rumble of a long, resounding fart came from within.

Chaya cranked her head around to look back at the shop. Was Hong Li in there? What if he had discovered the telephone?

She heard a phlegmy cough, a feminine croak, followed by the slurp and splash of the bucket and dipper putting the finishing touches on the job. The door opened and Hong Li's mother stepped out and grinned ludicrously at Chaya. She muttered something in Chinese, which, by the accompanying flapping and flailing of hands, Chaya took to mean, "Hurry up. Do your business, then get back to the shop. There's work to be done."

With the door latched, Chaya reached up to the top of the wall and felt around for the phone. This was her chance to try calling her dad again. An icy hand gripped her stomach as she realized it wasn't there. What had happened to it? Had it fallen on the other side of the wall? If so it should still be there, as the wall only consisted of one thin layer of concrete.

She unlatched the door and did a hasty search of the outhouse perimeter, with no luck. Back inside, she checked every square inch of the tiny space, even inside the bucket, to no avail.

She slogged back down the path to the tire shop, where Hong Li's mother sat rolling won tons at the makeshift table. Chaya took up the task of chopping carrots and onions, which would join the won tons in a watery soup for the evening meal. She could only hope that Hong Li, who was in front of the shop discussing business with a truck driver, had not found the phone. That would mean big trouble.

Someone had to have found it. The communal toilet served at least four houses. But why would someone take it, anyway? Practically everyone over ten in this village had their own phone. Perhaps an animal, a packrat maybe, had carried it off.

Outside, the truck engine started and gears ground as it inched away from the hovel. Then Hong Li blustered through the door with fire in his eyes. With a suddenness that caught her off guard, he smacked her across the face with the back of his hand and followed up with a punch to the stomach that caused her to double over and drop to the hard dirt floor. She saw him draw his foot back, ready to kick.

She coiled into the fetal position and whimpered "No. No, please."

His sandaled foot smashed into the side of her ribcage. He then stomped around the one-room hovel ranting and knocking things over like a madman. He returned to Chaya, bent over her and shouted streams of Chinese invective while holding the phone in front of her face.

Chaya whimpered and lay motionless as Hong Li stormed from the shop still raving.

His mother came to her. She helped Chaya to her feet and walked her to the edge of the bed, where Chaya sat heavily. The mother dampened a towel with water from the kettle and dabbed at Chaya's reddening face.

***

Two hours later, Biyu came to the tire shop and sat with an arm draped over Chaya's shoulder. Tears traced tracks down Chaya's cheeks as Biyu hugged her tighter and cooed, "He's a proud man. You've hurt him. Like every other man in this village, he has a temper and he can be violent. Do you want to go for a walk, Chaya?" Off in a corner, the mother of Hong Li sat silently and rolled won tons.

They walked in silence to the edge of the village, where the dirt road met the highway. Biyu said, "Let's cross. There is a path to a little waterfall on the other side."

Mists swirled as they trod mutely toward the waterfall on a lushly forested path, lined with bougainvillea and cucurbita.

For twenty minutes they plodded up the muddy trail, and then Biyu asked, "Did you have a boyfriend in Phnom Penh?"

"My first boyfriend was Kosal. I thought he loved me," Chaya said with a sob. She stopped walking and sat on a wet boulder beside the stream. "He brought me to Nanning, then left me at the so-called beauty shop." Tears again streaked down her face. "I just want to go home." She pictured the comfort of her bedroom in the spacious penthouse suite in Tonle Bassac. Nicely furnished with rich accents and luxurious bedding, it had been her sanctuary, the place where she retreated with her iPhone to exchange texts with her girlfriends.

Her brothers, four and six years older, had been both her companions and her nemeses during the years when they all lived under the same roof. They had teased her, as older siblings do, but they had also been solicitous and protective of her as she grew toward pubescence. They tolerated no harassment of their little sister from their geeky friends. Last year Chann, the younger one, entered the Royal University of Phnom Penh. With his older brother, he had moved into a rental house on Russian Federation Boulevard. Chaya missed them both but she relished the weekends when they dropped in at home to eat a meal or two and have the servants do their laundry.

Now, sitting on a damp rock next to a babbling creek somewhere in southeastern China, she wished she had heeded their warnings that she was too young to be wishing for a boyfriend.

"I thought I was in love with Kosal, but now I know what a mistake that was. When I get home, I don't want to be around any men other than my father and my brothers. Hong Li is an animal. I can't stand him."

"Chaya, I shouldn't do this. But I'm going to let you use my phone. We have a strong signal here. Get a message to your father and tell him that this village is sixty-three kilometers southeast of Nanning's Outer Ring Road, on Highway G325. Tell him you are living in the tire repair shop."

***

Colonel Khlot sat in a sidewalk coffee shop on Tran Phu Street in Hoi An, speaking to his wife on his phone while simultaneously admiring the young Vietnamese women in tight jeans and high heels passing by. The call waiting function on his phone chirped.

"Kalliyan, wait. I have another incoming call." He triggered the hook flash button, said "Khlot," and then listened intently but expressionless.

A minute later, he disconnected without returning to the connection with Kalliyan. He rose and threw some Vietnamese currency on the table. Then he strode three blocks to Green Gecko's office.

CHAPTER THIRTY-ONE — CATHERINE TRUTCH

Alexandre was on a ladder lighting incense on the family shrine, a plywood ledge on the kitchen wall, when Catherine and Pete Trutch entered his bistro for a late breakfast. "Oh, good morning," he said, then switched to Vietnamese, "*Chào buổi sáng.*"

"Good morning," Catherine said. "I'm glad to see you paying homage to your ancestors. May we have two *café sua* when you have a chance?"

"Of course, Madame." He descended and grabbed two glasses as Catherine and Pete seated themselves on a rattan settee facing the whipped surf of the South China Sea.

"This is so peaceful," said Catherine.

"Particularly at this time of day," Pete agreed, "before the crowds of expats show up to drink beer."

"We haven't had much time to ourselves for the past few days. I'd like to talk about Lien. Since she and I had our coffee date a week ago, I've been worrying about her."

"Oh?" Pete turned to face her, his expression open. "In what way?"

"She's putting on a brave front, but I think she's more tender than she's letting on. I suspect she's really still quite wounded. I don't want any GG cases to expose her to more depravity."

"Really? I'm inclined to think that as long as she believes that helping other victims will help her, she should have the opportunity. She has emotional support from the GG staff and their psychologist, what's her name … Hartzog? She's available for counseling sessions and further assessments."

"When did our roles reverse?" Catherine asked. "When we walked in the park a few weeks ago, you were the cautious one and I was saying she's mature and capable and that GG wouldn't put her in harm's way. Now, I'm not so sure. I think she's fragile. I don't want to see her PTSD aggravated — or worse."

"Nor do I, but I can't interfere if she's determined to pursue this. If she thinks it will help her heal, if it gives her *purpose,* we should support her. Besides, you heard that psychologist's recommendations, she said it could be therapeutic. I think the expression she used was it could serve as a *desensitizing* thing from her experiences in Cambodia."

"Yes. I remember that, but how could it serve to desensitize her if she sees more of the same? More of what she experienced in Svay Pak?"

Trutch's phone rang. He looked at the display, then said, apologetically, "It's Stewy Fitzsimmons. I'd better take it."

He listened with only the occasional "hmm," or "I see," until, about four minutes into the conversation he first turned red and then, a moment later, the color receded and his face became deathly pale, like wood ashes. Catherine felt her own color rise as she watched him.

With a final, "I see," he shut down the phone. His hand moved unconsciously to the scar on his left cheek and he stroked it involuntarily; his color remained as pale as a bed sheet.

Catherine reached for his hand. "Pete, what is it?" His skin felt clammy. She stroked his palm. "What is it, darling?"

He looked out toward the Cham Islands, undulating lumps of green, nine miles offshore. "Colonel Khlot, from Phnom Penh, is in town. His daughter has been kidnapped. They've located her in China. That bastard wants GG to rescue her."

"Colonel Khlot? The policeman who … who … was Lien's first abuser?"

"The same, and the asshole who tried to thwart my efforts to find her when I searched for her in Cambodia." He knit his brows together until they furrowed, forming a deep V on his forehead. He slammed his fist on the rattan tabletop. "That bastard!"

Catherine squeezed Pete's hand. "Oh my God. What if Lien meets up with him while he's in Hoi An?"

"It's already happened," Trutch growled. "They met inadvertently yesterday afternoon in the GG office. Stewy had no idea. Apparently, the minute Lien laid eyes on him, she really lit into him — verbally. Catching him so off guard, he peed his pants. I hope that was the only fucking pair he had with him."

"But she's okay?"

"Yes. According to Stewy, the outburst was good for her. She blew off some steam."

"Oh my God," Catherine repeated, "The poor dear. Let's go to her right now. Make sure she's okay."

"Stewy assures me she's fine. She came to him this morning and said if a rescue is planned for Khlot's daughter in China, she wants to be part of it."

"That's just astounding. Incredible. I can't believe she'd want to do that." She lay her hand on Trutch's arm. "Well, yes I can. To Lien, it probably doesn't matter that this is Colonel Khlot's daughter, she's just another young woman in peril."

"They've pinpointed her location to a village southeast of the Chinese city of Nanning. But they don't really know what her situation is — whether she's been forced into prostitution or what."

Catherine took a sip of her now-cold *café sua* and brushed a wisp of reddish-gray hair off her forehead. With a mix of confusion and trepidation, she wondered about the wisdom in Lien's going on the raid. Just how dangerous might it be? When Pete's phone rang again, she feared the worst as he answered.

But his eyebrows lifted almost immediately. "Lien, how are you, sweetheart?"

Again Catherine watched him closely, looking for clues to the content of this call, while he listened and answered with the occasional "Uh hum," or "Okay."

Finally he said, "Okay, sweetie, see you then, but just make it something simple." He set the phone on the table. To Catherine he said, "She wants to cook for us in the group house tonight. I suspect she wants to talk about the rescue gig to China."

CHAPTER THIRTY-TWO — LIEN

My feelings had gone back and forth since my surprise encounter with Colonel Khlot the previous day. At night I rolled around in bed, feeling again the horror in Svay Pak and the trauma of the first night he took me. During what little sleep I had, he appeared in my dreams, standing naked in front of me. I awoke to my own screams as one of my roommates came to my bed to comfort me.

I cried for much of the morning until my mood swung back to anger and I stormed for half an hour until I calmed down again. That's when I went to Stewy and told him I wanted to go on the China rescue trip. I hated Colonel Khlot, but I believed his daughter deserved to have choices in life. I wanted to help rescue her — not in spite of Colonel Khlot, but because she had no choice about being his daughter.

As I started the food preparation for *Ông* Pete and *Bà* Catherine, my fury returned. The fish for tonight's soup lay on its side, its mouth agape, angry-looking little teeth grinning at me, an unseeing glassy eye staring straight up. I grabbed the cleaver and with a violent swing chopped off its head. I continued to savagely slam the blade down until I had hacked the creature into bits and pieces.

"Hello, Lien," Catherine called from the front door.

I took a deep breath in through my nose and exhaled it through my mouth to regain control. "Come in. Come in," I called as I walked toward the front door, wiping my hands on a towel.

Catherine wanted to help with the dinner but I assured her that I wanted to do it myself. Preparing the meal focused me and helped divert my mind from the shock of the unexpected encounter with Colonel Khlot. Catherine looked over my shoulder as I peeled and chopped ten garlic cloves.

"Whoa, that's a lot of garlic," Catherine said. "What are you preparing that's so rich?"

"It's a fish soup. I've never made it before but I watched my Grandmother Quy make it many times. One of her sayings was, 'Most men have never met a garlic they didn't like.' So I hope *Ông* Pete will love this. I've made a green papaya salad to go with it."

"That sounds delicious. What's in the papaya salad, besides papaya?"

"Lime juice, palm sugar, fish sauce, dried shrimp and, of course, more garlic."

Grandfather Pete entered the small kitchen, "Did someone just use one of my favorite words?"

Thirty minutes later, the three of us sat on little red plastic stools around the circular metal table in the living room. I spooned a portion of the piping hot fish soup into each of our bowls and presented the green papaya salad on side plates. Grandfather Pete finished his soup first, and, skilled with chopsticks, started on the salad. Catherine had less chopstick experience and asked for a fork.

Finally, I said, "I want to be on the team that goes to China to rescue this girl, Colonel Khlot's daughter. Her name is Chaya. She's only fourteen."

Grandfather and Catherine looked at each other. Then Catherine said, "Are you sure, Lien?" Grandfather just touched the scar on his left cheek and looked at me with wide eyes.

"Yes, I'm sure. Helping to rescue enslaved girls is what I want to do and it doesn't matter that she's Colonel Khlot's daughter. She's only fourteen and she's being ... I think the word is ... *exploited*. Even though I've never met her, I know what she feels. I know she is alone and afraid."

Grandfather's expression was thoughtful. He said, "Since we know now that Chaya is in a village, and not a city, she's probably been sold as a bride. Her situation may not be as terrifying as if she were forced to be a prostitute."

"*Điên quá đi!*" I shouted. "That is a stupid thing to say. Even if she is a bride she is a fourteen-year-old girl being forced to have sex with a strange man. She is a prisoner in that village just like she would be in a brothel. We need to rescue her and I want to help."

Grandfather Pete dropped his jaw and stared at me. Catherine jumped back at first, then reached over and stroked my arm. "We understand, Lien. Pete's not trying to belittle the seriousness of the situation. He's merely trying to reassure you that perhaps Chaya isn't in as much danger as you were. Just the same, I think I know how you feel. Even if she is a bride, we know she is an unwilling wife, and since her … uh …husband probably bought her, she could be in an abusive situation."

Tears flooded my eyes. I couldn't believe I had shouted at my grandfather — the man who had rescued me and funded my education. The man who had traveled to Vietnam twice a year for the past six years because he loved me. I put my hand on his arm. "I'm so sorry," I sobbed. "It's just that I think she deserves better than to be raped. I want to help rescue her."

Catherine said, "I too think she should be rescued as soon as Green Gecko can put together a plan, but we're very concerned about you going along on a rescue attempt. Sweetie, this could be dangerous, and it could cause you to relive many ugly things from your own experience."

I looked back and forth from Pete to Catherine, then I buried my hands in my face and mewled like a kitten. I whimpered, "I relive them every day. I don't know what's happening to me. One minute I'm angry. The next minute I'm sad. I want the past to be the past and to move forward, but I can't forget." I blubbered, "I can't shake it, I can't shake it."

Abruptly, I pushed my chair back and rose. I moved to my grandfather and threw my arms around his neck. I put my head on his shoulder and moaned, "I will never marry, don't you see? This is the only way forward for me. It is my karma. I must do this. Please support me."

CHAPTER THIRTY-THREE — LIEN

It was going to happen! Stewy Fitzsimmons and Jacqueline Hartzog, the psychologist, had sat with me to explain that I could go on the rescue to the village of Xing Xiang Tun as an observer, to help where I could while Tam and Mai did the real work. I'd also be the communicator on the team, staying in touch with Stewy's office by cell phone while the mission was in progress.

My Vietnamese passport had already been couriered to the Chinese embassy in Hanoi with an application for a tourist visa. We expected it to be returned with the visa stamp by tomorrow. "I'm *pumped*," I said, having heard Stewy say the same at times.

Now the five of us — Stewy, Tam, Mai and I — were in the lounge at GG, planning the mission. The policewoman Nga had joined us to provide her input.

Tam stood before a large-scale map of southeastern China. "Xing Xiang Tun is here." He used a ruler to point to a spot on the map. "The village is sixty-three kilometers southeast of the city of Nanning. According to Chaya's brief conversation with her father, she is an unwilling bride living in the village tire repair shop. The plan is that in three days the three of us will fly to Nanning posing as tourists, Mai and I as a married couple and Lien, as Mai's younger sister. We'll pick up a rental car at the airport in Nanning."

"Do we know exactly where this tire repair shop is?" Mai asked.

"No," Stewy said. "Here comes the shaky part. We know that Chaya called using the cell phone of the village schoolteacher, a young woman who speaks English. Her name is Biyu, and we have her cell number. On the assumption that she is cooperating with Chaya, you are to call her number once you're in a hotel in Nanning and coordinate the details with her for locating and snatching

Chaya."

I wanted the others to know that I would be of value on the mission because of my sharp mind, so I asked, "What if she's not so cooperative? She could tell Chaya's husband or other villagers that a rescue attempt is about to be made."

"That's a risk all right, but since she loaned her phone to Chaya and provided directions to the village, we have to assume that she'll be of assistance."

"Once we have Chaya in the car," Tam said, "we could head for one of two border crossings —Mong Cai, which is here," he pointed to a city along the border at the Northeastern most corner of Vietnam, "or here, at Lang Son." His ruler moved left, to a spot further inland.

"These are our only two choices because we've developed a good relationship with the Chinese border police at both crossings over the past several years. They will be cooperative in helping us through to the Vietnamese side."

"What about police on the Vietnamese side?" I asked.

"The same thing," Nga said. GG is known to the Vietnamese police at these two crossings. They cooperate. Anywhere else along the China-Vietnam border is questionable."

"So, how do we know which crossing to head for?" asked Mai.

"That depends on the situation," Stewy said. "There's a possibility, you'll be pursued." He glanced at Lien. "If the villagers are angry enough when they discover you've snatched Chaya, they could make phone calls to the police or to the person or persons who arranged to sell Chaya to them. Those persons could, in turn, get criminals or the police involved in trying to recapture Chaya. They might set up roadblocks, so Tam will have to make the decisions, on the go, as to where you cross and how you get there."

My concern must have shown on my face because he added, "Lien, we've never had anyone hurt in these rescues. I'm just giving you what we call the worst-case scenario. Tam and Mai are both experienced at this. You'll all be ready for any contingency."

Nga lightly touched my forearm. "Lien, rescuing these kids who've been trafficked is important. They have a right to a childhood and to a future with choices. You're very brave to do this. GG is experienced. You'll be okay."

I liked Nga. I could see she really cared, so I put on my brave face to hide my uneasiness and said only, "Okay. I know."

"This will be the first rescue I've been on where we use a rental car," Mai said. "Do we bring it across the border into Vietnam, just ditch it near the border, or what?"

"The plan," Tam said, "is to leave it on the Chinese side of whichever crossing we use then walk across the bridge into Vietnam. Again, both the Chinese and Vietnamese border police will cooperate with us at either crossing. Once we're back into Vietnam we'll call the rental car company and tell them where the car is. We'll also pay any extra charges for dropping it remotely. We want to remain on good terms with the Chinese car agency."

"I have another question," I said to Stewy. "You said the traffickers usually choose girls from poor families because they think the parents are uneducated and ignorant. They're not powerful. So why would this trafficker — this Kosal — why would he choose a girl whose father is so powerful in the police force? Isn't that stupid?"

"Good question," Stewy said. "Sometimes criminals like the challenge of tempting fate. They want to see if they can outsmart the authorities. Sometimes it's called matching wits. It's like a game to them. Do you see what I mean?"

" I … I guess so." But I really didn't.

"We have hotel rooms booked for one night in Nanning," Tam said. "We'll check in after we pick up the rental car. Hopefully we'll be on our way to the village the next morning, depending on how successful we are in reaching and obtaining the cooperation of this Biyu woman. If all goes well, we'll be back in Vietnam by that evening. We'd only have spent one night in China."

Mai said, "How many hotel rooms? If you and I are supposed to be married maybe we should be in the same room. I'll want twin beds though," she joked.

To demonstrate my cleverness, I made a joke myself. "And if we have three beds, I'll be the chaperone."

Everybody laughed. But having hinted, even indirectly, at sex, I felt a bit queasy. Bad joke.

***

When the meeting broke up I remained in the lounge to telephone Pha. She answered on the first ring. We exchanged pleasantries, and I asked about her cooking class. Then I got to the point. "I'll be away from Hoi An for a few days. Can we get together next week to go to the beach and watch for the men who sent you to Singapore?"

"Okay, as long as you're with me."

My next call was to Paul Pham, the Vietnamese-American monk. He didn't answer and he had no voice-mail message, so I hesitated for a moment, wondering why I wanted him to know, and then I sent him a text. *Paul. Its Lien going away 4 a few days can we meet for that tea next week?*

I wasn't admitting any attraction to him, but he was cute and funny and I felt safe around him.

CHAPTER THIRTY-FOUR — CHAYA

Hailstones, some the size of hens' eggs, battered the corrugated metal roof of the tire shop. The rattle and clatter, accompanied by the hoarse rumbling of thunder, was deafening. Hong Li's mother wobbled about the room assembling meager ingredients for the evening meal, adding the jangle of dishes and pots to the clamor.

Chaya sat unfazed on the little plastic stool, her expression stony. Beset by a fleeting shiver, she snugged up the cheap burlap shawl she wore loosely over her shoulders. Beneath the plywood table, a rat, beady eyes ablaze, scouted for scraps and diverted her attention. Enraged, she snatched one of Hong Li's tire tools from the floor in front of her and flung it in the direction of the rodent. With a screech, the rat disappeared through a slit in the rough-hewn wall behind the table.

She had connected with her father via telephone a full six days ago. He was her only hope in an otherwise black future. But when would he show up? With Hong Li still indignant over the cell phone incident, life had become even less tolerable than during her first two weeks in the village. No longer trusting her, Hong Li had virtually imprisoned her, allowing her out of the hovel only to use the biffy or to go on short errands to the market, usually with Hong Li's mother and sometimes with Biyu.

He sat smoking a foul-smelling cigarette in an opposite corner of the shop, where he stared sullenly at a rivulet of muddy water coursing under a wall and across the hard-packed dirt floor to escape beneath the door. He looked up at the metal roof and cursed the infernal weather. Few trucks would travel the treacherous mountain roads in these conditions.

Bastard, she thought. Why couldn't he go outside and be killed by a hailstone? When her father came, surely he would kill him anyway.

Abruptly, Hong Li rose from his stool, muttered something in Mandarin to his mother, and then approached Chaya, his expression of lust and fury telling her that she was about to be raped again. As the corners of his mouth curled into animal rictus, his brows hooded the malevolence in his eyes. He grunted. Mother drifted outside.

Chaya stood and hissed like a cornered animal. She flailed her arms, fingers spread and curled, nails ready to gouge and slash his idiotic face. But with one swipe, his meaty hand connected with the side of her face and put her on the floor. He grabbed her by the wrists and flung her onto the platform bed. As hail and thunder continued to thrash the metal roof, he pinioned her with his body weight and opened the front of his trousers.

***

When morning came, Chaya again sat morosely on the plastic stool staring down at her hands while Hong Li snored contentedly on the platform bed. The desultory light of a gray day seeped in through the windows and gaps in the siding. Outside, the village stirred as people made their way on bicycles and on foot toward the small public market at the north end of the settlement, their chatter chirpy and effusive.

The rickety door opened and Biyu stuck her head in and looked around. She held her eyes for a second on Hong Li's slumbering form then whispered, "Chaya, come outside with me, quickly. It's important."

Chaya stepped out into the road, still sodden from the storm. The gloomy sky above was the color of pewter, the razored mountain tops beyond the village tangled in fog. Mud squished up over the top of her sandals and through her toes. Biyu took Chaya's upper arm and urged her farther away from the tire shop.

Fifty yards up the road they neared the market, a warren of makeshift stalls separated by strands of rope. Biyu spoke in a low voice. "Fifteen minutes ago some people from Vietnam phoned me. They're on the way here from Nanning. Your father sent them to rescue you."

Chaya's pulse quickened. "My father sent them? How will they get me? Who are they?"

"One of them is named Lien. She wants you to call them back right away and they'll talk about how you go with them. Take my phone. The number is

152

right here under "recents," just press the button.

Chaya had hardly hit send before a voice on the other end said, in English, "Hello, this is Lien."

"This is Chaya. My father is with you?"

"No, Chaya. There are three of us. We are with Green Gecko, a group that rescues trafficked children. We're here to take you to Vietnam."

"Vietnam? But I want to go home to Phnom Penh. What will happen in Vietnam?"

"We'll talk about the details later, Chaya, but after we get you to Vietnam we'll take you to your father. You and he can talk about going back to Phnom Penh. If you're seriously sick, or in shock, you have an option to stay in Vietnam for treatment. It's called rehabilitation. But that would be up to you and Colonel Khlot to decide."

Chaya's hands trembled. "What do I do? How can you get me?"

"We're on the side of the road, Highway G325 about five kilometers from your village. We can be there in about ten minutes. Can you be somewhere easy for us to find?"

"I can be at the market. It's at the north end of the village near the highway."

"Okay, Chaya," Lien spoke rapidly, her voice telegraphing eagerness. "We'll be there in about ten minutes. We're in a red Taurus — that's a kind of car. It's new and shiny. There are three of us in the car."

"You'll be the only new car in the village. I'll see you."

"We're on the way, Chaya."

Seconds later, a red-faced Hong Li appeared, his lips pursed, his brows knitted. His entire body shuddered as he grabbed Chaya by the throat and threw her to the ground. He twisted her arm into a hammerlock and then jerked her back to her feet, all the while spewing a fiery stream of Chinese curses.

Biyu jumped back as the telephone dropped into the mud. Market vendors and patrons stared open-mouthed, some moving closer for a better look at the spectacle.

Hong Li ignored them all. With one hand firmly leveraging the hammerlock and the other holding her head back with a tight clutch on her ponytail, he propelled her down the muddy street toward the tire shop.

Chaya screamed for help in Khmer, then in English, "Biyu, help me."

CHAPTER THIRTY-FIVE — LIEN

We pulled into the village and found the market. Tam stopped the car, but no one approached. Something was wrong. Where was Chaya? The villagers in the market appeared agitated, with much hubbub and aggressive gesturing. Several pointed toward our car. A tall young woman clutching a cell phone approached us. Tam put down the driver's window. Fetid air and market smells of bloody meat and overripe vegetables rushed in.

The woman shouted, "I am Biyu! We talked on my telephone." She spoke rapidly, in quick clipped phrases while gasping for breath. "He took her. Hong Li." Her head jerked to the left, indicating a direction. "The husband is beating her. The tire shop. On the left. Go there. Get her."

Tam looked to Mai on the passenger side of the front seat and then to me in the rear. "Do we do this?" he asked in Vietnamese. "Are you ready?"

Numerous people in the market now approached our vehicle, gesticulating and excited. I couldn't tell if they were angry or curious.

Mai said, "Let's go."

"Yes, go," I said.

Mud splashed on the windshield and through the open driver's side window as Tam sped toward the tire repair shop, a dilapidated shack fronted by a stack of wheel rims and old tires. We skidded to a halt, opened our doors and leaped out. Tam yanked open the shop's feeble door, almost pulling it off its hinges, and disappeared inside. As I approached the doorway after him, Biyu came running up the muddy street toward us. "Be careful. Be careful," she shrieked.

I rushed through the doorway, followed by Mai, and almost fell over Tam, who lay face down on the muddy floor. He raised his head and said, "I'm okay. Tripped over some kind of equipment." He rolled on his knees and pulled himself up.

Across the room, a young girl, obviously Chaya, was on her knees. A disheveled man with chin whiskers stood over her with a firm grip on her hair, holding her head motionless. He glanced our way and sneered.

"Stop," Tam said. "Let her go, please."

As the man roared in Chinese at Tam, Chaya reached under a table, just a sheet of plywood resting on wheel rims, and brought out a tire iron. She swung it in a wide arc and connected with the left side of the man's knee. There was a crack and the man released his hold on Chaya and fell onto his side. Without a moment's hesitation, Chaya forcefully swung the tool into the side of his head. With the crunching sound of metal to bone, the man became motionless. Blood gushed from above his ear. An older woman on the other side of the room wailed and covered her face with her hands. Tam and Mai stood motionless, frozen in their tracks.

Biyu came breathlessly into the room and took in the scene. Eyes wide with horror, she said something excitedly in Chinese.

Tam responded, also in Chinese. Then he switched to English. "Let's go, we've got to get out of here."

I took a whimpering Chaya by the arm, led her to the open back door of the car and pushed her in.

As Tam and Mai climbed in the front, Biyu stood by the driver's side speaking rapidly in Mandarin.

"I know. I know," Tam said in English. "We're off. Thanks for your help Biyu."

***

Minutes later we raced south on highway G325, a winding, mountainous road. Except when farm traffic or the occasional ox cart slowed us, Tam was able to maintain a speed of about fifty kilometers an hour, and the villages and tiny farms blurred past the windows as Chaya cried and shook violently beside me. I had my arm around her shoulders to steady her when she leaned forward and vomited on the floor. The car filled with the sour smell of bile. "It's okay, Chaya," I said.

I helped her clean her mouth and chin with a tissue, but as we rocked and swayed through a rough section of the road she gagged and vomited again.

She removed the threadbare burlap shawl she was wearing over her

155

shoulders and put it on the floor to cover the puddle of vomit. Now she wore only a thin blouse, buttoned to the top.

I reached into my backpack and pulled out a light flannel shirt I had brought as protection against cold nights in case we had to stay longer in China. I wrapped it around Chaya's shoulders and again enfolded her in my arms. "It's okay, Chaya."

"Did I kill him? Did I kill Hong Li?" Her voice was tremulous through her tears.

"I don't know. Don't think about it now. We're taking you to safety."

Tam turned his head and said over his shoulder, "In about six kilometers, I can get on Highway G75, the Nanbei Expressway. It's four lanes, a straight shot to Qinzhou, sixty kilometers. From there another expressway will take us to Dongxing, the city on the China side of the crossing into Cong Mai."

Mai said, "So we're crossing at Cong Mai? Shall I call Stewy and ask him to alert the border police there?"

"Good idea. Tell him we expect to cross at Cong Mai in about two and a half hours. But there's always the possibility that we may have to divert over secondary routes to Lang Son. If so, no telling when we'll reach the border."

I asked, "Where will we go after we've crossed? We won't have a car if we leave it on the China side."

"We'll take a train or a bus to Hanoi," Mai said. "Stewy might meet us in Hanoi along with Chaya's father. Or he might just want us to get a flight from Hanoi to Da Nang. He'd meet us in Da Nang with a car and drive down to Hoi An."

At the mention of Colonel Khlot my stomach felt as though it had been gripped by a frosty hand. I took a couple of deep breaths and held Chaya tighter. She had stopped trembling and now seemed numb, silent as she stared straight ahead. We pulled onto the expressway and accelerated to about sixty-five kilometers per hour.

Mai clicked off her phone and announced, "Okay. Once we're across the border, Stewy wants us to make our way to Hanoi. He and Colonel Khlot will meet us there. We are to call him again as soon as we clear into Vietnam."

The ride to the outskirts of Qinzhou was uneventful, and we made good time, averaging over seventy kilometers per hour. From there, we made a graceful turn through a modern interchange onto the expressway G7511. Tam said, "Just over an hour to the border. Everything is going well so far."

I silently prayed that it would stay that way.

**

The Qinzhou-Dongxing expressway, a broad four-lane divided highway, coursed through dense tropical forests and scattered farms. The occasional village, cleared of trees, allowed us views of the rugged mountains to the north. Traffic was heavier on this wide belt of asphalt, but with no slow-moving farm vehicles or animal-drawn carts to slow us, we made good time.

As Chaya dozed with her head on my shoulder, I felt an odd tenderness toward her, despite my ever-present awareness that she was a monster's daughter who reminded me of that horrible building in Svay Pak, with its "working rooms," or, more aptly, rape chambers. For the rest of the drive, I struggled with the notion that the mind is a prisoner of memory, burdened by the thoughts and images that anchored past events.

Then Tam announced, "The expressway ends in about five kilometers. That leaves us ten kilometers from Dongxing. We'll take a random route through secondary roads until we're close enough to the border to park the car and walk across. I think if the villagers in Xing Xiang Tun had alerted the police, they'd have caught up to us by now, but still, we're better off on the secondary roads for the last few kilometers."

Chaya, awake by then, said with panic in her voice, "I don't have my passport. I left it in Kosal's car."

"Shouldn't be a problem," Mai said. "Green Gecko is known to the border police on both sides at the Mong Cai crossing. They cooperate in getting trafficked children out of China. Stewy would have notified them by now that we're coming."

"Will ... will my father be waiting on the other side?"

It was difficult for me to think of Colonel Khlot as anyone's father. To me he was still a fiendish, sly animal. But I said gently, "Maybe you didn't understand Mai earlier. We will take a bus or train to Hanoi and your father will meet us there." Even as I reassured her, I hoped to never lay my eyes on that beast again. I wondered how I could avoid it.

The expressway ended and we spent the next twenty-five minutes navigating a jumble of one- and two-lane country roads until we entered the built-up area of Dongxing, where Tam skillfully piloted us through the city streets and alleys until we were within several hundred meters of the border crossing. He selected a remarkably clean alley behind a six- or seven-story glass-clad office building to park the Taurus.

"We still need to be careful," he cautioned, as he hid the key fob under the front floor mat of the vehicle. "This is a city of about seventy thousand. The people are prosperous compared to those in the surrounding countryside, but there's plenty of opportunity to make money at a key border crossing into Vietnam."

I held Chaya's hand as we made our way on foot toward the crossing. Tam, Mai and I all carried light backpacks, but Chaya had only the threadbare clothes on her back, along with my light flannel shirt over her shoulders. Her palm perspired in mine, and her breath came in quick, nervous huffs as we approached the long concrete building with the Chinese flag fluttering atop.

Through a wide portal in the central part of the building cars, trucks and motorbikes entered and exited in a slow trickle. In a side parking lot, other vehicles waited to enter the portal. They crept forward one at a time, tiny clouds of dust as fine as talcum powder wafting from beneath their wheels.

Tam confidently led us to the pedestrian entrance just to the right of the vehicle portal. We entered a large, ugly room with cinder block walls painted the color of boiled cabbage. The smell of cigarettes hung in the air. In one window, a portable air conditioner hung pitifully, its electric motor humming in a futile attempt to remove some of the smoke and humidity, a puddle of condensation beneath it on the stained tile floor. Only two of the five wickets were staffed.

We lined up behind a Vietnamese family of five — a mom, dad, two girls and a boy, all returning from a shopping trip. Within minutes, an official motioned us forward and Tam presented our three passports and rendered an explanation, in Mandarin, of Chaya's presence. Tam and Mai stood side by side, smiling at the official, while Chaya and I stood directly behind them. Beads of perspiration had formed on Chaya's temples, and her wide eyes searched the room. Clearly she was terrified that the police were after her for killing Hong Li.

Although I had no idea whether it was true or not, I squeezed her hand and whispered, "It's okay."

The guard tapped computer keys and focused intently on his screen. He glanced up at the four of us, then back to the screen as he keyed in something else. Then, without warning — whap. Whap. Whap. He stamped our three passports. Chaya jumped, and then he waved his hand toward the exit on the other side of the building.

We passed two other border guards at the doorway as we exited, and then we started up the sidewalk toward the bridge over the Ka Long River. The bridge itself was graceful, about three hundred meters across, with broad sidewalks for pedestrians on either side of the traffic lane, and lamp posts set about fifty meters apart. Two by two, the four of us started across the bridge, Tam and Mai in front and Chaya and I behind. To the right and left, hundreds of barges and sampans idled through the muddy water on both sides. Ahead about a hundred and fifty meters, the exact border between China and Vietnam was marked by signs in the center of the bridge. Just past those signs about ten Vietnamese policemen and policewomen stood at the border, dressed in their distinctive pea-green uniforms.

"They're waiting for us," Tam said. "As soon as we step across they'll escort us the rest of the way and process us through customs and immigration. We've done this so many times, the Vietnamese police like to make a ceremony out of it every time we rescue someone from China."

Then we heard shouting behind us. I looked back and saw three Chinese border police rushing toward us. "Halt!" they yelled in English, and then again in what must have been the Chinese equivalent. All three screamed at us; two had their guns drawn and were waving them.

"Run," Tam shouted, unnecessarily.

I was already galloping toward the center of the bridge, Chaya's hand in mine. She struggled a little, but fueled by adrenaline, she loped along like her life depended on it, which it likely did.

The Vietnamese police shouted encouragement and gestured for us to race as fast as we could, but seconds seemed like minutes and hours as we dashed toward them. I risked a peek over my shoulder and noted with panic that the Chinese border guards had gained on us, even as everything before us moved in slow motion. The lamp standards came at us at a snail's pace and the border seemed to be moving slowly away as we approached it. Vehicular traffic in both directions had stopped. Some of the motorbike drivers shouted encouragement as well.

"Keep going. Keep going," Tam yelled.

Ahead, I could now see the whites of the eyes of the Vietnamese police, so I assumed we were gaining ground as all nine of them continued to gesture and shout. The ponytails of two female officers bounced and flailed as they jumped up and down, waving us on.

Behind me, the heavy footsteps of the Chinese police gained on us. One seemed so close I imagined his breath on the back of my neck when he shouted something at me. Then another one yelled in a high tenor voice. Amidst the jumble of Mandarin, I discerned the name Chaya. Chaya tightened her grip on my hand.

All at once, the sound of running feet behind us slowed and stopped. Tam and Mai slowed to a walk and then stopped. Chaya and I doubled over with heaving chests. We had crossed the border. I dropped Chaya's hand and turned to face her. One of the Vietnamese policewomen approached and placed her arm around Chaya's shoulders. The other took her hand and led her toward the Vietnamese shoreline. To my delight, Nga, the anti-trafficking policewoman, greeted us at immigration. We had made it.

BOOK THREE

CHAPTER THIRTY-SIX — THE PIED PIPER'S MAN

A handsome young Vietnamese man with a well-trimmed pencil moustache strode casually along the side of Highway TL-609 in the hamlet of Xuan Phuoc, scanning the villagers for prospects. A teen-aged girl caught his attention. She wore peasant attire — loose black pajama pants, a cheap floral-print blouse, buttoned to the top, and a conical hat made of rice straw — and squatted on her haunches outside a cinder block hovel, helping her mother do laundry in a plastic basin. A flimsy metal cart on the porch displayed sundries for sale: soda pop, rice wine, cigarettes. He considered two courses of action as he watched the pair. He could approach the mother with his proposition or he could wait for an opportunity to speak to the girl alone.

Opting for the first option, he politely approached. "Hello, Auntie, may I speak with you?"

"You want to buy cigarettes? Rice wine? Whiskey?"

"Oh no, but you look like you're having a hard day." He proffered a twenty-thousand dong note. "Let me help out with some money."

"Thank you." Without making eye contact, she took the money and stuffed it into a hip pocket.

"Your daughter is very beautiful," said the man. He squatted next to her so their eyes would be at the same level. "How old is she?"

"I'm sixteen," the girl said as she wrung out a denim shirt.

He pulled his smartphone from his pocket and held it in front of the mother. "Will you look at this picture? I think this young man is very handsome. Don't you?" An Asian man of about thirty, wearing a crisp white shirt and blue striped tie smiled out from the photo.

The mother's eyes moved to the picture for only a second then she dropped her head again to concentrate on several garments she was agitating by hand in the gray water of the basin. "I guess so."

He showed the picture to the daughter. "Don't you think he's handsome?"

She giggled.

"He's a wealthy businessman in Singapore who wants a Vietnamese wife. The girl he chooses will have a whole new life, lots of money, nice clothes, even servants. And this man will love her." He set his cell phone to the camera function. "May I take your daughter's picture and send it to him? I think he'll like her."

"No," the mother said emphatically.

"Oh, why not? Your daughter is very beautiful. This man — his name is Wang — he'll love her. She'd have a good life. Wang lives in a big house and even has a car."

"No."

"But Singapore is an exciting city, full of fun. Everybody has plenty of money. You could even visit your daughter there. Have you ever been on an airplane before?"

The woman rose, stood on her toes for a moment to stretch her legs, tortured from a long squat, then turned her back on the man and trod into her house on bare feet.

The man looked inquiringly toward the girl, who merely shrugged.

Seconds later, the woman returned. She thrust a booklet at the man.

Puzzled, he took it from her and thumbed through the pages, a combination of photos, illustrations and print using simple language. Some of the illustrations were like cartoon strips, where the people in the pictures had speech bubbles above their heads. He understood immediately that it was an anti-trafficking brochure distributed by Green Gecko.

He threw the brochure down into the dust and made his way to a dilapidated coffee shop with a mishmash of plastic stools and scarred tables. As he sat and pulled out his cell phone to dial his boss, he noticed another copy of the brochure resting on a smudgy glass-topped table across the room. In brilliant red and blue, its glossy front featured a montage of happy children.

The proprietor, a balding man in his forties, approached with a coffee.

"Where did you get that booklet?" the man asked.

"From my son's school. There was a meeting last night, with parents, policemen and teachers. Volunteer young people from Da Nang or Hoi An made a presentation. They even had a projector."

"That must have been an interesting meeting."

"It was. I hope it will help keep our children safe. There's another meeting tomorrow night at the pagoda in Thuc Khe. Do you want to attend?"

"Maybe so."

***

The Pied Piper took the call from a beach chair in front of the Hai Cua bistro. "In Xuan Phuoc? They're really becoming a thorn in our side." He paused to listen for a few moments.

"Tomorrow night?" He listened again for a couple of seconds. "Okay. I'm sending Vang up there to join you. Before that meeting I want you to hurt those GG volunteers. *Hurt,* do you understand? Enough to scare the shit out of them and send a message to Green Gecko. Those villages out there and all the way to Quang Ngai are ripe for the picking. We need to keep those bleeding hearts out of them."

***

Late in the day the little coffee shop across the street from the district administration building was abuzz with the banter of the many patrons, farmers, laborers and a smattering of youthful employees of the People's Committee. The working people drank plain coffee or tea while the government office workers drank expensive cappuccinos.

In one corner the man with the pencil moustache sat with Vang. He said, "The meeting at the temple starts in one hour. I've learned that four young people from Green Gecko slept in the school last night and will walk to the meeting. We'll hit them on the temple grounds. What did you bring in the way of a weapon?"

"An axe handle."

"Good, and I have a policeman's baton. We'll send a strong message to GG, but be careful. No hitting them on the head or neck. We want them to have bruises, but nothing broken."

"I understand."

As the two left the café, the sixteen-year-old who'd helped her mother with the laundry the day before walked past. She carried a basket filled with vegetables, apparently headed home from the market. The man with the moustache handed the girl a slip of paper with his mobile number and said, "If you change your mind, call me."

The girl said nothing and avoided eye contact, but she put the paper in her pocket.

The two men walked ten minutes to the adjoining village and sat on a stone bench on the pagoda grounds. They concealed their weapons in shrubbery behind the bench and waited, their posture erect, their hands resting on their knees, palms up and cupped, eyes straight ahead but unfocussed. For all appearances they were just two good Buddhists, meditating.

The man with the moustache, more inclined to slouch in the saddle of his motorbike than to sit with his back straight for any length of time, soon felt fatigue in his lumbar region. Moments later it morphed into pain in his sciatic nerve and radiated down his leg. He squirmed and shifted his feet and legs but found no relief. Just as he was about to stand and attempt to extend his back muscles, Vang jabbed his elbow into his side. Two young men and two young women had entered the pagoda grounds, no doubt the young idealists from Green Gecko.

Since they'd arrived well before any of their audience members, likely to set up and test their audio/visual equipment, there would be no witnesses. Both men reached for their weapons.

And then two uniformed policemen followed the young people through the gate.

The man with the moustache and Vang hastily resumed their meditative poses.

The GG volunteers followed one officer up the broad stone staircase and entered the pagoda, but the other officer remained watchful at the foot of the stairs.

"Let's go," said the man with the moustache. "We'll find the school where they're sleeping and get them when they return." As they rose, he turned and bowed toward the shrine with steepled hands. "So we look more like legitimate worshipers," he murmured to Vang.

CHAPTER THIRTY-SEVEN — LIEN

I had been back from China for three days and had slept soundly each night — hurray, no nightmares. The mission had been a success, despite some tense moments in the village and at the border, and I felt particularly joyful, almost at peace for the first time in a long while. I pedaled toward An Bang Beach, where I would meet *Ông* Pete and *Bà* Catherine at Hai Cua bistro, eager to tell them all about my adventure in China and about how the rescue of Chaya worked out.

I hadn't told them about the bicycle yet, but I hoped they would approve. It had been more than five years since I had ridden, perhaps since I rode my bike to and from school in the village of Tuy Phuoc, before my Uncle Vu betrayed me. But it was a real rush to be cruising along on a sturdy bicycle now with good brakes and a comfortable saddle, the breeze in my face.

The previous day, the man in the bicycle shop on Cam Chau Street had fitted me with a good helmet and had adjusted the seat, handlebars and pedals to fit me perfectly. He sold me the bike, slightly used, for only thirty-five US dollars, but not before cautioning me to always think of safety. Be aware of everything going on around you, he said, and told me that Hoi An, with its heavy truck and bus traffic, could be a dangerous place to cycle.

But traffic was light, and the morning beautiful and sunny. Only a few puffy clouds drifted across a brilliant blue sky, and birdsong had replaced the roar of busses and trucks. Emerald-colored rice paddies grew so close to the roadway that it was like gliding over a sea of green, as free as the wind.

At the bistro, I secured my bike to a palm tree with a chain and padlock, and was greeted by Alexandre. "*Xin chào*, Lien. Welcome." He gave me a quick, hesitant hug, as though unsure whether it was appropriate or not.

I didn't resist. I didn't feel repulsed. I didn't really feel anything. I didn't find Alexandre attractive but I was not afraid of him. I suppose I had what we Buddhists call a neutral feeling, neither pleasant nor unpleasant.

Looking a little embarrassed, he said, "Pete and Catherine are in one of the beach gazebos." He pointed to one of four little thatch-roofed sun shelters on the sand near the surf, each furnished with beach chairs and a small bamboo table. "Brother Pham — Paul Pham —is with them. Come, I'll take you down there."

"Paul's with them?" Although I wasn't drawn to Paul either, I found him kind of cool to be around.

They all rose from their lounge chairs as I stepped into the gazebo, and Grandfather and Catherine each embraced me warmly. My grandfather actually had tears in his eyes. I could see he was proud of me.

Paul just stood there, before the backdrop of ocean and the distant Cham Islands, shuffling from foot to foot with an idiotic grin on his face, his hands thrust deeply into hidden pockets in his wine-colored robes. One of the islands looked as though it was perched atop his gleaming shaved head. I smirked, and wondered why he always looked so funny.

After an exchange of pleasantries my grandfather turned serious. "Lien, Paul was just telling us about four GG volunteers who were beaten up last night in a village in the foothills to the west of us. What was the name of the village, Paul?"

"Xuan Phuoc."

"Oh no." A wave of panic squeezed my heart. "How badly were they hurt? Who did it?"

"One girl is in hospital in Da Nang with a fractured tibia and possible internal injuries. The other three are bruised and battered, but otherwise okay."

I felt sick to my stomach. "Who would do that?'

"More than likely a couple of goons working for the Pied Piper," Grandfather said. "That's what we're calling whoever's running this ring of traffickers taking young women and girls to Singapore as brides."

"Paul just mentioned this a few minutes ago," Catherine said. "I'm still in shock and very worried about you working for Green Gecko, Lien. Are you sure you want to continue?"

"I've never felt better about myself than I do right now working for GG.

This was what I wanted to do. For the first time in five years I feel like I'm someone good — not a … bad girl." I had almost said "whore." "I have a purpose, I'm working with good people and I can do good."

"Of course you can, sweetheart. I just … I mean … there's risk in doing this. We don't want to see you hurt."

"I know there's a danger, but someone must face that danger. Green Gecko is making a difference. I think working for them, even with danger, is my karma. It's giving my life meaning. Also, I've seen Dr. Hartzog four times now, and I think that talking things out with her is helping me recover from what she calls PTSD."

"I agree that it's PTSD," Grandfather said, "and whatever helps, you should continue, as long as you're certain it's what you want. I wish I could stay and discuss it further, but I have my next meeting about security with Stewy in about thirty minutes. This development puts a new urgency on it." He rose from his beach chair. "I must excuse myself to get downtown now, but Lien, please stay and visit with Catherine." He bent to give me a hug and Catherine a kiss on the cheek.

Paul stood also. "I should go too. Too much beach time and I might be tempted to order another cheeseburger." He smiled at me, and then set off towards his parked bike.

Catherine and I had a few seconds of awkward silence before I broke the ice. "Now that we're alone, *Bà*, I want to tell you how ashamed I feel for yelling at Grandfather the other night when we had dinner at my group home."

Catherine put her hand over mine and said, "I think Pete understands, dear."

"But *Bà*," I said, my voice tremulous, "in my culture we're taught to respect older people. By getting angry, I dishonored him and shamed myself."

Now she squeezed my hand. "With all you've been through, I think everyone can forgive the occasional time you raise your voice."

"I don't remember ever in my life feeling angry before my … before I went to Svay Pak. Ten days ago I had a … tantrum, I think you call it … with Colonel Khlot. I don't know this about myself … this anger. Even though I'm having a good day today, I don't like myself very much for being mean to other people, especially to my grandfather. I know he loves me, and I love him," I stammered, a stranger to the intensity of my remorse.

168

"I think maybe your feelings of anger are part of the PTSD. Have you talked about this with Dr. Hartzog?"

"No. I guess I haven't felt that I could talk with her about it. Will you come with me on my next visit with her? I think you could help me express these feelings that are so foreign to me. I'm afraid of what comes out of my mouth now. I'm not in control of this anger. It's upon me before I know it."

"Would your counselor be okay with my being there? Usually sessions are private between therapist and client. You know that I'll support you in any way I can, so I'm happy to do it if it's allowed."

"Oh, *Bà* Catherine, it would be so nice if you could come. Sometimes it's difficult to express myself and you seem to know without words what is in my heart. There's a form I can fill out that says I'd like to have an advocate with me."

"Then I'll be there," she said.

CHAPTER THIRTY-EIGHT — TRUTCH

Trutch thought it was a chorus of crickets at first. But Stewy pulled his smart phone from his shirt pocket, glanced at the caller ID and said, "Excuse me, Pete, I'd better take this. It's one of our volunteers in Xuan Phuoc. He's talking with the police about a lead."

The two of them were alone in the lounge at the GG office; they had just concluded their meeting about security. "Of course," Trutch said. "I'll use the loo."

When he'd finished in the restroom, Stewy was still on the phone so Trutch went to the large open work area where several young GG staffers sat at a long table strewn with files and scraps of note paper, a room that must have been the living room when the building had been a house. All three young people were speaking on telephones — one on a landline, the others on their mobiles. Impressive, dedicated young people, Trutch thought, people making a difference.

Through the arched doorway, in the next room, a gray-haired Caucasian woman and three young Vietnamese women sat around a low coffee table, open notebooks and papers strewn in front of them.

Stewy joined him and nudged his elbow. "That's our contract psychologist, Jacqueline Hartzog," he whispered. "You met her a few weeks ago. The woman on her left is one of our staffers. They're conducting a reintegration interview with two recently rescued trafficking victims."

Trutch nodded. The two men turned in unison and walked back to the lounge. "What's a reintegration interview?" Trutch asked.

"Jacqueline's determining what their needs are — how damaged psychologically they may be, how ready they may be to go home to their families. Alternatively, if they need to and are willing, they may go into rehabilitation counseling. If they come from a dysfunctional family, are in danger, or are severely damaged, placing them in a shelter is also an option. Sometime reintegrating them with their family is a bad idea, particularly if a family member duped them or sold them to the traffickers. Unfortunately, that's often the case in the poorer villages, among marginally educated families."

"I understand," Trutch said. "Five years ago I visited one of those shelters in Phnom Penh while I was searching for Lien. Meeting some of the girls in rehab was so moving, I left in tears."

As they resumed their seats, Stewy said, "That call was from one of my staffers in Xuan Phuoc. We could have a lead as to the identity of one or more of the Pied Piper's gang members."

"Oh?"

"Yeah. The *Cong An*, the local district police, have a cell number. A trafficker approached a sixteen-year-old girl a day before our volunteers were beaten up. He gave her a slip of paper with his phone number on it in case she decided she wanted to go to Singapore. She gave it to the local constabulary."

"Well, that could be a break for you. Are the police pursuing it?"

"Yes, but it's not a quick and dirty process. The local cops in the villages and districts are not very sophisticated. At the urging of our volunteer, they've passed it up to the *Canh Sat*, the national police, at the province headquarters, where there's more know-how and better technology. Unfortunately, because of bureaucratic inertia it could take hours, even a day or two before they know anything."

"Can we do anything to expedite the process? Would the anti-trafficking police move it along faster if we called Nga at her Da Nang office?"

"It's worth a try, but I doubt it. We have so many overlapping layers of police in this country — national, provincial, district and village, special units like border police. None of the various agencies have uniform or coherent procedures, they all make their own rules and policies without the benefit of coordination. There are only about fifty trained anti-trafficking officers in the entire country, and they're mostly regarded by other jurisdictions as elitist and unapproachable. So there's not a lot of cooperation, but I'll ask Mai to call Nga and see if there's anything she can do."

When Stewy's phone once again chirped like crickets in the night, Trutch stood, but Stewy waved him back to his seat. "It's okay, stay. This might be interesting."

Stewy spoke for nearly six minutes, and then he hung up and said to Trutch, "That was a colleague from another anti-trafficking NGO in Hanoi. An English-speaking liaison officer with the Sapa police, in the northwest, just called to tell her that in the past three days four teen-aged girls from that area were kidnapped and spirited across the border. The local police are asking for NGO help in recovering them."

"Can the Hanoi foundation help?"

"Not unless they have a concrete idea of where the victims are. We get these calls all the time. China is a huge country and the traffickers' network moves fast to get their victims to market — and that could be anywhere in the country. If one of the victims happens to get access to a cell phone and is able to call her parents or a friend, then maybe an NGO can act, as we did in Chaya's case."

"Sounds like Sapa is ripe for some of the awareness training your volunteers have been doing in local villages."

"We actually sent a team up there last year. They visited for a month, made presentations and distributed materials to parents, schools, the local police and anyone else who would listen. But if a fourteen-year-old girl becomes enamored of a handsome sixteen-year-old boy with a shiny motorbike, chances are slim she'll think about our warnings. She'll willingly hop on the back of the bike and the next thing she knows she's crossing a river, probably blissfully unaware she's just left Vietnam." He reached for the desk phone. "Let me get Mai to place that call to Nga."

***

The following morning Trutch received a call from Stewy. "Two things I thought you might want to know, both bad news."

Trutch sat back in his chair. He had just finished speaking with Lien minutes before, so at least he knew that she hadn't met with some sort of misfortune.

"First, the Pied Piper and his crew have been busy. We've just learned that two seventeen-year-old girls from the commune of Cam Chau have been lured onto an airplane to Singapore with stars in their eyes. Their parents are frantic. Cam Chau is the neighborhood immediately west of downtown Hoi An."

"Damn. And the second thing?"

"Dead end on the cell phone number. It was from a throwaway phone."

CHAPTER THIRTY-NINE — CATHERINE

Jacqueline Hartzog, greeted Catherine cordially. Professionally attired in a pair of tan linen slacks with a softly tailored cream silk blouse, her gold jewelry — a choker and dangling earrings in the shape of a graceful, *ao dai*-clad Vietnamese woman — shone as the two shook hands. The office, like its owner, reflected calm, tastefully decorated in muted blues and soft greens. Jalousie windows dominated one wall and allowed a breeze off the Bay of Da Nang to waft through the room. A lithograph, featuring a sampan with red sails on an azure body of karst-studded water, occupied the opposite wall. Catherine sat with her and Lien in a semicircle of armchairs that picked up the wall colors.

Before them was a low glass-topped table. From a yellow teapot Jacqueline poured a fragrant potion into small ceramic cups. "I'm glad you could join us today, Catherine," she said. "Lien is making good progress. She's a strong young woman who's open and honest in these sessions. It also helps that her English is so advanced. I'm afraid my Vietnamese is abominable."

"And mine is non-existent. Thanks for including me. It's good to know that Lien is making progress. Now that you've had an additional four weeks to work with her, what do you think is the long-term outlook for her PTSD? Do you think it will eventually run its course?" Catherine reached over and placed her hand on top of Lien's.

"Well, Lien and I have discussed that, haven't we?" Jacqueline glanced at Lien, who sat straight in her chair, hands resting on her knees. "Lien, do you mind if I share with Catherine?"

"No, that's why she's here." Lien shifted slightly in her chair and crossed one ankle over the other. She had chosen to wear a knee-length shift rather than her usual blue jeans.

"Okay. I'll try not to be too technical here, but essentially it's difficult to be prognostic about Post-Traumatic Stress Disorder. PTSD is a label that attempts to encapsulate a broad, amorphous spectrum of symptoms and behaviors. It can be of short duration after a traumatic event is experienced, or it may be long term."

"Yes, I know that much," said Catherine. "Pete suffered mild PTSD after his combat duty."

"I'm glad it was mild. Generally speaking, if symptoms last longer than a year or two, they're likely to go on indefinitely if left untreated. Like other mental disorders, however, PTSD can respond well to treatment. There's no sure-fire cure for it, but the symptoms can be effectively managed such that the patient returns to normal, or near normal, functioning."

"That's a relief. Do you mind if I interrupt with questions as you go forward?"

"Please do. The point I'm trying to make is that every case of PTSD is unique. Its symptomatology and duration can be different with each person. We have a variety of treatment approaches, including medication and any of several approaches to therapy. There's no right or wrong treatment strategy and some individuals respond better to certain treatments than others."

"Just as an aside," Jacqueline continued, "I'm not a fan of antidepressants or anti-anxiety drugs because of their side effects. I prefer to try behavioral therapies first. The effectiveness of any treatment depends on numerous factors including personality, intelligence, educational level, socioeconomic status, nature of the trauma, severity of the symptoms and the presence of a support network. So we can't predict with certainty the course of this disorder. I think it's safe to say, however, that in Lien's case the combination of cognitive behavioral therapy, coupled with her work at GG and the strong support network she has through her family and her peers at GG, is helping to manage the symptoms. Do you agree, Lien?"

"Oh yes. I don't have nightmares or flashbacks as often as I used to, but I'm still afraid to be alone in the dark. That's when I feel mixed up, like I'm not sure who I am. And I'm cautious around men unless I know them, and unless I trust them."

"It may take a long time to get over those effects," Jacqueline replied, "and I'll be frank, you may never work your way through them completely. Who are some of men you feel you can trust?"

Lien laced the fingers of her hands together. "My father, my grandfather … Stewy Fitzsimmons, Tam, Alexandre at Hai Cua and … uh, Paul Pham, I guess are some."

"And other than your father, you've only come to know these men since after you were … after you left Svay Pak. Did you trust them right away?"

"No," Lien said emphatically. "I was terrified the first time I saw my grandfather. I didn't trust any of the others at first, but gradually I realized they were nice men."

"May I intervene with a question here, Jacqueline?" Catherine asked.

"Of course."

"I'm wondering, Lien, why do you trust these men? What is it about them?"

Lien chewed lightly on her lower lip as she thought about her answer. "I don't know. I think there's something different in their eyes. I don't have the English to explain it. They don't look at me the way the men in Svay Pak did, and they're nice to me."

Another pause. Both Catherine and Jacqueline remained silent.

"Yes," Lien said. "It's something in their eyes."

"What is it you see in their eyes?" asked Catherine.

Lien's eyes shifted down and to the left and then upward and to the left as she searched for her answer. "I think their eyes are soft when they look at me. Their eyes are kind, too, like puppy eyes. I don't feel threatened by their eyes. Their eyes seem to tell me that they won't hurt me. I don't know how to explain it more than that."

"That's good, Lien," Jacqueline said. "A month ago you told me you were sad because you believed you could never have a loving relationship because of what happened to you. Do you still feel that way?"

"I'm confused about that now, because I think the monk, Paul Pham, likes me. But even though he's Vietnamese, and a Buddhist, he's also American. I don't know if a real Vietnamese man can ever love me. I'm not attracted to Paul in … you know … in *that* way. But I really do trust him."

Catherine asked, "Why is it you trust him, Lien? Is there another reason beside what's in his eyes?"

"Maybe the robes. The shaved head. He's a monk, even if only a temporary monk. I grew up to think that monks are good, kind, thoughtful people. Paul is all those things, but he's also funny … in a cute kind of way. He seems to want to be friends."

Now Jacqueline took the reins again. "I think there are good, kind men out there that can love you because of what's in your heart, regardless of what's happened to you, but I think you'll find that out for yourself in time."

Lien asked, "Can we talk about anger? I don't remember being angry as a young girl, but sometimes now I get so mad at someone, I don't know myself."

"I think," Jacqueline said, "that because of the PTSD, you're sometimes subconsciously keyed up and on edge or irritable. That's not uncommon. If you reach a point where the tension is exacerbated — we call that a trigger — you may act out. A trigger can be anything that reminds us of our trauma and brings back the bad memories."

"I recently had a fit of temper with my grandfather over something he said that I didn't agree with. I'm so ashamed for that. I love my grandfather and I'd never do anything to hurt him. I also had a fit of rage when I met Colonel Khlot. I really let him have it. I even used swear words in English and Vietnamese. At the time, it felt good to get so angry with him. Now when I think about it, I'm ashamed that it felt good. Vietnamese girls are not raised to show anger.

Catherine attempted some humor. "My goodness, Lien, where did you learn English swear words?"

Lien smiled briefly, then frowned. "I learned some of them from the gross men who came to the brothel in Svay Pak, and I've also heard English swear words in the coffee shops here in Hoi An and even at Hai Cua on An Bang Beach. English videos and movies also taught me swearing."

Jacqueline said, "Anger can be difficult to manage and it may not always be good to suppress it. No one can fault you for attacking Colonel Khlot. Maybe you should give yourself a free pass on that one, Lien. Everyone experiences anger from time to time, but just recognizing that anger is not always appropriate goes a long way toward getting it under control. We'll work on identifying the triggers for your anger, then figure out how to reframe it into a more constructive emotion."

Catherine said, "Lien, it may interest you to know that your grandfather experienced many of the same symptoms that you describe, including anger, following his experiences in this country during the 60s and 70s." She glanced at Jacqueline, "Let me tell you one story about Grandpa Pete's anger. It's actually kind of funny."

When Jacqueline nodded Catherine said, "We were in Hawaii shortly after Pete's second tour in Vietnam, driving a rental car down Ala Moana Boulevard in Waikiki. Your grandfather was eating a huge chocolate ice cream cone as he drove. We stopped at a traffic light, preparing to make a right turn. The light was red but free right turns are okay in Honolulu, so your grandfather was licking his ice cream cone while he waited to make his right turn. A very impatient young man in a Corvette convertible came up behind us, with his blond girl friend sitting beside him. He honked his horn and gestured for Pete to make his turn. Your grandfather looked into the rear view mirror and made a shrugging gesture. The young man behind us then laid on his horn and gave us the finger."

Lien's mouth fell open. "What happened then?"

"Your grandfather put our car into park. He set the emergency brake and turned on the four-way flashers. Then he tore open the driver's door and marched back to the Corvette. I said, 'Don't Pete,' but he didn't listen. He just stomped back there, still gripping his chocolate ice cream cone." Catherine watched Lien's eyes widen.

"When he got back to the Corvette, he bellowed, 'Look punk' — actually he said, 'Look *asshole*, if it's all the same to you, I'll be the judge of when it's safe for me to make my right turn. Meanwhile you just sit here honking your horn and stewing in your own juices.' With that he smashed the ice cream cone on the windshield of the young man's car, smeared it around, and returned to our car. I looked back and saw the ice cream melting down the windshield. The guy just sat there stunned. Seeing him behind the windshield, it looked like he had chocolate streams dripping down his face. The last thing I remember as we drove off was hearing that punk's girl friend laughing at him and calling him a lolo."

Lien couldn't stop laughing. "My grandfather did that? *Trời ơi,* that's so funny."

"Sometimes," Catherine said, "being angry is okay."

"Good point, Catherine," Jacqueline said. "And I think rape-related PTSD is very similar to that suffered by soldiers who've experienced battle."

"Yes, and like you said, anger is often appropriate. Your flare up with Colonel Khlot, Lien, means you're no longer a victim. You were in charge of that situation. At last you could tell him that his behavior was not okay. That he harmed you. Obviously, you got to him. He certainly reacted as if you hit a tender spot."

"Thanks, Catherine." Lien leaned in and hugged her.

"This is our first session since you returned from China," Jacqueline said, shifting gears slightly. "How was that experience for you?"

Lien looked directly at Jacqueline. "Mostly, it was very good. I think it was what you Westerners call a mixed sack ..."

"You mean a mixed bag?" Catherine gently corrected.

"Yes, a mixed bag. It felt really good to be rescuing a girl from something similar to my own experience. My Grandmother Quy used to say that if someone else is drowning, you have to give a hand. That's what we did. It was exciting, but it was scary too. First I was afraid of the villagers and later of the border police."

"And how did it affect you that the girl you rescued was Colonel Khlot's daughter? Did you, or do you, have any feeling about that?"

"Yes." Her sigh was almost a sob. "It seemed weird to be embracing and comforting this girl while knowing her father was the first man to rape me. I've tried to sort out my feelings about that over the past few days. Yesterday I even called Chaya in Cambodia to see how she's doing. She's temporarily living in the Phnom Penh Women's Shelter. It's a rehab place for girls who've been trafficked. I wanted to talk to her without letting her know how I know her father. She's doing okay, but she's having nightmares. She's worried sick that she may have killed her 'husband,' Hong Li."

"Can you tell us how you feel now about that? About her being Colonel Khlot's daughter, I mean," said Jacqueline.

"Since I met Chaya and know that Colonel Khlot was behind her rescue — that he came to GG for help — I think it's possible someday I can stop hating him. Maybe one day I'll even feel sorry for him." She hesitated. "But right now, he still makes me sick to my stomach just to think of him. I may never forgive him for what he took from me."

"Hmm. That's certainly understandable, Lien. But we'll work on ensuring that your feelings about him don't consume you."

"I have a question," Lien said. "Should I do something for Chaya?"

"What did you have in mind?" Jacqueline asked.

"The woman in the village who helped Chaya is named Biyu. Her phone number is still in my phone. Do you think I should call her and find out whether Hong Li died? I mean do you think Chaya should know?"

Jacqueline took a sip of her now tepid tea. "I think that's a good idea, Lien. One way or another it will give Chaya closure. If this Hong Li is still alive, it could relieve her anxiety, and if he's dead she'll have to deal with that psychologically. Maybe knowing the answer to that question will help her deal with it rather than keep stewing about it. Let's do it now. Why don't you see if you can reach this woman and put your phone on speaker?"

Catherine wasn't sure this was good advice. What if the man was dead, she wondered. Would Lien feel like an accomplice to a murder? She considered raising this point with Jacqueline, then dropped the idea. What better setting to deal with any resulting emotions than here in her psychologist's office with her step-grandmother also here for support?

Lien placed the call. Biyu answered on the second ring. Lien identified herself. She made it clear that Chaya was safe and in a shelter in her home city. She asked if Biyu was, likewise, fine. Then she enquired as to Hong Li.

Biyu's voice rattled through static. Catherine, Lien and Jacqueline each looked at the others for comprehension. "Can you say that again, Biyu?" Lien asked. "I couldn't hear you."

"Yes. … (static) …will be okay … a … in his head is broken and … brain… bruised … in hospital … will be okay."

Jacqueline whispered, "I think she's saying that he has a skull fracture and that his brain is bruised. That means he has a concussion. There might be swelling, but usually it resolves."

Lien nodded impatiently. "Did you say they think he will be okay, Biyu?"

"Yes."

"We're glad to hear that. Chaya will be glad as well. Are you okay? Are you being punished for helping us?"

"Hong Li's mother … (static) … angry. I am okay now …."

"Thank you Biyu. This is Lien's grandmother speaking. Your help saved a young girl's future."

Lien smiled and said, "I think that news will be a relief to Chaya." After a moment of silence, she added, "It makes me feel better about everything too."

CHAPTER FORTY — LIEN

The monsoon season brought cooler temperatures, and for once Hoi An had not been hit with heavy winds, rains and flooding. We made it through November without the flooding that sometimes forces the closure of streets in the old town. But now, from where I sat with Pha on a bamboo mat near Cua Dai Beach, clouds and rain moved our way from the Cham Islands. Not a fierce storm, just a squall, and so far nobody had left the beach to avoid it.

We had come to the beach, for the third day in a row, to see if any of the female vendors were being approached by men who resembled the ones who had talked Pha into going to Singapore to be a bride. Because of the Pied Piper's recent violence, I was a little nervous. In fact, Stewy really didn't want me to be involved in watching for the Piper's men, but I had assured him that if we saw the men, we wouldn't approach or confront them in any way. We'd simply observe and report back to him. Though I was a little edgy, I had been sleeping well, and adrenaline rushed through me at the thought of doing something positive at the beach.

Pha continuously rubbed her thumb across the knuckles of her opposite hand, revealing her nervousness as well. She wore no makeup and was garbed in peasant pajama pants and a green T-shirt. An oversized rice-straw conical hat and dark glasses shaded her face to keep any of the vendors from recognizing her.

Nearby, Western tourists were being pampered around the pool and on the lush grounds of the Hotel Victoria, where two security guards stood in khaki uniforms, one at each end of the hotel's beach frontage. Their job was to keep the young vendors of sunglasses and trinkets away from the hotel so that white tourists would not be pestered, but the youthful hawkers were persistent and resourceful. Often, using street smarts and teamwork, they'd create a diversion of some kind to capture the guards' attention while several others made it onto the hotel grounds. There, with their trays and baskets of made-in-China baubles, they boldly approached the lounging tourists and launched their appeals. "You buy? You buy? Look, jade necklace. Very cheap. Yo-yo for baby, very good. Sunglasses. You see? Genuine Ray Ban. Two dollah. Very cheap."

As we watched the beach, we played *Tien Len,* a Vietnamese card game. We shuffled the grimy cards and dealt our two hands face down on the mat as we looked about for men intent on making their living by creating misery for young girls. When a gust of wind ruffled the cards, and lifted three off the mat to deposit them a few yards away, I splayed my open hands across the remaining cards while Pha jumped up to retrieve those that had flown away.

As she sat back down she said, "Maybe we should stop for the day." She looked seaward toward the advancing line of clouds. "If the rain comes, the tourists will go inside and the vendors will go home. The men will not come today."

"Let's give it a few more minutes. If we see the vendors leave, then we'll leave too." I reshuffled the deck of dog-eared, soiled cards. "I don't remember whose cards are whose, so let's shuffle again."

I dealt our two hands and picked up mine. I glanced at Pha, who sat motionless, staring off into the distance, not toward the clouds but toward the street that runs parallel to the beach. I turned and followed her gaze, but saw only the usual traffic of motorbikes and taxis. Nothing seemed out of place.

I tapped her hand. "Do you want to play this hand, Pha?"

She said, "Do you see the man sitting on a blue motorbike under the palm tree by the tea stand?"

I moved to turn around.

"No. Don't look now," she whispered decisively. A muscle was twitching in her jaw. "He's been watching the girls. He could be one of the men. I can't see his face with his helmet on, but he might be the one with the thin mustache, the first one to talk to me."

I adjusted my position and scooted around on the mat until I sat next to Pha, no longer across from her, so I could watch the man without being conspicuous. But I waited to look in his direction. "What's he doing?" I whispered.

"Just sitting there on his bike, watching. Now he's lighting a cigarette. I still can't see his face clearly … the helmet."

When I risked a look, he was taking a deep draw off his cigarette. He exhaled a burst of white smoke, which quickly separated into threads in the breeze. He pulled a cell phone from a pocket and stared at the screen for a few seconds as if he might be reading a text message. Then he appeared to tap out a return message, the cigarette dangling from his lips.

Another gust lifted the unplayed cards and scattered several of them in the sand. I dashed after them and chanced a longer look at the man on the motorbike. He had finished with his message and was again scanning the beach.

When he looked at me, I diverted my eyes and quickly picked up the remaining cards. I glanced his way as I sat and saw with horror that he was still watching me. A shudder ran up my spine. Did he think I was a prospect? I had deliberately dressed a little shabby this morning so as to blend in with the beach people. Was that a mistake? Had he singled me out as another poor girl from one of the villages?

I reached into my little backpack and put on my sunglasses. Maybe I could keep my eyes on him without his noticing. I glanced toward Pha. Her hands trembled as she pulled the conical hat lower over her eyes. The man was smiling now, and I prayed he wouldn't come over to talk to me.

He stayed seated on his bike, possibly looking past me to smile at someone else. But then he flicked his burning cigarette into the sand and with one hand reached up and unsnapped the chinstrap of his helmet. He lifted it off his head and hung it from the handlebars.

Wanting to get a picture of him if I could, I fumbled in my backpack for my cell phone. I barely heard Pha whisper something.

Then she said with urgency, "It's him. It's the moustache man." I heard real panic in her voice when she said, "Oh no. He can't recognize me."

I retrieved my phone and fumbled with the power button, my hands all thumbs. When the screen lit up, I had trouble finding the camera icon. I scrolled left and right through the screens trying to recognize the button as they all blurred together into a collage of color. I looked up. The man with the moustache had dismounted.

"Oh no. Oh no." Pha said.

"Don't worry," I whispered, though terrified myself. "I think he wants to talk to me. Not you. Just try to look plain, like maybe you're my little sister."

I located and touched the button for the camera function as he walked toward me. I didn't want to raise the phone to where he could see what I was doing, so I held it in my lap and aimed it toward his face — I hoped. I couldn't see the screen, so I didn't know if I was pointing correctly. I took about six pictures, changing the camera angle slightly each time.

He came straight to me.

Pha had leaned forward to stare into her lap, so the conical hat concealed her entire face. I had that horrible feeling in the pit of my stomach, like someone was squeezing it, and the skin on my neck felt prickly.

"Hello," he said. "Are you married?"

"No." I suppressed a gag.

"I'd like to show you a picture of a handsome man who's looking for a beautiful Vietnamese girl like yourself." He opened his phone and showed me the image of a young man in a business suit. "He's very wealthy and lives in Singapore, a modern, clean city. Would you like to fly there and meet him?"

"No."

"I can fly you down first class."

"No. Please leave me alone."

He smiled again and handed me a scrap of paper. "This is my phone number. Call me if you change your mind. But the number is only good for twenty-four hours."

I tried to control my trembling hand as I took the paper. Anything just to get him to leave us alone.

He glanced toward Pha. "What's the matter with your friend. Is she shy?"

"Yes, she's shy," I said with a little too much enthusiasm. But it was enough to get him to walk back toward his motorbike. I took a deep breath and let out a long sigh. "He's leaving, Pha."

I scrolled through the pictures I had taken. In two of them only the lower half of his face showed and in two more his face was missing entirely. But one of them was a perfect frontal image, silly little moustache and all.

Then the squall was upon us, pelting us with rain. I tucked the camera into my pack. We both rose and trudged toward the taxi stand at the Hotel Victoria, leaving the sodden cards and the tatami mat on the ground.

***

I showed Stewy the photo. "Pha recognized him. She said that he was the first man to approach her on the beach and take her to tea."

"That's a clear photo, Lien. This might give us the break we need. I doubt this was the Piper himself, but if we can identify this guy, he may lead the police to the head man or woman."

I pulled the slip of paper out of my pocket and offered it to Stewy. "He said to call if I changed my mind, but that this number is only good for twenty-four hours."

"Yeah, he's likely using disposable phones, so that number probably won't help, but I'll pass both the photo and the number on to Nga at the anti-trafficking police. Hopefully the photo will get us somewhere."

CHAPTER FORTY-ONE — NGA

As Nga prepared for a meeting with the Pied Piper, she wondered how she had got involved in this nasty business to begin with. This was the day she would tell him that she wanted out. For the thousandth time, she wished she had never been sucked in.

On the beach three years ago she had been attracted to his accent, his quick wit and his handsome stature. He had been keen on her wholesome laugh, her smooth conversational ability and her athletic figure. When he learned she was a policewoman, he became even more interested. He said he was a businessman but didn't disclose the exact business. It didn't matter, Nga was smitten. They became lovers and met several times a week, alternating whose house they slept in.

When Nga received orders to go to Hanoi for the three-week training course that would qualify her to join Department C-45, the anti-trafficking police, she hated to leave him. But it was a plum job within the Ministry of Public Security and she would return to Da Nang to work in her new specialty.

But in Hanoi, on April 30, 2015, an event occurred that changed the course of her life.

It had been a good day. She had watched the Reunification Day Parade as it moved triumphantly along Hung Vuong Boulevard to the accompaniment of fireworks, sirens, whistles, flags and the always present military. The celebration marked the fortieth anniversary of the day that Saigon and the government of the South fell to the advancing North Vietnamese Army troops, ending the long American war. Celebrations occurred simultaneously all over Vietnam, but the one in Hanoi was the grandest, the parade an elaborate affair featuring many floats, performers and marching bands. Symbolizing the Communist victory and mirroring the flag of the Socialist Republic of Vietnam, the color red dominated many of the floats and costumes.

In an ebullient mood, Nga pulled her motorbike from the parking spot behind the Imperial Citadel, planning to attend the Reunification Day music festival to be held in Thong Nhat Park. She had just paid the parking attendant, and with a swipe of her long sleeve, had erased the chalk marks on the saddle when her cell phone rang.

She took the call. Instead of heading for the music festival, she rode straight to Viet Duc Hospital. There, her distraught mother was weeping at the bedside of her father. He had been complaining of abdominal pain but had resisted going to the *bac si* until this morning, when the pain became so severe he couldn't get out of bed. Nga's mother had called an ambulance.

Incoherent, her mother couldn't explain the situation to Nga, so the attending nurse summoned a doctor. Stage four pancreatic cancer. Terminal. Maybe two or three weeks to live.

Emotionally, her father's impending death devastated both her mother and herself as an only child. Beyond that, when her father's paltry pension as a retired government functionary ended with his death, her mother would have no means of support. On a policewoman's salary, Nga could do little to help with the bills, particularly as she lived and worked in Da Nang, nearly eight hundred kilometers away. Nga's mother was not in the best of health herself and would soon need home nursing.

Nga returned to Da Nang crushed and depressed after her father's death. The first night she cried herself to sleep without sharing the scope of the problem. But on the second night she bared her soul while she lay in her boyfriend's arms. He said nothing at first, just lay there smoking while she sobbed, her head on his chest. After a few minutes, he said, "I know how you can earn enough money to support your mother."

For a year and a half she had been feeding information to him. But each time she did, her crisp uniform and the status that went along with it felt like a disguise, shrouding her dark soul. She was able to support her mother, but she felt dirty. She *was* dirty, a dirty cop, aiding and abetting these vile men as they took advantage of young girls. She had been an innocent once herself and knew how easily she could have been lured into slavery. Love and fealty demanded that she provide for her mother, but her work for the Piper was chipping away at her moral fiber. The good karma of helping her mom was surely erased by her treachery.

***

Now Nga sat before him in the clay house in the village of Tra Que, between Hoi An and An Bang Beach. "This is a picture of your man Vinh, snapped at Cua Dai Beach yesterday. Green Gecko is onto him. They want the police to act."

The Piper studied the picture. "He's a moron. How'd they get onto him? How did someone get his picture and who was it?"

"Yes, he is rather stupid. He went back to the same beach where he's operated several times before. A girl named Lien took this picture. She's the one who rescued Pha from Singapore and helped in the rescue of a girl sold as a bride into China a short time ago. Lien was sold into Cambodia herself a few years ago. She's a recovering trafficking victim. I have to say, she's very brave."

"So, she works with Green Gecko."

"Yes."

He rubbed his chin with the palm of his hand. "What do you think we should do about this?"

"For starters, you should have a serious talk with Vinh. Tell him not to be so stupid, to avoid having his picture taken, and for God's sake, change his appearance by getting rid of that mousy moustache. Come to think of it, both Vinh and Vang — or maybe they should be Yin and Yang — should modify their appearance frequently. Change hairstyles, use different combinations of facial hair, dark glasses, and so forth."

"Yeah, yeah, but what will the police do about it, now that GG has officially complained and provided evidence of one of the culprits?"

"I've told Green Gecko that we're on it, that we've put out a bulletin with the picture, that a search for him is underway. That's not true, I've not initiated any of that." Her voice softened. "But I have to tell you, this tears me up. I feel dirty every time I do something that's likely to hurt more girls like Lien and Pha. Meeting them and knowing what they went through rips me apart. It sears my heart like a tongue of flame."

"You're going soft on me?"

"I don't like what I do for you, I never have." She stifled a sob. "It's a betrayal of my Buddhist principles and of my oath as a policewoman." Now her voice took on more resolve, "This is wrong. I'm sorry I ever agreed to this."

"You're in it, Nga. Fully. We count on you for information. You count on me for the means to support your mother. One hand washes the other. In nature that's known as a symbiotic relationship."

"I want to quit. I'll find another way to support my mother."

"You can't quit, Nga. I've got you squirming on my hook. You can't turn the police on us. If you did, I'd make sure that you took a hard fall. It would be the end of your career and would probably mean jail time for you. How would you support your dear mother then?"

Nga turned her head and hastily wiped away a tear. She stood to leave.

"Wait, you little bitch. Here's something else you should know. You'd better harden your bleeding heart because I'm about to send another message to Green Gecko. That cocky little Lien will be punished for taking that picture."

Nga's eyes widened and she gulped. Then she stared him down. "You bastard."

***

Seated in a wooden armchair in the living room of her two-room flat in Da Nang, the lights off, the door and window both shuttered, Nga stared morosely at her lap. She had to make one of two choices, both bad. Angry with herself, she stood and strode to the tiny efficiency kitchen. With a violent swing of her arm, she swept a pair of dishes and two empty bottles off the counter and onto the floor where they shattered, sending spinning shards across the room. She slammed a pan on the countertop with a shriek, then leaned on the counter with her elbows, placed her face in her hands and cried. Wasn't this the definition of insanity — thinking you have absolutely no options and nowhere to turn?

She returned to the rosewood chair and kicked a shard of china across the room. She sat down hard and leaned her forehead against her hand, elbow on the arm of the chair. Why had she gotten herself into this? She could have remained in Hanoi after her specialty training and shared accommodation with her mother. She could have looked after her whenever she wasn't working. But no, she'd been infatuated with this so-called businessman and had wanted to get back to the Da Nang-Hoi An area to pursue the relationship amid the beachside amenities of one of Vietnam's nicest spots. How damned selfish. She stomped her foot on the floor. She should have put family first.

During the specialty training in Hanoi, she'd read and viewed videotapes of many case studies regarding trafficking victims. Her heart went out to these girls and she frequently found herself fighting tears as she sat in the classroom learning about their suffering. By the end of the first week, she knew she wanted to work in this area, where she could make a difference. She would commit herself to the protection of vulnerable children and the apprehension of the animals who lined their pockets with the proceeds of depravity. But the Piper had promised he would support her mother. The exchange of a little information every now and then had seemed innocuous at first. She reported the outcome of certain meetings she sat in on and the content of certain planning and policy documents that crossed her desk. These actions didn't contribute directly to the abuse of children. After all, it was only information, and the Piper paid well.

Full awareness of how this information was put to use crept over her gradually, as she sat in on meetings with the Piper and his goons. Pha was the first victim she had met face to face and that one interview had wrenched her gut and eaten at her soul. She couldn't live with herself if she continued abetting this scourge, but what other choice did she have? Who would support her mother if she went to jail?

For a fleeting moment she contemplated suicide. But that wouldn't solve anything. It might unburden her conscience, but it wouldn't help keep her mother.

And now the Piper had thrown in a new wrinkle — Lien. Nga trembled at the thought that this man, who had been her lover, might hurt this tender young woman, only now finding her footing after her own horrendous experience. She needed to find a way to warn Lien.

Taking another tack, she wondered if she might anonymously tip off her colleagues in the anti-trafficking unit. What if she gave them the Piper's identity and the scope of his nefarious activities? Would that put him away and reduce the threat to girls in central Vietnam, Lien in particular? After a moment's thought, she rejected the idea. The police would want specifics. They'd want concrete evidence. They'd need more than an anonymous tip. To provide them with sufficient information to act would require her to admit her own complicity. That would be the end.

Nga looked up at the ceiling and let out a wail, her mind swirling. Although it was now dark, with light rain falling, she slipped into her sandals and left the apartment. Only when she became conscious of the absence of heavy traffic did she realize the time, three in the morning. Apart from intermittent light from the occasional motorbike, the only illumination came from the mercury vapor streetlights.

She walked steadily along Vo Van Kiet Street toward the Han River, with her head down. Reflections on the glistening street momentarily diverted her attention — like fairies dancing around a fire, she thought, and soon enough the bright blue, red and green LED lights of the famous Dragon Bridge dominated her field of vision. The three gold arches of the six hundred-meter long bridge had been designed to suggest the undulating back of a swimming dragon, with a head on the west end and a tail at the east end.

She trod up the approach to the first span where the refracted images of the multicolored lights bobbed and jittered on the ripples of the river, adding a ghostly dimension to her dismay. By the time she reached the middle span and paused to lean on the rail, she believed the flickering lights beckoned her. She watched the dark current and the trembling rainbow of lights and attempted, as she had been taught in meditation classes, to suspend all thoughts or judgment … just breathe … count the breaths … in … out … simply breathe … concentrate on the lights … let them course through your body.

After about thirty minutes the germ of an idea wriggled into her mind. Vague and indistinct at first, it gradually crystallized in bits and bites until eventually it surfaced fully, allowing her to submit it to the test of logic. It wasn't a permanent, or even a perfect, solution. It couldn't solve the whole problem, but it might afford her some breathing room concerning the Piper's threat against Lien. She took a deep breath and walked the two kilometers back to her flat.

***

She waited until 7:30 a.m. to make the call. Most offices in Vietnam are open by seven, but Stewy was, after all, a westerner. Who knew when he would be at his desk?

"Mr. Fitzsimmons, this is Policeman First Class Nga."

"Good morning, Nga, and as I've told you before, please call me Stewy."

"Okay. Do you have privacy?"

"Yes. I'm alone enjoying coffee in the garden."

"And you're on your cell phone, right?"

"Yes."

"I need to alert you, as you westerners say, to something important, but I must ask you to keep the method by which I learned what I'm about to tell you strictly confidential. You must not tell anyone. Okay?"

"This sounds serious."

"It is. I believe one of your staffers is in danger, but you must tell no one how I found this out. Not your colleagues, not your staff, not other police people. Can you promise that?"

"Okay. Who's in danger and how?"

"For the past couple of months, I've been under cover. At the direction of my supervisor, I've infiltrated the Pied Piper's gang …"

"Isn't that dangerous? Who is he, or she, or they?"

"Not so fast. Yes, it's dangerous. I'm as good as dead if my cover gets blown. You must not reveal this to anyone."

"Yes, I understand. But who's in danger?"

"Lien."

"How do you know?"

"I was in a meeting yesterday. The Pied Piper knows Lien took a picture of one of his men on the beach. The man with the moustache saw Lien working the camera from her lap. Now the Piper intends to send GG a message by harming her in some way."

"Whoa. Slow down. How would he know her name?" His tone signaled disbelief.

"The Piper's gang in the Hoi An area is small. This man was probably one of the ones who bombed your staff group home and who beat the volunteers in Xuan Phuoc. I'm sure they know many of your staffers and their names."

"What do you think I should do?" He sounded wary but ready to take action.

"Just protect her. Give her more security. That's all I can suggest. Meanwhile, I'm trying to learn enough to bust this gang."

She rang off, satisfied that she had taken appropriate action to protect Lien, but with her conscience still in agony.

CHAPTER FORTY-TWO — LIEN

By 3:00 a.m. I had given up on sleep, the image of the moustache man stuck in my mind, his breath hot and putrid in my face. I had tossed and turned ever since. By six, my sheets were twisted and soaked with sweat. My pillow was missing. My heart pounded in my chest, and the metallic taste of fear filled my mouth. My nightmares were back.

The day before, Stewy had called me into the lounge and cautioned me to be extra careful. "We had a threat from an anonymous caller," he said.

"What kind of threat?"

"It seems someone is really angry about the picture you took of the moustache man. I don't want you going anywhere away from the group home or the office by yourself. Always have someone with you. Even if you use your bicycle, please ride with someone else. Make sure you carry your cell all the time, and I want you to wear this around your neck." He handed me a whistle on a chain.

"It's a police whistle," he said. "Very loud. If you feel threatened by someone use it."

He didn't mean to alarm me, he said. The threat might amount to nothing, maybe a prank call. But still, prudence required that I take it seriously. He asked if I wanted to leave Hoi An for a while, maybe go to Saigon to visit my father and my grandmother. Green Gecko would fly me down if I wanted.

I hadn't seen Grandmother Quy in almost a year and I missed her love and wisdom. I hadn't seen my father for a year either. But I remembered something else Grandmother Quy had said, so I repeated it to Stewy, "No. The ox stands its ground."

"I didn't think you'd want to go," he said. "You'll be okay here if you take precautions. We have security both here and at your house. I'm telling the others as well, but I wanted to warn you first. Just use good judgment when you travel between home and work, or from home to visit Pete and Catherine. And vary your routine. Don't leave home at the same time every day and use different routes to and from the office."

"If we're afraid of these predators and they know it, then they win," I said, unsure how I knew that expression or why it happened to surface in my mind just then. Maybe it had something to do with the threat of terrorism that dominates the news on TV.

But after a night of bad dreams, I didn't feel so brave. I sat on the edge of my bed, my heart throbbing so hard it shot pains down my spine and up into my neck. As dawn surfaced, I stared at a gecko clinging to the whitewashed cement wall of my bedroom. Soon he would retreat to whatever crack he lived in and wait out the day. What a simple existence, just hanging out, eating bugs all night, then sleeping all day. I wished I could climb into a crack as well.

I startled at the sound of something squealing downstairs and then felt foolish; one of my roommates was making morning tea. I felt another surge of adrenaline when I detected street noises outside. Had a motorbike just stopped at our house? I twitched. Was that a car door? This was what Jacqueline Hartzog called hypervigilance. It went with my PTSD.

Rain tapped on the roof, lightly at first, and then seconds later it grew into a deluge with millions of drops pounding like hoofbeats on the metal roof above my head. My roommate awakened and sat up on the other bed, across the small room from mine. She blinked and wiped the sleep from her eyes, then looked at me with alarm. "Lien, you look terrible. What's the matter? It's only a squall."

The rest of the morning went pretty much the same way, with me anxious and wary, keenly sensitized to every sound and sudden movement as Mai and I bicycled to Green Gecko later, when the rain let up. In the office, too, I jumped at the sound of a ringing phone and looked up every time someone moved from one room to another.

At one o'clock, Tam asked me to join him for a bowl of pho at Nha Hang 31, in a little alley off Le Loi.

"Of course," I said. "And let's ask Mai too." If two was good security, three would be even better.

We sat on low red plastic stools around a battered metal table on a covered patio. While we waited for our lunch, we asked for hot tea, but rather than sip it, we used the boiled liquid to sanitize our plastic chopsticks. Although the food was fine if it was served good and hot, one could never be sure about the cleanliness of the utensils.

We discussed our mutual experience rescuing Chaya from the village south of Nanning. It felt good to remember how we came together as a team and got the job done. Tam said in English, "Together everyone achieves more. Get it? T-E-A-M." We high-fived each other and the easy banter eclipsed my anxiety.

The food arrived, three simmering bowls of rich broth with thinly sliced beef, rice noodles and pieces of bok choy. The fragrance of cilantro and garlic rose with the steam. Saucers of mung bean sprouts, fresh mint leaves and wedges of lime had been served on the side and we each busied ourselves adding these toppings to our bowls with our chopsticks. The intoxicating aroma of this Vietnamese favorite hovered over our table as we slurped the broth with wide spoons and lifted noodles and beef with our chopsticks, speaking little as we ate enthusiastically.

When we got down to the dregs, Mai said, "Speaking of Chaya, do you know what day she was married to that monster Hong Li?"

Tam and I shook our heads.

"The thirteenth day of the tenth lunar month in the year of the Dragon. November 8. Do you know what else happened on that day?" Her tone of voice suggested that whatever it was, it too was bad.

Again, Tam and I both shrugged.

"The Americans elected this man named Donald Trump."

I didn't know much about American politics but I knew that my Grandfather and Catherine were not happy with America's recent choice of president. Apparently neither were Mai or Tam, judging by their facial expressions. I wondered why they should care as Vietnamese, but they both had more education than me, so maybe they were able to see a picture of where the world was headed that I could not.

I thought about this as we walked back along Tran Hung Dao Street to Green Gecko — and then my mind snapped back into fearful anxiety. Two men sat astride stationary motorbikes across the street, staring at me.

From the corner of my eye, I watched them and made sure I stayed close to Tam and Mai. They followed me with their eyes, but didn't do anything else.

***

Mai and I waited until 6:15 to leave the office. We normally left at around five, but heeding Stewy's warning, we agreed that I should change my time and not bicycle home alone. Just as we made the right turn off Tran Hung Dao to Hai Ba Trung one of the two men I had seen at lunch appeared beside me on his motorbike. He turned to smirk at me, a long filtered cigarette hanging from his lips. I looked straight ahead, then slowed my pedaling, hoping he would proceed past me, but he slowed his motorbike and stayed beside me.

I shouted to Mai, who was ahead of me and unaware of the stranger at my side. "Mai, slow down, stay with me."

But she couldn't hear me over the traffic noises. Motorbikes and buses full of tourists clogged the roadway in both directions, and still the man stayed alongside me. I sped up again. He stayed with me. "Mai, wait," I yelled.

She still couldn't hear me. I pedaled steadily, despite the bus and bike traffic, so conscious of the man keeping pace with me that I concentrated more on him than on the other traffic. When I stole a sidelong glance to my left, he was staring straight ahead with a little smile on his face, cigarette still dangling.

He shouted something. I jumped at the sound of his voice, and my right foot slipped off the pedal but I got it back on. He shouted again. I sneaked another peek at him and noticed that he wasn't shouting at me, as I had thought, but was shouting into a cell phone.

I screamed at Mai again. This time she heard, and noted the panic in my voice. She turned, saw what was happening and slowed.

"Get on my right," she shouted, bravely motioning for me to catch up with her and steer my bike to her right so she'd be between the man and me.

As she slowed I caught up to her and guided my bicycle to her right. Now we were pedaling fast. I spotted the Yamaha dealer where we needed to turn left coming up about two hundred meters ahead. I couldn't imagine how we would make that left turn with him on Mai's left side. Could we both suddenly slow down and then turn behind him to get onto the side street? What about the oncoming traffic? I prayed there would be a gap at exactly the right time.

Without warning, the man slowed briefly, cut behind us, then came up on my right side, within inches of me, turning his bike toward us, inching closer. I eased my bike to the left, trying desperately to leave space between us, terrified that he'd reach for me and cause me to fall. Mai saw what was happening and squeezed left as well, giving me more room but triggering a thunderstorm of blaring horns from behind us.

Our street came up and Mai shouted, "Turn with me. Now."

The traffic was heavy in both directions, so I hesitated to abruptly turn into it, but Mai swerved to the left and I did the same, amid the screech of brakes and more thunderous horn honking.

We made the ninety-degree swing onto our side street, but just as I felt some relief, the man again appeared at my right side. Somehow, he had also made the turn and had stuck with us.

Mai turned left onto the sidewalk in front of the house. I instinctively stuck with Mai rather than get caught alone with this person. I pedaled onto the sidewalk and stopped, gasping for breath, beside Mai. I had such a huge lump in my throat I felt strangled as I awaited the inevitable with my eyes closed, the same bitter taste in my mouth as I had whenever I was beaten or tortured in Svay Pak and Poipet.

Seconds passed and nothing happened. I opened my eyes and turned my head to see him accelerating down the street, his motorbike trailing a thin stream of blue exhaust.

CHAPTER FORTY-THREE — LIEN

After yet another night of demons, I woke just past daybreak to a cockcrow on the edge of the countryside. If I went to the roof of our house I could see the mists just beginning to lift off the rice paddies, the sun a dull, burnt-orange disc claiming its place in the gray morning. The morning haze had not yet burned off and the sounds of busy traffic remained muffled. It would be hot and humid today. I wanted to pull the covers over my head and stay in bed.

The motorbike incident yesterday afternoon had triggered too many memories. My skin prickled and a throbbing headache pushed from the back of my neck up toward my temples. Stewy's words rung in my ears: *Lien, I want you to be extra careful. We had a threat from an anonymous caller.*

I reached over to the small table by my bed and groped for the whistle he had given me. Its cold metal failed to reassure me. Nevertheless, I put it around my neck even before I took off my pajamas. My hands trembled as I fumbled into blue jeans and T-shirt. I needed to regain control, calm down, so I sat on the edge of the bed, cupped my hands and rested them face up on my thighs. I closed my eyes and took deep rhythmic breaths, counting each one.

After ten minutes of deep breathing, my heart rate returned to normal, although the fear remained at another level of my consciousness, pushing, clawing.

Mai entered the room and sat next to me on the bed, offering a cup of chamomile tea. The first sip was light and airy, with hints of apples and flowers. I knew she meant it to calm me, but also that it would be only a Band-Aid; my raging anxiety could still burst through its subtle, soothing effect.

When I finished, we rose and treaded lightly down the stairs to the kitchen where another of the girls was already eating *bánh bèo*. I had no appetite, but I sat at the table with them and sipped tea. Then a commotion at the front door and a female shriek sent my body into full blown panic.

The shriek was followed by a man's gruff voice, scuffling noises, and then a crash as a piece of furniture fell over. Nausea seized me. I dropped my teacup into my lap, but I felt no scalding.

The same man from the motorbike crashed into the kitchen and shoved toward me, his face inscribed with malice. He gripped my shoulders and jerked me from my chair and into the living room. Time slowed as it had on the bridge in China, and I remember thinking that I must be in another nightmare. As he yanked me into the reality of the present, I felt as if I had a bone stuck in my throat. I gagged and kicked without connecting, heaving my feet at thin air as he propelled me toward the front door. Several of my roommates yelled and tried to stop him by pushing and hitting at him, but he lumbered through the door still firmly gripping me by the shoulders.

I couldn't fully comprehend what was happening. But even in my fuzzy, bewildered state, I recognized the second man who now approached from a motorbike parked on the sidewalk. Moustache man.

I screamed and continued kicking wildly, trying to connect, but moustache man reached down and grabbed my ankles. He lifted my feet off the ground and controlled my flailing feet and legs. Continuing to scream, I twisted and struggled as the two men forced me to straddle the motorbike seat.

Once they got me over the seat, the man with the moustache held me tightly around the waist. He shouted, "I've got her, Vang! Get on and drive." He mounted the seat behind me, wedging me tightly, like meat in a sandwich, between the two of them. The one called Vang hit the electric start and the bike buzzed to life. I saw a tattoo of an anchor on the back of his hand.

"Help! I'm being kidnapped!" I screeched, my situation now abundantly clear. Moustache man's hot foul breath swept across my neck as he pressed me forward against Vang's oily, sweat-stained T-shirt. I howled, pinned, until a maroon cloud obscured my vision.

I thought I must be passing out, but the cloud became a real thing, a coarse cloth furiously flung over Vang's head and shoulders. The bike tipped to the left and Vang let out a yelp followed by a curse as the bike went down, its weight pressing my left leg onto the pavement. Vang jumped free of the motorbike, his head and shoulders still shrouded in the wine-colored cloth as someone spun him around.

I turned my head to see a man twisting and wrapping the purple cloth tightly around Vang's body. He hurled Vang to the ground and turned to us.

Paul Pham moved fast, bare-skinned from the waist up, wrapped from the waist down in his sarong-like *antaravasaka*, his muscular torso glistening. He made straight for moustache man, who had pulled himself to his feet. With flat, straight fingers, Paul slammed the edge of his hand into the man's throat, and my captor crumpled to the ground. With a quick look my way, and a reassuring smile, Paul turned his attention back to Vang, now freeing himself from the folds of Paul's *kashaya*. Wham! A karate chop to the side of the neck and Vang went down.

Paul turned to me and lifted the bike off my leg.

"Are you okay?" he asked, his gentle voice a contradiction to the aggression of seconds before.

"I think so," I managed, my voice trembling.

He put his arm around my shoulders and threw a cursory glance back at the two prostrate forms on the pavement. "Let's get back in the house and call the police to collect these two thugs."

Within minutes, three officers arrived on motorbikes. My roommates and a cluster of neighbors gathered and all started chattering at the same time to report what had happened.

Inside, Mai wrapped a blanket around me and offered more chamomile tea, guiding the cup to my lips. Paul fussed over me as if he were my grandmother. "Should I call a doctor? Do you want me to call your grandfather and Catherine? Are you warm enough?"

I choked back a couple of sobs that pushed their way up from my diaphragm. "I'll be okay, Paul. How did you happen to come by at the perfect moment?"

"I was on my way to Hai Cua at the beach." His cheeks glowed with embarrassment. "I ... um ... sometimes pedal by your house in the hope I might see you. Just as I was passing I saw the two men hand some cash to the security guard, so I stopped my bike by the Yamaha dealer to see what was happening. When the guard climbed on his motorbike and left, one man went to the door and the other stayed on the street. I knew something was wrong as soon as one of your roommates shrieked."

"The loudest shrieks you heard were probably mine," I told him, my thin, quaking voice belying the words.

CHAPTER FORTY-FOUR — NGA

Nga stood before the small altar in her modest apartment near Da Nang's Dragon Bridge. She pulled three incense joss sticks from a drawer beneath the altar and lit them with a disposable flint-wheel lighter. She blew on the smoldering tips and then placed them between her hands, fingers extended and joined in prayer. Lifting her hands to her forehead, she faced the photo collage of her ancestors and bowed reverently three times.

She placed the burning joss sticks into a small pot of sand that shared space with the offerings on her altar, several pieces of ripe fruit, a capped bottle of La Rue beer and a plateful of dried squid. She raised her eyes to the cluster of black and white photos depicting both sets of her grandparents and her recently deceased father. With closed eyes, she bowed once more to the pictures. Then she set off for her office, where she expected a quiet day, a chance to reflect.

She spent most of the fifteen-minute motorbike ride through Da Nang's busy streets proudly admiring the relative cleanliness of the city, its broad sidewalks devoid of the litter and detritus that characterizes many other Vietnamese cities, its four-lane roads beautified with wide center islands of green, graced with Areca palms and small, sculpted trees. Still, by the time she reached the Tam Chinh police station on Hanoi Street, her focus had shifted back to her unsolved problem. Warning Lien, through Stewy, had only solved part of her dilemma. Still nagging her troubled conscience was the issue of how to disentangle herself from the Piper's grip, and how to do this in such a way that it wouldn't jeopardize her job as a policewoman, and, by extension, her mother's welfare.

She still chewed on these questions as she settled in behind her gray metal desk in the crowded squad room. Her desk butted face to face with that of a young gum-chewing policeman with the physique of a body builder and the cherubic face of a fifteen-year-old. "Good morning, Dong," she said.

"Morning, Nga. Captain Minh wants to see you in his office."

Her stomach did a flip-flop. Captain Minh had been transferred to their Da Nang detachment from Saigon a few days earlier, and she had yet to meet him. She had been told to watch for his Mercedes SUV, and that he had a reputation as an inveterate smoker whose office always smelled foul, a man who was tough on criminals and subordinates alike. It was rumored that, as a senior police officer in Saigon, he had played both sides of the street, abetting some traffickers for his own financial gain while coming down hard on others. Lives had been lost as result of his duplicity.

She stopped briefly in the women's room to spruce up. The image that peered back at her did her no favors; she had worry lines around her brow, tightness in the corners of her mouth and faint shadows under her eyes. A splash of cold water on her face and the application of light lipstick did little to improve her appearance, so she tugged on the shoulders of her uniform tunic and pinched the creases in her trousers to crisp them up. She swiped her hand across her eyes one last time and surrendered to whatever fate awaited her down the hall.

"*Moi vao. Moi vao,*" he said, in response to her light knock.

Nga stepped into a dense fog of swirling cigarette smoke. The cramped room contained two chairs and the ubiquitous gray metal desk, adorned simply, with in and out boxes, and an enormous metal ashtray fashioned from the shell casing of an artillery round. Windowless, illuminated by a single fluorescent tube on the ceiling, the room had one other decoration, the obligatory portrait of Uncle Ho, which hung on the wall behind the desk. Below it sat Captain Minh, his sparse hair closely cropped into a buzzcut.

"Sit down, Policewoman," he said, his voice gruff. He peered at her over prominent eyebrows, his jowls slack. A double chin and a roll of flab around his waist attested to a comfortable lifestyle.

"The local *Cong An* in Hoi An have arrested two men — suspected traffickers — who attempted to abduct an eighteen-year-old girl from inside her house. I want you to go to Hoi An and take over the investigation from the locals. I believe you know the intended victim. Her name is Le Nguyen Thi Lien."

Nga tried to mask her dismay, but her hand moved abruptly to cover her mouth as she waited to learn whether or not Lien had been hurt in the attempt. An abduction attempt would surely have intensified her distress. The girl would need help.

But the two arrested men were no doubt Vinh and Vang, the Piper's chief goons, who knew her well. Thoroughly familiar with the extent of her complicity, their testimony would spell her end as a policewoman.

"Uh, I'm working on an important case here in Da Nang right now, sir," she lied. "It's at a critical juncture. It goes to trial tomorrow. I think I should stay in the city for now."

"Which case is that?"

"It's about the prosecution of a female trafficker, Vu Ha Thi Van, who was caught at the Chinese border trying to smuggle three underage Vietnamese girls into sex slavery." In reality, a colleague would be testifying on behalf of the police, but if Captain Minh bought this, Nga hoped she could worm her way onto the file and go to court the next day.

"I'm familiar with the case. I've just been briefed on it. The trial has been delayed. You get down to Hoi An, *today*."

"Yes, sir." Nga returned to her desk and sat heavily in her chair, her mind working furiously.

"What's the matter with you?" her colleague asked as he popped his gum. "You look ill."

"Leave me alone. I have to go to Hoi An and I need to think for a few minutes."

An image of the inside of *Chi Hoa* prison, in Saigon, with its dingy, vermin-infested cells, swam to mind. She had toured the prison once as part of her training and had concluded at the time that it was an easy place to die.

She pictured her mother parked in a wheelchair in the care facility in Hanoi. She put her face into her palms and rested her elbows on the desktop, overwhelmed with regret and sorrow. She was trapped.

Only two courses of action were open to her. She could go to Hoi An, where she would certainly be exposed by the Piper's men, who would seek leniency by cooperating with authorities, or she could march back to Captain Minh's office and tell him what she knew about the Pied Piper's activity. In so doing, she would confess to her own involvement. Either option would spell the end of her career and probably result in jail time, but either option would also shut down the Piper's nefarious enterprise, as Vinh and Vang would surely finger the Piper themselves in their bid for mercy.

The higher moral road would be to tell Captain Minh her story and perhaps get some credit, and maybe leniency, for confessing. She lifted her face and steepled her fingers against her forehead. She stood, squared her shoulders and walked back to Captain Minh's office.

CHAPTER FORTY-FIVE — LIEN

The anxiety made me ill. At first I was cold. My roommates piled extra blankets on me but I couldn't get warm. And then I was hot. Gentle hands mopped my body with a damp cloth but the sweat continued to rush out of my pores. Then I got cold again and shivered under the layers of blankets. They tried to spoon warm soup into my mouth and encouraged me to drink tea, but I had neither appetite nor thirst, only dry heaves. I retched for hours, expelling nothing more than a dribble. Exhausted, I refused to sleep. I didn't want to live in the nightmares anymore. I had no options. The demons ate away at my sanity.

Memories of Svay Pak constantly pushed themselves to the surface of my mind. I relived the moment my friend, Diamond, returned to our attic quarters from one of the rape chambers below, her white silk pants stained with virginal blood. Her eyes were glazed; she didn't speak. The other girls attempted to comfort her with murmurs and coos. They placed a cup of warm tea to her quivering lips, but she seemed unaware it was there.

I relived the time Thanh came back from the torture room in the basement, where she had been punished for resisting the "duties" expected of her. Her fingers were pulpy and bloody where the nails had been ripped off. I saw the empty place on her shared pallet bed the morning after she disappeared from the brothel.

Through the floor came the grunts and coarse laughter of rough men taking their pleasure from girls young enough to be their granddaughters. I knew it would be my turn soon. I clutched the Buddha I wore around my neck, closed my eyes and willed myself back to the peaceful village of Tuy Phuoc.

But they always returned. The horrible men, mostly vulgar, with foul breath, bad teeth and stupid, leering expressions on their faces. Some, like Colonel Khlot, came across as more refined, but in the end they all wanted the same thing — to satisfy their lust with the rape of young girls. We were less than human to them. We didn't have feelings. We couldn't think. We were supposed to do whatever they wished, submit to their violence and dominance as though that were the only reason we existed. We were little more than objects with warm places for them to stick their stiff appendages. Predators, pedophiles, they were worse than animals.

Again, I calmed myself by breathing through the panic. Inhaling through my nose and exhaling through my mouth, I concentrated on counting the breaths as I was taught in the rehabilitation center in Ho Chi Minh City. Inside, I went to my peaceful place, a shaded forest glen with a rapidly moving stream that sounds like the laughter of children. Two girls I helped to rescue, Pha and Chaya, joined me. They took me by my hands and the three of us danced to the music of the babbling creek. Tiny spotlights of yellow sunlight penetrated the forest canopy in places and made circles of light on the forest floor. We danced in and out of the circles and giggled like schoolgirls. We lay on the soft green carpet of grass and rolled over and over.

When the vision faded Catherine was at my side, gently stroking my forearm. "Lien," she said. "Precious Lien. Everything will be okay."

And deep inside me, I knew the love of this sweet woman and my grandfather would help me heal. Perhaps the image of the forest glen had refreshed me because I resolved that I wouldn't allow myself to be a victim of the men.

CHAPTER FORTY-SIX — PETE TRUTCH

Pete Trutch stepped out of the shower in the villa at An Bang Beach and trod into the living room with a towel wrapped around his waist. Catherine sat on the edge of the couch, a cup of tea before her and a cell phone to her ear. "Pete, it's Stewy. He's asked us to come into his office this morning. Here, you'd better talk to him."

"Stewy, what's up?" Trutch put the iPhone on speaker so Catherine could hear.

"A new development, mate. The Pied Piper has been apprehended boarding a plane to Singapore with an underage girl from Cam Thanh. The police bagged him."

"That's good news. How did this develop?"

"It's an interesting story. Nga, the anti-trafficking policewoman, was instrumental, but in a rather irregular manner. If you and Catherine can come in, I'll tell you the whole story."

"Give us forty-five minutes."

"Good. I also want to give you a heads up. There's an unbelievable twist of irony in the scenario. The bust was made by a Captain Minh, recently transferred to Da Nang from Saigon. I believe you had dealings with him five years ago in Saigon."

Trutch almost dropped the phone. *Captain Minh.* "The asshole who demanded a bribe from me to share his knowledge that Lien was in a brothel in Cambodia. A crooked cop, that one. We later learned that he was on the payroll of the traffickers who took Lien to Svay Pak."

"The very one, reputed to have been corrupt for many years. I think his transfer to Da Nang was orchestrated to spare the top brass in Ho Chi Minh embarrassment. Word was probably getting around that he'd been lining other pockets in the police bureaucracy. Everyone in anti-trafficking knows how difficult this scourge is to defeat, with so many officials in on the action. Cops, border guards, military officers, even the judiciary in many countries."

Catherine chimed in, "Not only was Captain Minh a threat to Pete five years ago, but he made a point of intimidating me at the Hotel Continental. He scared me half to death."

"Yes, Catherine, a bad apple. But come on in to GG and I'll fill you in on the rest of the story. It's extraordinary."

***

Concrete walls, three meters in height, surrounded a small, leafy courtyard at the rear of the GG office. In the small murky pool there, half a dozen golden koi glided languidly among several lotus flowers, delicate in full bloom. A little Asian-style footbridge crossed the pond and led to the seating area, where Trutch, Catherine and Stewy perched on mahogany lounge chairs and sipped tea.

"This is our Zen garden," said Stewy. "It's one of the few places in this city where one can enjoy the sound of silence. We're well insulated from the noise of motorbikes, roosters, karaoke and funerals by the buildings all around us. Just enough sunlight finds its way in for the plantings to stay fresh and healthy."

"It's a lovely spot," Catherine agreed.

"I encourage my staffers to come back here and recharge their batteries anytime. But let me get to the situation that's unfolding, with all its unexpected twists and wrinkles. I didn't tell you on the phone that the Pied Piper is someone we know."

"Who?" Trutch and Catherine said simultaneously.

"Alexandre, the proprietor of Hai Cua."

"What?" Trutch said. "He seems like such a nice guy."

"A gentleman," said Catherine. "I thought."

"Apparently he had a lot of people snookered. He's been luring girls into marriages in Singapore and whorehouses in Cambodia for several years. Your old friend Captain Minh made the bust based on a tip from an insider. He knows of GG's reputation and concern about trafficking, here and in neighboring provinces, so he called me this morning to brief me."

"What strange reversals," Trutch said. "Alexandre, whom we thought was a nice guy, is the culprit. And Captain Minh, my nemesis, makes the arrest. Jeez, do you have any other surprises, Stewy?"

"Yes. One more. I told you that Nga, the policewoman, was instrumental in collaring him. But she was actually a mole — she provided sensitive information to Alexandre about police progress on investigations as well as insight into our trafficking prevention. Evidently, the glib, smooth-talking Alexandre coerced her into this role."

He explained Nga's need to support her indigent mother in Hanoi, and how she had gone to Captain Minh to spill the beans about the identity of the Piper, admitting her role. "It was a courageous thing for her to do," he said.

Silence fell over them as a female staffer came into the courtyard and demurely refilled each of their teacups. Several splashes in the pond suggested the koi also expected a handout.

"What will happen to her?" Catherine asked. "I haven't met her but I know Lien thinks highly of her."

"She's being held in detention right now in Da Nang, but I believe she genuinely hates the whole ugly scene of child trafficking," Stewy said. "Alexandre exploited a vulnerability because he's a vile man. What happens to her is ultimately up to Captain Minh, but I suspect she will face a judge and go to jail."

"What an absolute shame," Catherine said.

"Yeah, they allowed her to call me this morning, right after Captain Minh briefed me. She's certain her career is over and she's worried that her mother will have no means of support and become a ward of the state. She'd have to live on less than four hundred thousand dong a month — less than twenty dollars."

Trutch touched the scar on his cheek with his forefinger and exchanged a glance with Catherine.

***

During the forty-minute taxi ride from Hoi An to Da Nang, as his driver careened through traffic, he exhibited what now struck Trutch as mandatory driving skills for Vietnamese taxis. The guy had little use for the brakes and drove principally with the accelerator and horn, dodging and weaving through more slowly moving motorbikes, trucks and bicycles. Trutch had securely belted himself into the backseat, but the shoulder strap cut into his flesh and every bump jarred his kidneys. There would be no tip.

Worse, he had had a tearful encounter with Lien earlier in the morning. "But why would Nga have to go to jail?" she had sobbed. "She did the right thing, and I know how much she cares about what she does. She believes that children should have a chance to be children. Grandfather, please. Can't you and Stewy do anything?"

Trutch agreed with Lien. He also believed that Nga had her heart in the right place. She had done wrong to provide the Piper with information, but she had also been seduced and then cruelly coerced. Why should Captain Minh, who had arguably done far worse for nothing other than personal gain, skate on through his career and get closer to a comfortable retirement while exercising the power to destroy a young subordinate?

At the police headquarters on Hanoi Street, the shabby lobby, with its cold concrete cinder block walls and floor of broken and chipped tiles, struck him as a near carbon copy of the one he had visited in Saigon five years earlier. On that occasion, Captain Minh had levied a "fine" on him for treading on police toes while Trutch had done his own research into Lien's whereabouts. He couldn't believe he was about to confront the asshole again, this time of his own volition.

As a surly sergeant unceremoniously ushered him into Captain Minh's office, he felt as if he'd walked into the past. The same billowing pall of smoke, the same overflowing ashtray, the same cheap gray metal desk and the same portrait of Ho Chi Minh staring imperiously at the opposite wall.

And the same beefy, arrogant prick. "Well, Colonel Trutch, long time no see. What brings you back to Vietnam and into my office? Have you been meddling again?"

Trutch remained mute as they stared silently at each other, his face no doubt reflecting the same distrust as Captain Minh's.

A phone faintly rang in another office, and then Minh spoke, "How do you like Da Nang, Colonel Trutch?"

"I like Hoi An better. How do you like Da Nang yourself?"

"I find it a bit provincial, as you westerners would say. Not as urbane as Saigon."

"But the ocean breezes are refreshing."

"That may be, but the people in Central Vietnam are simple minded."

"Perhaps you made a mistake of some sort that resulted in your transfer to Da Nang?" Trutch asked carefully. "Maybe someone looked out for you and did you the favor of sending you here instead of ending your career?"

Captain Minh's ears reddened slightly and he lowered his brows. "Some years ago when I had a conversation with your wife, she asked me to clarify my *agenda*. I didn't know that word at the time, so she told me. Exactly what is *your* agenda today, Colonel?"

"I think you can help someone who's made a mistake." Trutch slid a fat envelope across the desk and into Minh's meaty paws

***

A full moon hung over the Cham Islands and bathed the frosted surf of An Bang Beach with an effulgence that struck Trutch as more than light. Its radiance had a life of its own; it could be felt as well as seen. As though he were checking the bouquet of a crisp Pinot Grigio, Trutch inhaled the fresh offshore breeze slowly and deeply through his nostrils. Beside him Catherine sipped from a glass of red wine, her face radiating contentment as the young people around them bantered and laughed among themselves, their camaraderie a tonic.

At another table, Stewy and several staffers played a Vietnamese game involving tiles, something that resembled an Asian version of dominoes.

Nga, in civilian dress, chatted with Lien as the two sat on a rattan settee. Lien's attention appeared divided, as she largely focused on Paul Pham. Wearing Levis and a T-shirt emblazoned with the words *Gooooooooood Morning Vietnam*, he stood beaming behind the bar as he poured Coke into tall ice-filled glasses. Every once in a while, his eyes strayed towards Lien and revealed his appreciation of how lovely and calm she looked, a beautiful lotus flower.

Hai Cua had been decorated for the occasion with a smattering of helium-filled balloons and a banner suspended from the bamboo poles, which served as rafters for the thatched roof that read: *Congratulations Paul.*

A new sign at the motorbike parking area, under the palms, read:

Welcome to Hai Cua
Paul Pham, Proprietor

"Did you ever think five years ago that we would be sitting here on the beach with a Vietnamese family?" Trutch asked Catherine.

"Absolutely not. I pictured us in our retirement traveling and volunteering for a few boards back in Seattle. I thought that you were a lunatic when you got yourself embroiled in the seamy realm of child trafficking, but the rewards have been worth all the worry."

"I'm glad you're seeing it that way. Speaking of rewards, let's suggest to Lien that when we leave for home we take her as far as Saigon to see her father and grandmother. It's a visit long overdue and I need to see my son."

"I agree Colonel Trutch." Catherine covered one of his hands with hers. "And are you pleased with your investment in the futures of these young people?"

"No question about it." Trutch swung his gaze back to where Lien chatted with Nga, her eyes still mostly on Paul Pham. Not long ago, Paul had confided in him that he was about to leave his monastic practice and rejoin the world, not in the U.S. but in Vietnam. Trutch had guessed that the reason might be his attraction to Lien. Fronting money to transfer the title of the bistro to Paul had seemed like a sensible investment.

And his "investment" in Nga was simply the right thing to do.

Karma, luck and the gods had favored this small family, thrown together by fate.

ABOUT THE AUTHOR

R. Bruce Logan is a retired U.S. Army officer. He served two one-year tours of duty in Vietnam during the 60s and 70s where his duties included command of an infantry platoon in combat and operations officer in a corps headquarters. Since 2006, he and his wife, Elaine Head, have engaged in humanitarian work among the marginalized in Vietnam. Together they have written an award-winning memoir, *Back to Vietnam: Tours of the Heart,* published in 2013, which describes their experiences in Vietnam spanning half a century. In 2016, *Finding Lien,* the antecedent to this novel, was published by Black Rose Writing. When not in Vietnam or Hawaii, which alternate as their second home, Bruce and Elaine live on Salt Spring Island in British Columbia.

www.rbrucelogan.com

ACKNOWLEDGEMENTS

First I wish to thank the organization known as Tours of Peace, Vietnam Veterans (TOP) for reintroducing me to Vietnam in 2006, after nearly a forty-year absence. Were it not for TOP, its founder, Jess DeVaney, and the veterans we've met on its tours, Elaine and I would not have come to know Vietnam as well as we do now after eleven years of lengthy visits.

Thanks also to Vu Duc Anh, a top-drawer tour guide and mentor of Vietnamese culture, who has become a close friend over the past eleven years and has helped us understand the contrasts and contradictions of his country.

I owe Steve Fitzsimmons, a frequent TOP traveler, my gratitude for allowing me to use his name for my character, Stewy Fitzsimmons. I hope you like your fictitious alter ego, Steve.

Thanks to my dear wife and soul mate, Elaine Head, who is always my first reader and constructive critic of any draft I produce. She is also the inspiration for the intelligence, wit and compassion of my character, Catherine.

My thanks to the Hanoi-based Blue Dragon Children's Foundation and its founder, Michael Brosowski, for familiarizing me with the work of an exemplary NGO involved in the rescue of child trafficking victims and in educational programs aimed at promoting awareness of this heinous practice. Thanks too to another NGO, Go Philanthropic, and its founders Lydia Dean and Linda DeWolf who have been supportive of our research and writing about Southeast Asia.

I'm grateful for the diligence, patience and honesty of five beta readers who gave me feedback and suggestions for improvement during the writing of this novel: Gail McKechnie, Roger Upton, Irene Frances Olson, Nguyen Minh Nguyet, and Dr. Elizabeth Nguyen Gutierrez. Ms. Nguyet ensured that my usage and spelling of Vietnamese words and phrases was authentic and helped me understand how the world is seen through the eyes of a Vietnamese teenager. Dr. Gutierrez was able to help with the Vietnamese perspective and also, as a child and adolescent psychiatrist, commented constructively on my take on

PTSD and the therapy process.

My editor, Pearl Luke, who divides her time between Chiangmai, Thailand, and Vancouver, B.C., has once again been valuable in counseling me on the effective construction of phrases and sentences and provided timely advice on the numerous revisions required to turn the manuscript into a book. Murray Reiss is a masterful line editor. He can clean and polish a draft manuscript practically overnight, as he did with this story.

My profound thanks and sincere appreciation to all of these people.

AUTHOR'S NOTE

Child trafficking is a monstrous social problem of global proportions. It is second only to drug trafficking as the world's definitive criminal activity. Research suggests that revenue from sex trafficking approaches 35 billion dollars a year. Although many nations have signed on to a UN Protocol to prevent, suppress and punish Traffic in Persons (TIP) and countless nongovernmental organizations (NGOs) around the world are combating this heinous practice, the scourge continues to grow at a rate of 3.5% per year.

What can you do? Learn as much as you can then use your voice. Buy more copies of this book and its antecedent, *Finding Lien*. Use them as gifts to promote awareness. All proceeds from the sale of both books are donated to NGOs involved in combating trafficking.

Make donations directly to any of these NGOs:
Children's Education Foundation – www.childrenseducationfoundation.org
Blue Dragon Children's Foundation – www.bluedragon.org
Go Philanthropic Foundation – www.gophilanthropic.

Purchase other Black Rose Writing titles at www.blackrosewriting.com/books

and use promo code PRINT to receive a 20% discount.

BLACK ROSE
writing™

CPSIA information can be obtained
at www.ICGtesting.com
Printed in the USA
FSHW02n1521190918
52226FS

9 781684 331024